The Butterfly Cemetery

Selected Prose (2008-2021)

Franca Mancinelli

Translated from the Italian by John Taylor

BITTER OLEANDER
P R E S S

The Bitter Oleander Press
4983 Tall Oaks Drive
Fayetteville, New York 13066-9776
USA

www.bitteroleander.com
info@bitteroleander.com

ISBN #: 978-1-7346535-4-0

Library of Congress Control Number: 2021952459

Front Cover Image "Congregation" (2014) by Kiki Smith: Jacquard Tapestry, 116"x76" courtesy of Magnolia Editions

Cover Design: Rod Martinez

Back cover photograph of Franca Mancinelli by Chiara Signoretti

Printed by McNaughton & Gunn, Inc.
Saline, Michigan 48176-0010
www.bookprinters.com

Distributed in the United States by
Small Press Distribution, Inc.
www.spdbooks.org

Manufactured in the United States of America

TABLE OF CONTENTS

Il cimitero di farfalle / The Butterfly Cemetery   9

L'amore del fuoco / How the Fire Loves   13

La forma di un dono / The Form of a Gift   15

Linfa / Sap   19

L'incanto della morte. Rosaspina / The Enchantment of Death: Briar Rose   25

Storia di un terremoto / An Earthquake Story   29

La bambina che imparò a volare / The Little Girl Who Learned How to Fly   33

Un letto di sassi / A Bed of Stones   35

Pareti, macerie / Walls, Rubble   45

Stazione centrale / Central Station   51

Sul traghetto Ancona-Igoumenitsa / On the Ancona-Igoumenitsa Ferryboat   55

Il ragazzo tra gli scogli / The Boy among the Rocks   57

Mare, treno / Sea, Train   61

Piazza XX settembre – Fano. Seguendo le ammoniti / Piazza XX Settembre
     — Fano: Following the Ammonites   65

Maria, verso Cartoceto / Maria, towards Cartoceto   71

Dentro un orizzonte di colline / Inside a Horizon of Hills   79

Abitare nella città ideale. Frammenti in forma di visione / Living in the Ideal
     City: Fragments in the Form of a Vision   87

La donna delle pulizie / The Cleaning Lady   103

Vigilando / Keeping Watch   107

Un verso è una vasca e altri appunti sulla poesia / A Line is a Lap and Other
     Notes on Poetry   109

Un rischiosissimo gioco / A Very Risky Game   115

Cedere la parola / Yielding Words   119

Poesia, lingua madre / Poetry, Mother Tongue   127

Un libro di poesia, una struttura vivente / A Book of Poetry: A Living Structure   143

Una pratica di autochirurgia interiore / An Act of Inner Self-Surgery   151

L'invisibile come testo a fronte / The Invisible as the Facing Page   157

"Franca Mancinelli: Facing the Invisible"
A Postface by John Taylor   160

Acknowledgments   174

Notes   177

The Butterfly Cemetery

Il cimitero di farfalle

Su un prato d'erba medica una bambina inseguiva le farfalle con le mani di retino aperte nell'aria oppure le prendeva per le ali, quando si fermavano sui fiori. Strette tra il pollice e l'indice, come un velo di zucchero colorato, avrebbe potuto mangiarle. Ma le bastava parlarci, muovendo appena le labbra o mormorando nel pensiero, fino a che queste, posate sulla spalla, non volavano più via: si erano affezionate a lei. E invece non molto tempo dopo, erano foglie indebolite e inerti. Dopo alcuni giochi in cui, come assonnate o addomesticate, rispondevano a tutti i suoi desideri, la bambina capiva che era venuta l'ora di seppellirle, nel sottoscala dove, dentro una corolla di sassi bianchi, ramoscelli incrociati e fiori mosci, si era formato un piccolo cimitero. Poi qualcuno le venne a dire della polvere che fa volare. O forse se lo disse da sola, nello stesso modo in cui era venuta a sapere che le farfalle, per affetto, si fermavano su di lei invece che sui fiori. La polvere restava sulle dita di chi toccava le farfalle: loro perdevano la leggerezza, si intristivano e poco dopo si addormentavano per sempre. Appena lo seppe smise il gioco e il cimitero sotto le scale scomparve, ricoperto dall'erba. Un pomeriggio però le sembrò di vedere, nella luce tesa come il filo per i panni, una bambina sul prato d'erba medica che rubava la polvere dalle ali azzurre e poi se la cospargeva sui palmi delle mani, sui polsi, lungo le braccia e su fino alle spalle, e iniziava a correre veloce, spiccando ogni tanto un salto, come un piccolo aeroplano che tenti il decollo.

Le ali delle farfalle non si potevano toccare, come gli arcobaleni. Un giorno una bambina più grande che era con lei sul balcone le aveva detto che c'era l'arcobaleno e, mentre lei lo cercava nell'azzurro senza vederlo, le aveva indicato il luogo preciso in cui doveva restare, la linea da non superare perché quei colori restassero sospesi. Le tornò alla mente una sera di quando era più piccola e, prima di dormire, aspettava che la madre venisse a salutarla. Era settembre e lei si era posata sul copriletto come una farfalla, con le ginocchia aperte. Quando la madre la vide le disse che non era più tanto piccola da potere stare in quel modo, che anche in spiaggia, ormai, non andava più senza costume e anche quando giocava doveva stare composta. Al suo *perché* rispose che non si fanno vedere le mutande e che i bambini non escono dall'ombelico. Silenziosamente si richiuse a dormire, nel baco dorato dell'estate. Le sue parole avrebbero nascosto la traccia sottile di una tomba di farfalla.

Quando tornò all'asilo si immerse nello sciame degli altri bambini, in quel disordine dove nessuno si sente solo. Soltanto un giorno le mostrarono un bambino che mangiava in cucina mentre tutti gli altri erano nella sala, sbattendo in coro le forchette e i bicchieri sui tavoli colorati. Glielo mostrarono ad esempio perché lui, con la compostezza e la calma di un adulto, mordeva un pezzetto di biscotto e poi beveva un sorso di latte, continuando così fino

The Butterfly Cemetery

A little girl would chase butterflies through an alfalfa field, with her hands open like a net in the air or she would catch them by their wings when they stopped on flowers. Held between the thumb and forefinger, they were like colored sugar coatings that she might have eaten. But it was enough for her to talk to them, barely moving her lips or murmuring in her mind, until the butterflies, resting on her shoulder, no longer fluttered off: they had become attached to her. And yet not long afterwards, they would be inert, enfeebled leaves. After playing some games in which they responded, as if tame or drowsy, to all her desires, the little girl understood that the time had come to bury them in a place, beneath a staircase, where, inside a corolla of white pebbles, crisscrossed twigs, and flaccid flowers, she had created a small cemetery. Then someone told her about the powder that makes one fly. Or maybe she said this to herself, in the same way that she came to know that the butterflies, out of affection, would alight on her instead of flowers. The powder would remain on the fingers of whoever touched the butterflies, which would lose their weightlessness, sadden, and soon afterwards fall asleep forever. As soon as she understood this, she stopped playing the game and the cemetery beneath the staircase disappeared, covered over by grass. One afternoon, however, she seemed to see, in light taut like a clothesline, a little girl in the alfalfa field who was stealing the powder from the sky-blue wings and then sprinkling it on the palms of her hands, on her wrists, along her arms and up to her shoulders, and she started running fast, leaping from time to time, like a small airplane trying to take off.

Like rainbows, butterfly wings could not be touched. One day, an older girl who was with her on the balcony had told her that there was a rainbow and, while she was looking for it in the blue sky without spotting it, the older girl had shown her the precise place where she had to stand, the line not to be crossed, so that the colors would remain suspended. An evening then came to her mind, when she was younger and, before falling asleep, was waiting for her mother to come and say goodnight to her. It was September and she had settled on the bedspread like a butterfly, with her knees open. When her mother saw her, she told her that she was already too big a girl to stay like that, that she no longer went even to the beach without wearing a swimming suit and that even when she was playing she had to stay calm and collected. To her *why*, the little girl's mother replied that panties must not be shown and that babies do not come out of a belly button. Silently she enclosed herself in sleep, inside the summer's golden silkworm. Her words might have concealed slight traces of a butterfly grave.

alla fine della colazione. Passavano i mesi con i grembiuli gialli, rosa e azzurri che ruotavano in una giostra, come petali illuminati; un ritornello portava uno dei bambini a turno nel centro del cerchio: per qualche minuto in lui si gravitava tutta l'attenzione, poi da stame tornava nella corolla del fiore.

Presto venne l'ultimo anno, quello in cui si parlava molto della scuola, di quello che avrebbero imparato e di come avrebbero dovuto comportarsi. Dissero che sarebbero stati tutto il tempo in un'aula, ognuno seduto al suo posto, con i libri e i quaderni, come facevano adesso per alcune ore, disegnando o riempiendo di colori le figure. Nella sua fronte entrò un pensiero improvviso, come uno di quegli insetti che entrano nelle case e restano poi a lungo prigionieri delle stanze, a volte morendo prima di tornare da dove sono venuti. Si chiese se si sarebbe visto, ora che ognuno era fuori dallo sciame, fermo in un rettangolo entro il quale rispondeva al suo nome, che lei era *diversa*. In quell'ordine, in quella linearità di fronte a un adulto, forse avrebbe dovuto nascondersi. Ma la sua colpa era già così sprofondata in lei da confondersi nella sua quiete. Molte farfalle che aveva preso tra le dita erano sepolte, ormai invisibili i perimetri di sassi bianchi, dissolte nella terra le ali, nel sottoscala.

When she returned to nursery school, she immersed herself in the swarm of other children, in that disorder where no one feels alone. But one day, they showed her a boy who was eating in the kitchen while all the others were in the cafeteria, banging in unison forks and glasses on the colored tables. They showed him to her as a model because, with an adult's calm and composure, he would bite into a piece of biscuit and then take a sip of his milk, continuing like this until the end of breakfast. Months went by with the yellow, pink and blue smocks which, like bright petals, would spin in a merry-go-round; a refrain would bring one of the children, in turn, to the center of the circle: for a few minutes all the attention would gravitate around him then, from the stamen, he would return to the corolla of the flower.

Soon came the last year, when much was said about grade school, what they would learn and how they should behave. It was said that they would be in a classroom all the time, each of them sitting at a desk with books and notebooks, as they did now for a few hours whenever they were drawing or filling in figures with colors. A sudden thought entered her forehead, like one of those insects that enter houses and then remain prisoners of the rooms for a long time, sometimes dying before returning to where they came from. She wondered if it would be noticed, when they all stood outside of the swarm, within a rectangle from which each one replied to his or her name, that she was *different*. In that orderliness, in that linearity facing an adult, perhaps she would have to hide. But her guilt had already sunk so deep inside her that it was blended with her quietness. The many butterflies that she had taken between her fingers were buried, by now the white pebble borders were invisible, the wings dissolved in the earth, beneath the stairs.

L'amore del fuoco

Dalla cena la bambina si era allontanata. L'intrico dei discorsi non la riguardava. Ne era fuggita facilmente, come un cane dalla rete rotta del giardino. Si era accucciata da sola sul divano. Il televisore spento, guardava il fuoco che tremava nel camino come se avesse freddo. Non può essere accarezzato da nessuno, il fuoco. Sempre un po' discosto dagli altri, in uno spazio suo. Accanto pezzi di legno e giornali. Saranno tra le sue braccia, fino alla cenere. Ama così il fuoco. La bambina prese un foglio di giornale. Così grande che avrebbe potuto avvolgerla tutta. Ma al pensiero di farlo si sentì subito addosso il freddo e l'odore di un pesce morto. Accartocciò il giornale dolcemente. Mentre si rimpiccioliva nelle sue mani prendeva le sembianze di un piccolo animale. Era proprio così: le sorrideva ringraziandola per averlo riconosciuto anche se non aveva gli occhi e il muso, e le zampe gli erano rimaste chiuse, legate dentro il corpo. Si dondolava, voleva essere cullato. I grandi iniziavano a stare in silenzio più a lungo, sempre più a lungo, ognuno nella propria sedia come braci che andavano spegnendosi. Al momento dei saluti trovarono la bambina addormentata sul divano stringendo tra le braccia un giornale stranamente accartocciato. Il fuoco si alzava ancora, debolmente, come una pianta che non ha abbastanza luce. La madre le fece lentamente scivolare il giornale dalle braccia. Proprio mentre il suo animaletto veniva gettato nel camino, la bambina si svegliò. Il fuoco si riprese a un tratto, si aprì nel suo ultimo germoglio e poi tornò a richiudersi in sé, più fievole di prima, tra le sue ceneri. La bambina sentì le lacrime che le si indurivano nella fronte. Non le uscirono dagli occhi, restarono sospese, come piccole, sottili, stalattiti.

How the Fire Loves

The little girl had left dinner. The intricate conversation did not concern her. She had escaped easily, like a dog through the broken chain-wire fence of the garden. She had curled up alone on the sofa. The television was turned off, and she was watching the fire in the fireplace, shivering as if it were cold. The fire cannot be caressed by anyone. It is always a little distant from the others, in its own space, alongside newspapers and pieces of wood; they will be in its arms, until they become ashes. This is how the fire loves. The girl took a newspaper page. It was so large that it could have wrapped her up entirely. But as soon as she thought of doing so, she felt the cold and the smell of a dead fish on it. She crumpled the newspaper gently. As it shrank into her hands it took on the appearance of a small animal. It was just that: it smiled at her, thanking her for recognizing it even if it didn't have eyes and a muzzle, and its paws had remained closed, bound up inside its body. The little animal was rocking, it wanted to be cradled. The grown-ups remained silent longer, longer and longer, each one sitting on his chair like embers that were going out, fragments of the tree trunk that they had been. When goodbyes were said, they found the little girl asleep on the sofa holding an oddly scrunched-up newspaper in her arms. The fire was still flickering up, weakly, like a plant that doesn't have enough light. The mother slowly slipped the newspaper from the arms. But just as her pet was thrown into the fireplace, the little girl awakened. The fire suddenly flared, opening in its last blossom and then again closing back into itself, weaker than before, among its ashes. The little girl felt the tears stiffening in her forehead. They did not come out of her eyes, but remained suspended like small, thin, stalactites.

La forma di un dono

I giorni che precedono il Natale hanno sottili fili argentati sparsi nella casa, luccichii sul pavimento. Sono le tracce delle grandi scatole di cartone e delle vecchie valigie che contengono il presepio e gli addobbi dell'albero. Transitano dalla soffitta alla sala dove vengono lasciati chiusi dal nastro adesivo e da vecchi lucchetti, con il loro carico conosciuto e misterioso. Oggetti che riemergono solo in questo periodo dell'anno, aspettano avvolti nella carta di giornale, di essere liberati: sospesi come frutti, doni lasciati sui rami, o appoggiati nel morbido del muschio.

Qualcosa cresce nell'aria. Qualcosa di cui non puoi indovinare i contorni, la consistenza. In questi giorni i desideri stanno prendendo la forma che la realtà ha deciso. Puoi intuirlo da alcune domande che si fanno spazio tra le tue parole in stampatello obbediente all'alfabeto da poco imparato: stanno andando a comprare i regali che hai chiesto nella lettera. Di questi natali dell'infanzia non ricordo nessuno dei miei desideri, ricordo soltanto la lettera in cui elencavo i regali per gli altri: una collana per la mamma, una penna stilografica per il babbo; per mio fratello qualcosa di semplice come un gioco.

Un anno, in uno dei giorni che precedono il Natale, aprendo per caso la porta a soffietto del ripostiglio nel sottoscala, apparvero quattro pacchetti chiusi in una carta splendente blu, rossa, dorata, argento. Così belli nei riflessi che mandavano dal buio, che richiusi quasi subito la porta. Nei giorni seguenti non tornai ad aprirla e se capitava di dovermi avvicinare a quel luogo, lo facevo senza mostrare alcun segno di quella sottile lotta tra il richiamo a entrare e scartare i pacchi, e l'attesa e il rispetto silenzioso che imponevano. Il patto si era stretto appena erano apparsi: quello che una fata ti ha concesso di vedere può svanire come un arcobaleno nel sole. Bisogna avere passi di farfalla, posarsi leggerissimi, chiudere a lungo gli occhi nel buio da cui è nata la magia. Dentro di me l'immagine dei pacchi nascosti si dilatava e cresceva, maturando il tempo della sua rivelazione. Quel tempo non venne. La notte di Natale i pacchi erano altri, nessuno assomigliava a quelli che avevo intravisto nella penombra del sottoscala. La fata li aveva ripresi con sé, ritratti nel buio, ferita dal mio sguardo come un animale a cui è stata scoperta la tana nel folto.

I regali si aprivano a mezzanotte sotto l'albero, lentamente, per non strappare la carta e il nastro, o spezzando ogni involucro e indugio. Quello che avevo desiderato per gli altri era stato esaudito: mia madre si provava la collana, mio padre aveva trovato la penna, mio fratello stava scoprendo il suo gioco. Il mio regalo era davanti ai miei occhi, ma non saprei dire che cosa fosse. Non era per me. Il regalo per me era dentro uno di quei pacchi che devono rimanere chiusi. Scartarli è una rovina. Non importa che cosa contengono; potrebbero anche essere vuoti. Il mio è stato consegnato così. Dalla distanza della sala

The Form of a Gift

The days before Christmas have thin silver ribbons scattered around the house, glitter on the floor. These are the traces of the large cardboard boxes and old suitcases that contain the nativity scene and the decorations for the tree. They journey down from the attic to the room where they are left taped up or padlocked, with their known and mysterious contents. Objects that emerge only at this time of year and wait wrapped in newspaper, to be freed: they are hung like pieces of fruit, left as gifts on the branches, or placed in the soft moss.

Something is growing in the air. Something whose contours and consistency you cannot guess. During these days, desires are taking on the form that reality has determined. You can intuit it from some questions that make room for themselves between your words written in block letters and obeying the recently learned alphabet: your parents are going to buy the presents that you have asked for in your letter. From these childhood Christmases, I remember none of my wishes, only the letter in which I listed gifts for the others: a necklace for my mom, a fountain pen for my dad; for my brother something simple, like a game.

One year, on one of the days before Christmas, when I opened by chance the folding door of the closet below the staircase, appeared four packages wrapped in shiny blue, red, golden, silver paper. They were so beautiful with their reflections shining out from the darkness, that I closed the door almost as soon. During the next few days I did not go back to open it, and if I happened to approach that place, I did so without showing any sign of that subtle struggle between the urge to go into the closet and open the parcels, and the waiting and the silent respect that they imposed. The pact had been sealed as soon as they had appeared: what a fairy has allowed you to glimpse can vanish like a rainbow in the sunlight. One must have a butterfly's footsteps, alight delicately, close one's eyes for a long time in the darkness from which the magic was born. Inside me the image of the hidden packages expanded and grew, making the time ripe for its revelation. That time did not come. On Christmas Eve the packages were different, none of them resembling the ones I had glimpsed in the dim light under the stairs. Wounded by my gaze like an animal whose lair has been discovered in the thicket, the fairy had taken them back with her, withdrawing them into the darkness.

The gifts are opened at midnight under the tree, slowly, so as not to tear the paper and the tape, or by ripping through all the wrapping and waiting. What I had desired for the others had been fulfilled: my mother tried on the necklace, my father had found the pen, my brother was discovering his game. My present was before my eyes, but I couldn't say what it was. It wasn't for me.

sapevo che era ricomparso con i suoi riflessi argentati nel buio del sottoscala. La fata era tornata a fidarsi di me.

*

Mia madre bambina giocava in un giardino di fianco alla strada. Una grande aiuola d'erba e alberi, poco lontano da casa. Portava con sé gli oggetti più cari –una fata le aveva detto di sotterrarli. Qualche centimetro sotto il terriccio scavato a mani nude o con una paletta da spiaggia. Avvolti in un fazzoletto di cotone con le sue iniziali ricamate, gli oggetti scendevano nel buio. Passava un tempo lungo come una notte o un inverno. Poi la fata tornava con un cinguettio di uccellino all'orecchio. La chiamava, la guidava verso l'aiuola. Le indicava il punto in cui avrebbe trovato un tesoro per lei.

*

Quel Natale mia cugina aveva deciso di non ricevere più soltanto doni, come una bambina piccola, ma di farli lei stessa ai suoi genitori. Voleva provare l'emozione di chi avvolge qualcosa in una carta splendente, la stringe con un nastro, fa un fiocco come su una scarpa, e poi aspetta di vedere l'espressione di chi la riceve, la soppesa tra le mani, la apre lentamente.

Per la madre comprò dei cioccolatini con gli spiccioli trovati nel posacenere, quelli che si lasciano per alleggerirsi le tasche. Per il padre dovette compiere una magia. Un giorno in cui lui era nell'orto e la madre di sotto in cucina, aprì la grande cassettiera di legno della camera da letto. Bastarono alcuni minuti per realizzare il suo dono. La notte di Natale il padre trovò avvolti in carta stellata un paio di vecchi calzetti.

The gift for me was inside one of those packages that must remain closed. Opening them brings on one's undoing. It doesn't matter what they contain; they could also be empty. Mine was delivered like this. From the distance of the room I knew it had reappeared with its silvery reflections in the darkness under the stairs. The fairy had trusted me once again.

*

When she was a little girl, my mother would play in a garden next to the road. It had a large flowerbed with a lawn and trees, not far from home. She would carry her most precious objects with her—a fairy had told her to bury them. A few centimeters under the ground, dug with her bare hands or with a beach shovel. Wrapped in a cotton handkerchief with her embroidered initials, the objects went down into the darkness. A long time went by, like a night or a winter. Then the fairy came back as a chirping in my mother's ear. The fairy called her, guided her to the flowerbed. She indicated the spot where she would find a treasure for her.

*

That Christmas, my cousin had decided not only to receive gifts, like a little girl, but also to give presents to her parents. She wanted to experience the emotion of someone who wraps up something in a shiny piece of paper, tightens it with a ribbon, ties a bow as on a shoe, and then waits to see the look on the face of the person who receives it, weighs it in his hands, opens it slowly. For her mother she bought some chocolates with the loose change she found in the ashtray, the coins her parents would leave there to lighten their pockets. For her father she had to perform a magic trick. One day when he was in the vegetable patch and her mother downstairs in the kitchen, she opened the large wooden chest of drawers in their bedroom. A few minutes sufficed to make the gift for him. On Christmas Eve her father found a pair of old socks wrapped in star-covered paper.

Linfa

Appoggiato al muro della soffitta, avvolto nel nylon, il piccolo abete sembrava il grosso baco di un insetto dormiente. Liberato dall'involucro rimaneva con i rami tesi e richiusi. Dovevamo ricollocarli uno per uno fino a che, riconquistato il suo aspetto, ritto nel piedistallo di finto legno, l'albero poteva finalmente respirare. Era come avessimo liberato dai lacci le ali di un grande uccello impagliato che restava a fissarci grato e insieme con una contrazione di tristezza, quasi fosse stato imprigionato proprio nel momento in cui avrebbe potuto spiccare il volo. La stessa cosa doveva accadere alle volpi imbalsamate con una zampa avanti e il viso voltato, come avvertendo un odore, un fruscio, e ai piccoli roditori fermi nell'istante in cui, soddisfatti, stringono una pigna. Il piccolo abete era ciò che restava di un abete vivo ridotto allo stato di mummia, ricoperto di una patina che si era indurita e volta nella rigidità della plastica e di altri materiali sintetici. Questo era quanto io e mio fratello avevamo appurato stringendolo e tastandolo dalla base del tronco alla punta dei rami. Quella sera, dopo averlo liberato, decidemmo di lasciarlo spoglio per la notte e di rivestirlo con le palline e i nastri il mattino seguente. Mancavano ancora alcuni giorni al Natale e il piccolo abete, con i rami aperti nel tepore emanato dai termosifoni, sembrava averci chiesto proprio questo: «una notte, lasciatemi almeno questa notte per ricordare la vita libera dai lacci». Più lo guardavamo più sembrava continuare, nella mestizia di quella sua posa costretta, in un'invocazione lamentosa che prendeva il tono secco e dimesso degli aghi uno per uno: «non resisto più a questa pagliacciata, non potreste finalmente finirla con queste vostre cosine colorate?». «Ma non ti piace essere adornato dalle nostre mani?» Pensavamo provasse qualcosa di simile al brulichio sottile che affiora sulla testa quando, in piedi alle nostre spalle, alto di fronte allo specchio, un grande ci pettinava i capelli. Ma il messaggio dell'abete era stato chiaro e continuava a esserlo, mentre lo guardavamo restare teso, senza alcun cenno di flessione nei rami. Gli scatoloni pieni di addobbi che avevamo trascinato nel pomeriggio dalla soffitta, avrebbero aspettato in un angolo della sala, chiusi dal nastro adesivo.

La mattina, appena svegli, scendemmo subito a vedere l'abete. Accoccolato attorno al suo tronco, dormiva il nostro gatto tigrato, Spaghetti. Intuì i nostri visi sporti sulla soglia e aprì gli occhi in uno scatto, il muso teso a registrare le minime vibrazioni. Il piccolo abete aveva qualcosa di diverso, ma non avremmo saputo dire che cosa. Sembrava reggere i rami in modo più convinto, anche se gli restava addosso una rigidità da spaventapasseri. Quando aprimmo gli scatoloni e ci avvicinammo per iniziare ad adornarlo, quell'inconfondibile odore che penetra immediatamente nelle narici e sembra incollarsi alla pelle

Sap

Leaning against the attic wall, wrapped in nylon, the little fir tree looked like the big silkworm of a sleeping insect. Freed from the wrapping, it remained there with its branches taut and closed. We had to pull them back out, one by one, until the tree, having recovered its appearance and standing on the fake-wood pedestal, could finally breathe. It was as if we had unbound the wings of a big stuffed bird that kept staring at us both gratefully and with a twitch of sadness, as if it had been caught just when it might have flown off. The same thing must have happened to the embalmed foxes, with one paw extended and their faces turned, as if sensing a smell, a rustling, and to the small rodents stopped at the very instant when, satisfied, they clasp a pinecone. The little fir tree was what was left of a live fir tree reduced to the state of a mummy, covered with a patina that had hardened and taken on the rigidity of plastic and other synthetic materials. This was what my brother and I had ascertained by squeezing and feeling it from the base of its trunk to the tip of its branches. That evening, after we had freed the tree, we decided to leave it bare for the night and to cover it with balls and ribbons the next morning. There were still a few days before Christmas and the little fir tree, with its branches opened to the warmth emanating from the radiators, seemed to have asked us precisely this: "Let me have one night, let me have at least tonight to remember my unbound life." The more we looked at it, the more it seemed to continue, in its sad constrained pose, a plaintive invocation that took on the dry discreet tone of the needles one by one: "I can't stand this silliness anymore. Can't you finally finish up with those little colored things of yours?" "But don't you like to be decorated by our hands?" We thought it was feeling something similar to the light tickling sensation on the head when an adult, standing tall behind us, in front of the mirror, combed our hair. But the message from the fir tree had been clear and it continued to be so, as we watched it remaining taut, without any sign of bending in the branches. The taped-up boxes full of decorations which we had dragged down from the attic in the afternoon would wait in a corner of the room.

The next morning, once we had awakened, we just as soon went down to see the fir tree. Nestled around its trunk was Spaghetti, our tabby cat, sleeping. He sensed our faces protruding in the doorway and opened his eyes in a snap, his muzzle jutting out to record the slightest vibrations. The little fir tree had something different about it, but we couldn't tell what it was. It seemed to hold its branches in a more convinced way, even though it still had a scarecrow-like stiffness to it. When we opened the boxes and brought them over to start decorating the tree, that unmistakable smell, which immediately

ci avvolse: Spaghetti lo aveva marcato, riconoscendolo cippo miliare, segna-confine del suo territorio. Era un impero vasto il suo, conquistato e difeso con battaglie da cui era sempre tornato incolume, a volte con un graffio sottile che ostentava, strusciandosi con il muso sulle nostre ginocchia, medicandosi nel nostro calore e insieme giustificando quelle lunghe assenze durante le quali lo immaginavamo percorrere i muretti di cinta, inoltrarsi nel folto delle siepi, sorvegliando i limiti estremi, per confermare quanto gli apparteneva. Ora che la sua traccia si era asciugata, condensando e irradiando la sua forza, nessuna caparbia azione di strofinaccio avrebbe potuto del tutto eliminarla: quella zona rientrava nel suo territorio. Consapevoli di questo, inginocchiati sulle piastrelle fredde della sala, iniziammo ad addobbarlo. Insieme alle palline che costituivano la maggior parte delle decorazioni, c'erano sempre state piccole candele, angioletti, degli uccellini, qualche minuscolo pacco regalo. Ci piaceva ritrovarli nella carta di giornale che li aveva protetti negli anni, riconoscerli tra le nostre mani, tornare indietro nei Natali fino a quando eravamo piccolissimi e le loro forme si confondevano con i bagliori che venivano dal camino, si allungavano e si muovevano insieme al respiro del fuoco. Ogni anno qualcuno degli addobbi che aspettavamo riapparire dal fondo dello scatolone, era scomparso: rotto o semplicemente sostituito con un altro che splendeva eccessivo, con riflessi estranei, come quelli delle vetrine dei grandi magazzini.

Abbandonato a se stesso, completamente passivo, il piccolo abete si prestava anche quell'anno all'ennesimo travestimento. A volte dovevamo strin-gere un fiocco, altre volte semplicemente infilare dalla punta dei rami un nastro sottile; «abbiamo quasi fatto, resisti» gli dicevamo. Venne il momento dei nastri dorati e argentati che devono avvolgerlo tutto, scendendo dall'alto, come scie di luce morente. E infine la stella, di cartone ritagliato con le nostre forbici spuntate; ben colorata di giallo, brillava ai margini di una polvere dorata. Per metterla dovetti salire in piedi su una sedia arrivando così all'altezza della cima. «Si tratta solo di pochi giorni» gli sussurrai. Il piccolo abete rispose con un silenzio contratto, come per un nodo alla gola. L'ultimo tassello era andato al suo posto richiudendo l'albero in un'inerzia totale, quasi fosse iniziata la sua stagione di pietra.

Nel pomeriggio, mentre eravamo seduti in giardino sotto la gabbia dei cocoriti, riapparve Spaghetti. Avanzava verso di noi lentamente, come volesse nascondere qualcosa. Una volta vicino tornò subito a strusciarsi alle nostre ginocchia e a tendere il dorso alle nostre carezze. Un battito sottile sopra le nostre teste ci richiamò: con i becchi contro le sbarre i cocoriti chiedevano che fosse loro riempita di nuovo la vaschetta dei semi. Ci dedicammo a quell'opera-

penetrates the nostrils and seems to stick to the skin, enveloped us: Spaghetti had marked the fir tree, recognizing it as a milestone, a boundary mark of his territory. His empire was vast, conquered and defended with battles from which he had always came back unharmed, sometimes with a mere scratch that he flaunted, rubbing his muzzle on our knees, both healing himself in our warmth and justifying those long absences during which we imagined him walking atop the boundary walls, entering the thicket of the hedges, keeping watch over the farthest borders, to confirm what belonged to him. Now that its trace had dried, condensing and giving off its strong odor, no stubborn action of a dishcloth could have completely wiped it away: that area was within his territory. Aware of this and kneeling on the cold tiles of the room, we began to decorate the fir tree. Along with the balls that made up most of the decorations, there had always been small candles, little angels, birds, a few tiny gift packages. We liked to find them in the newspaper wrapping that had protected them over the years, recognizing them in our hands, to go back to Christmases when we were very young and their shapes would blend with the glow that came from the fireplace, would become longer and move with the breathing of fire. Every year some of the decorations that we expected to see reappearing from the bottom of the box, had disappeared: they had been broken or simply replaced with another one that was too shiny, with extraneous reflections, like those of department store windows.

Left to itself, completely passive, the little fir tree lent itself to still another disguise that year. Sometimes we had to tighten a bowknot, at other times simply to thread a thin ribbon from the tip of the branches. "We're almost done," we would tell it, "hold on." The time came for the golden and silver ribbons that must envelop the entire tree, descending from above like trails of dying light. And finally the cardboard star, cut out with our blunt scissors; a vivid yellow, it had edges glittering with golden dust. To place it atop the tree, I had to stand up on a chair to reach the top. "It will last only a few days," I whispered to the fir tree. The little tree replied with a strained silence, as if with a lump in its throat. The last piece had been put in place, closing up the tree into total inertia, as if its stone season had begun.

In the afternoon, while we were sitting in the garden under the parakeet cage, Spaghetti reappeared. He progressed slowly towards us, as if he wanted to hide something. Once he was nearby, he immediately again rubbed himself against our knees and stretched up his back to our caresses. A slight beating of wings above our heads beckoned us: with their beaks against the bars, the parakeets were asking that the seed tray be refilled. We devoted ourselves to

zione, cambiando anche l'acqua e lasciando appese due foglie di insalata e due fette di mela. Quando rientrammo nella sala Spaghetti era intento a dare piccoli colpi con le zampe alle palline più basse dell'abete, come un boxeur di fronte al suo bersaglio. Era già riuscito, in questo modo, a farne cadere e rompere due. Appena si accorse della nostra presenza si rifugiò difilato sotto al divano. Inutile richiamarlo, provare ad attirarlo facendo rotolare una pallina verso di lui, allungandogli le crocchette. Ci rassegnammo ad andarcene ma, proprio mentre eravamo sulla soglia, ci venne l'idea di nasconderci dietro la porta. Dopo pochi minuti tornava a dirigersi verso l'alberello e a colpire con le zampe le palline rimaste in basso. Stavamo per venire fuori dal nostro nascondiglio ma qualcosa ci trattenne. Con una soddisfazione che gli usciva dalla punta della coda Spaghetti passava lentamente accanto ai rami sfiorandoli appena, lasciandosi accarezzare. Poi, in un attimo, prese lo slancio per compiere un salto che lo portò a raggiungere il centro dell'albero. Stette per un poco così, come cercando un incavo tra il tronco e un ramo; infine riuscì a sbilanciare il piedistallo e a fare cadere l'abete sul pavimento. A quel punto accorremmo, per soccorrere l'albero. Sul freddo delle piastrelle splendeva di un verde intenso che non gli avevamo mai visto. Lo tirammo su e lo tenemmo tra le braccia: un forte odore di resina ci raggiunse. I suoi aghi, ora tesi a cercare il nutrimento dell'aria, ci piccavano le guance e il palmo delle mani. Spaghetti ci seguiva a pochi passi mentre io e mio fratello portavamo il piccolo abete fuori. Lo sistemammo accanto al vecchio tiglio e al pino, dove avrebbe trovato uno spazio di luce sufficiente per crescere. Presto avrebbe allungato i suoi rami, avrebbe sentito nascere le prime pigne. Si era rotto l'incantesimo che lo imprigionava di nastri e lo chiudeva in soffitta. La sua linfa sarebbe tornata a scorrere come prima.

this task, also changing the water and suspending two salad leaves and two apple slices. When we returned to the room, Spaghetti was intently giving little punches, with his paws, to the lower balls of the fir tree, like a boxer striking his target. He had already managed, in this way, to knock down and break two of them. As soon as he noticed our presence he took refuge under the sofa. It was needless to call him back out, to try to attract him by rolling a ball towards him, or by tossing him some croquettes. We resigned ourselves to going away but, just as we had reached the doorway, we had the idea of hiding behind the door. After a few minutes he again headed towards the little fir tree and struck the remaining lower balls with his paws. We were about to leave our hiding place but something held us back. With a satisfaction emanating from the tip of his tail, Spaghetti passed slowly by the branches, barely touching them, letting himself be caressed. Then, in an instant, he gathered his momentum and made a jump that landed him in the middle of the tree. He stayed like that for a while, as if seeking a nook between the trunk and a branch; finally he managed to knock the pedestal off balance and make the fir tree fall over on the floor. At that point, we rushed over to rescue the tree. On the cold tiles it was shining with an intense green that we had never seen before. We pulled it back up and held it in our arms: a strong smell of resin hit us. Its needles, now sticking outwards to seek nourishment from the air, pricked our cheeks and the palms of our hands. Spaghetti followed us for a few steps while my brother and I carried the little fir tree outside. We placed it next to the old linden tree and the pine, where it would find enough room and light to grow. Soon it would make its branches grow, hear the first fir cones being born. The spell that had bound and closed it up in the attic had been broken. Its sap would again flow as before.

L'incanto della morte. Rosaspina

Negli anni in cui le parole scritte erano segni indecifrati, consegnati a un mondo che non potevo raggiungere neanche sulle punte dei piedi, un libro si apriva soltanto per i disegni che conteneva o perché la voce di mio padre lo attraversava, per strade del tutto sconosciute, anche se il suo indice sembrava tracciarle, lasciando brevi scie in cui i caratteri neri, come oggetti in una notte magica, prendevano vita, all'unisono sillabavano silenziosi la stessa storia che mio padre teneva sul petto, aperta, pronta a voltarsi e a cambiare figure. Era la sua voce a portare le storie, semidistesi nel grande letto dove mio fratello più piccolo vegliava, con orecchie minuscole che si richiudevano presto, contenendo qualche scia di suono e senso nel silenzio caldo. Quando il sonno aveva preso entrambi nella sua rete, un traghettatore invisibile ci lasciava oltre il corridoio, nei nostri letti. Oppure a volte, arrampicati uno su una spalla e uno sull'altra, come due piccole scimmie bilanciate, ci portava attraverso le due rampe di scale e ci depositava direttamente nella nostra camera. Un registratore sul comodino avvolgeva e riavvolgeva cassette gialle e azzurre che si compravano in edicola, insieme a un libretto illustrato con le storie che la voce sul nastro raccontava. Mentre al piano di sotto gli adulti sostavano al fruscio della televisione o al tramestio dei piatti, noi oltre il territorio impervio delle scale, in una piccola valle in alto, eravamo abbandonati alla stanza, consegnati alla notte, mentre la voce del nastro muoveva in figure le vene e i nodi dell'armadio, attraversava in un soffio di vita i vestiti appesi, risvegliava dal torpore gli oggetti che non erano in pace, che slittavano e scricchiolavano ancora prima di raggiungere le loro coordinate spaziali.

Di tutte le storie che sostarono in quegli anni nella nostra camera, una si fermò dentro di me, intrappolata nell'incavo della cassa toracica, lì dove si spezzava ogni tanto il respiro, costringendomi a inseguire l'ultimo sbadiglio, a tendermi con la bocca spalancata, come se l'aria non riuscisse a saziarmi. Una mattina mia madre nel corridoio di fronte all'ombra di una donna dice con orgoglio: «sa a memoria la favola di Rosaspina. Raccontala Franca». E così uscì da me per la prima volta, attraverso il filo di voce che avevo intessuto, una parola di seguito all'altra, liberandosi, infrangendo un silenzio fitto di spine, oltre le porte del castello addormentato, la storia di quella ragazza dal nome dolce e appuntito.

Ogni bambino che impara a memoria una storia impara la sua storia. Non lo sa, eppure parla in lui, nelle forme della fiaba, la vita annodata nel sangue che si scioglierà, negli anni. Ci vuole tempo perché si allunghino i capelli alle ragazze imprigionate nella torre, accovacciate all'ombra delle pareti, con l'unica compagnia di una mano che porta i pasti e scompare. Molto tempo perché i capelli, intrecciati, attraverso l'unica piccola finestra, scendano il muro

The Enchantment of Death: Briar Rose

In the years when written words were indecipherable signs, entrusted to a world that I couldn't even reach on tiptoes, a book would be opened only for its illustrations or because my father's voice was passing through it, over completely unknown roads, although his index finger seemed to trace them out, leaving short trails in which black letters, like objects in a magical night, came to life, silently spelling out in unison the same story which, open and ready to shift and change its pictures, my father was holding on his chest. It was his voice that brought the stories to us as we three were half-lying in the big bed where my little brother was staying up late, with his tiny ears that would soon close, containing a trail of sound and sense in the warm silence. When sleep had taken both of us into its net, an invisible ferryman would leave us across the hallway in our beds. Or sometimes, when we had each climbed up on one of his shoulders, like two small monkeys balanced on them, he would take us up the two flights of stairs and deposit us directly in our room. A tape recorder on the bedside table would wind and rewind blue and yellow cassettes that were bought at newsstands, along with the illustrated booklet comprising the stories that the voices on the tapes told. While the adults downstairs were at a standstill over the crackle of the television or the clatter of the dishes, we, beyond the inaccessible territory of the stairs, in a small valley on high, were abandoned to our room, handed over to the night, while the taped voice turned the veins and knots of the wardrobe into moving shapes, went through the hanging clothes in a breath of life, awakened from torpor the objects that were not at peace, that were still shifting and creaking before reaching their spatial positions.

Of all the stories that stopped over in our room back then, one halted inside me, trapped in the hollow of my ribcage, right where my breathing would break off every now and then, forcing me to keep chasing after the last yawn, to stretch out with my mouth wide open as if the air couldn't fill me enough. One morning my mother, standing in the hallway in front of a woman's shadow, said proudly: "She knows the tale of 'Briar Rose' by heart. Tell it to her, Franca." And so the story of that girl with the sweet, thorny name came out of me for the first time, through the thread of a voice that I had woven, one word after another, breaking free, shattering a thorny silence, beyond the doors of the sleeping castle.

Every child who learns a story by heart learns his or her own story. Unbeknownst to the child, it speaks inside her, through the forms of the fairy tale, the life knotted in her blood that will dissolve over the years. For the girls imprisoned in the tower and crouching in the shadow of the walls, with the company only of a hand bringing meals and vanishing, it takes time for their

fino a sfiorare la terra. Allora un figlio di re andato a caccia nei boschi, arriva in quel luogo sperduto, e aiutandosi con i capelli come fossero una corda di seta, sale. Questo motivo presente in molte fiabe, come ad esempio in *Raperonzolo* dei fratelli Grimm, narra di un periodo di isolamento e di maturazione necessario alla ragazza prima del suo incontro con l'altro e del suo ingresso alla vita come donna. Anche le parole crescono nella solitudine prima di ritrovare l'uscita, di aprire la nostra prigionia al mondo. Se il contatto con l'altro avviene prima del tempo, la ragazza si ferirà e cadrà come morta, cercando di recuperare nel sonno la crescita che le è stata spezzata. Così le parole pronunciate prima che abbiano affondato le radici nella nostra voce, sono strappate, non possono compiersi in una frase o in un verso, chiedono solo di continuare a dormire.

Nel momento in cui pronunciavo per la prima volta la storia di *Rosaspina*, mi accorgevo di averla in me, nel nastro buio e frammentato della memoria. Un prodigio semplice e misterioso come quello che mi portava in bicicletta da sola, con due rotelle piccole aggiunte ai lati. Pronunciavo la mia morte e la mia rinascita, la mia segregazione e la mia uscita dalla torre… ero già salva! Il principe che viene al risveglio siamo noi stessi, armati di coraggio e di spada, noi stessi decisi a bucare il silenzio, pronti a parlare. Allora il roveto si apre ai nostri passi, non è nient'altro che un cerchio fitto di rose presto sfiorite.

hair to grow long. Much time so that the braided hair can go through the unique small window and down the wall until it touches the ground. Then a king's son, who has gone hunting in the woods, arrives in that remote place and, using the hair as if it were a silk rope, climbs. This motif present in many fairy tales, such as in the Brothers Grimm story of "Rapunzel," tells of an isolation and maturation period necessary for a girl before she meets the Other and enters life as a woman. Words also grow in solitude before finding a way out, to open our captivity to the world. If contact with the Other takes place ahead of time, the girl will be wounded and fall as if she has died, trying to recover, in sleep, her growth that has been broken off. The words spoken before they have taken root in our voice are thus torn out, cannot be brought to completion in a sentence or poem, and only ask to continue sleeping.

At the very moment I was reciting the story of "Briar Rose" for the first time, I realized that it was inside me, on the dark, fragmented ribbon of memory. A simple mysterious miracle like the one bearing me forward alone on my bicycle, with two small wheels added to the sides. I was pronouncing my death and my rebirth, my isolation in and my exit from the tower. . . I was already saved! The prince who comes to reawaken us is ourselves, armed with courage, a sword, and determined to pierce the silence, ready to speak. Then the thorny bush opens as we step forward: it is a mere circle thick with roses soon to wither.

Storia di un terremoto

Atterrati sul mondo a breve distanza l'uno dall'altro, riuscivano ormai entrambi a muoversi sui piedi, aggrappandosi a qualcosa. Era finito da poco il tempo delle strisciate sul pavimento freddo, facendo leva sulle mani restando seduti, in quello strano modo che aveva adottato il più piccolo per spostarsi. Insieme alla sorella aveva imparato a salire gattonando le scale e poi a lasciarsi scivolare giù, con le gambe diritte, gradino dopo gradino, affidandosi al morbido del pannolone, in una discesa interrotta da brevi pause. In seguito sarebbero calati l'uno dopo l'altro come inaspettati pompieri sul passamano di legno, lenti e cauti all'inizio, poi precipitando festosi. La casa era un parco giochi che diventava di giorno in giorno più grande, con il giardino, il garage, e la cantina che di lì a pochi anni si sarebbe lasciata scoprire fino agli angoli più riposti.

Un pomeriggio, mentre giocavano nella sala tra le mattonelle gialle e il divano, una sagoma scura lanciò l'allarme gridando: «I bambini! ci sono i bambini!». La nonna nel suo grembiule nero a fiori tornò a pronunciare quella frase, con un tono che si faceva sempre più acuto, implorante. Seguendo la scia di quel richiamo i due fratelli si trovarono trasportati verso il parallele-pipedo del corridoio dove movimenti immensi scuotevano l'aria inclinando le pareti ora da un lato, ora dall'altro. Si fermarono tra le ante di una porta a vetri che creava una sorta di anticamera, da cui potevano guardare. All'altro capo del corridoio, il padre e la madre lottavano. Scosso dalle fondamenta, il mondo tremava. Mentre la minaccia si espandeva nell'aria, tornò di nuovo acuta, incrinandosi nel finale la frase: «I bambini! Ci sono i bambini!». Quelle parole venivano dal corpo della nonna, avevano tutta la sua materia solida, come se si fosse messa in piedi, con il suo grembiule, a dividere i due contendenti, a sbarrare ai nipoti la visuale. E invece, con l'irresistibile forza di un precipizio, il suo grido aveva portato i bambini proprio lì, sulla soglia, nello spazio-tempo in cui avrebbero dovuto non essere. Ritti uno di fianco all'altro, esposti a quel lungo lampo che iniziava a disegnare la loro sagoma, erano come ombre immerse nel buio del negativo. «Ci siamo. Non possiamo più scomparire» –la bambina sentiva la concretezza delle gambe che la tenevano in piedi, accanto al fratello più piccolo, funambolo vacillante, ma in piedi. «Siamo un errore, ma non possiamo più scomparire», le disse una voce che non pensava, che leggeva soltanto le cose che vedeva come sillabe che si stampavano nella mente. E mentre continuava all'altro capo del corridoio la lotta, con gli spettatori accecati dall'occhio di bue capovolto, «staremo con l'uno o con l'altra, forse saremo divisi» disse ancora la voce che leggeva la realtà alla bambina: un libro senza figure, che non avrebbe voluto sfogliare. E immaginò che il fratello, così piccolo, nel suo scomposto alfabeto, fosse protetto e confuso da qualcosa di opaco, non capisse. E con la polvere magica del suo pensiero gli donò due foglie che gli coprissero gli occhi.

An Earthquake Story

Having landed in the world at a short distance in time from each other, they were now both able to get around on their own two feet by holding onto something. The period had just ended when they would edge themselves across the cold floor by using their hands as levers while remaining seated, in that strange manner that the littlest one had adopted to move around. Along with his sister he had learned to crawl up the stairs and then to let himself slip back down, his legs straight, stair step by stair step, relying on the softness of the diaper, in a descent interrupted by short halts. Later, one after the other, they would climb down the wooden handrail like unexpected firemen, slowly and cautiously at first, then rushing down joyfully. The house was a playground that was getting bigger day by day, with the garden, the garage, and the basement whose most remote nooks, in a few years, would let themselves be discovered.

One afternoon, while they were playing in the room between the yellow floor tiles and the sofa, a dark silhouette sounded the alarm, shouting: "The children! The children are here!" Wearing her black, flowered apron, their grandmother came back to utter these words in a tone that became more and more shrill, pleading. Following in the wake of the call, the two siblings were drawn to the parallele-piped of the hallway, where vast movements were making the air shake and tilting the walls from one side to the other. The children stopped between the panels of a glass door that created a sort of anteroom, from which they could watch. At the other end of the hallway, their father and mother were fighting. Shaken at its foundations, the world was trembling. As the threat spread through the air, it came back acutely again, the words cracking at the end: "The children! The children are here!" The words came from the grandmother's body, from all her solid matter, as if she had stood up, wearing her apron, to divide the two contenders, to block the view from the grandchildren. And instead, with the irresistible force of a precipice, her shout had led the children right there, to the threshold, into a space and a time in which they should not have been. Standing side by side, exposed to the long beam of light that began to outline their shapes, they were like shadows immersed in the darkness of a photographic negative. "Here we are. We can no longer disappear"—the little girl felt her solid legs, which kept her standing next to her younger brother, an unsteady tightrope walker, but standing. "We are a mistake, but we can no longer disappear," said a voice that was not thinking, that was only reading the things it saw as syllables printed in the mind. And as the fight continued, at the other end of the hallway, with the spectators blinded by the turned-around spotlight, "we will be with one or the other, perhaps we will be separated," said the voice that was reading the reality to the little girl: a book without illustrations, which she would not have wished to leaf through. And she imagined that her brother, so small, with his halting

A un tratto la lotta si fermò: la fronte della madre si era aperta in un piccolo taglio fiottante. Poco dopo arrivò la zia e i bambini sedettero entrambi dietro l'auto che accompagnava la madre al pronto soccorso. Voltandosi verso di loro la zia disse subito *non è niente. Non si è fatta niente. Litigano ma si vogliono bene*, come mettendosi a carponi per parlare attraverso una porta minuscola.

Le parole dicevano il contrario di quello che la bambina aveva visto; con un tono persuasivo e fermo le imponevano il silenzio, stendevano su quella sequenza di immagini un lenzuolo, come si fa con i morti.

Passarono gli anni e quel cadavere che non mandava odore sembrava dimenticato, così bene mimetizzato in tutto quanto può sembrare, o sforzarsi di essere, la vita di ogni giorno. Ma un pomeriggio, in uno dei primi anni di scuola, mentre la bambina camminava verso casa con una compagna di classe, sentì chiedersi se era vero che i suoi genitori si stavano separando. Rispose subito che no, non era vero. Lei non sapeva niente… Ma mentre pronunciava quella parola l'odore dolciastro di morte era nel frattempo salito e iniziava a pizzicarle il naso; allora chiese «chi te l'ha detto». «I miei genitori» rispose sicura la compagna. Ne stavano parlando e lei dalla stanza vicina aveva sentito. Due rondini stridendo si abbassarono con i pensieri: «Mi hanno ingannato… senza neanche dirmelo… e non pensano a me, a noi…». E poi, sfiorata la terra, tornarono subito in alto. Vide la sequenza in cui qualcuno, con fare da gnomo, si sarebbe chinato verso lei e il fratello a dire che uno dei suoi genitori sarebbe andato a vivere in un'altra casa, ma avrebbero continuato a volersi bene e, naturalmente, a volere bene a loro. Prima che questa scena si avverasse e la più terribile scarica di terremoto devastasse il mondo, aveva ancora tempo per fare qualcosa. Li avrebbe tenuti sotto stretta sorveglianza, per verificare se era vero (ma era vero) che non erano uniti. Avrebbe guardato anche dietro il lenzuolo delle parole che stendevano attenti sopra la cancrena e, al primo indizio, mentre l'odore dolciastro avanzava, avrebbe lottato per reclamare la sua presenza. Le comparve subito l'immagine del fratello piccolo, così buffo e perso nei suoi giochi che decise che non lo avrebbe svegliato: avrebbe rinunciato ad averlo al suo fianco, avrebbe colpevolmente taciuto, ma si sarebbe battuta anche per lui.

words, was protected and confused by something opaque, and that he did not understand. And with some magical dust from her mind, she gave him two leaves to cover his eyes.

Suddenly the fight stopped: the mother's forehead had been opened into a small gushing cut. Shortly thereafter, their aunt arrived and the children both sat in the back seat of the car accompanying their mother to the emergency ward. Turning around towards them, their aunt immediately said *it's nothing. Nothing has happened to her. They argue but they love each other*—as if she were getting down on her hands and knees to talk through a tiny door.

The words said the opposite of what the girl had seen; in a firm, persuasive tone, they imposed silence on her, spreading a shroud over that sequence of images, as is done with the dead.

Years went by and that corpse that didn't smell seemed forgotten, so well camouflaged in all that everyday life can seem, or try, to be. But one afternoon, in one of her first years at school, while the girl was walking home with a classmate, she heard the classmate asking if it were true that her parents were separating. She answered immediately that no, it wasn't true; she didn't know anything. . . But as she was uttering these words the sweetish smell of death had, in the meantime, risen and started to tingle her nose; then she asked: "Who told you that?" "My parents," said her classmate confidently. They were talking about it and she had overheard them from the next room. Two squealing swallows flew down with these thoughts: "They've tricked me. . . without even telling me. . . and they aren't thinking of me, of us. . ." And then, having swept low over the ground, they suddenly flew back high. She saw the scene where someone, acting like gnome, would bend over to her and her brother to say that one of their parents would go to live in another house but they would continue to love each other and, naturally, to love them. Before this event came true and the most terrible earthquake devastated the world, she still had time to do something. She would keep a close eye on them to see if it were true (but it was true) that they were not united. She would also look behind the shroud of words that was spreading carefully over the gangrene and, at the first clue, while the sweetish smell was advancing, she would fight to claim her presence. The image of the little brother suddenly appeared to her, so funny and lost in his games that she decided that she would not rouse him: she would give up on having him by her side, she would guiltily remain silent, but she would fight for him too.

La bambina che imparò a volare

Sul davanzale tornava a posarsi un uccellino che batteva i vetri con il becco, li sfiorava con le ali, e poi volava via. I fruscii e i piccoli colpi che faceva sembravano le lettere di un alfabeto da decifrare. Veniva in ore diverse, a volte svegliandola la mattina, altre nel pomeriggio, mentre china su un foglio disegnava. Un giorno che aveva piovuto e lei era scesa nel giardino per guardare dentro le pozzanghere, vide riflesso quell'uccellino che veniva alla finestra. Si voltò indietro, guardò sui rami più alti degli alberi fino alla cima, sul prato e in mezzo ai cespugli, ma non lo vide. Tornò a guardare nella pozzanghera più grande: era lì, posato su qualcosa di invisibile. Non poté fare a meno di sfiorarlo, piano con un dito, per non farlo volare via. Ma appena infranse la superficie dell'acqua, lui scomparve. Non sapeva più dove cercarlo, se sul tetto o negli angoli più nascosti del giardino. Mentre pensava a dove potesse essere, iniziò a sentire sulle spalle un'inquietudine sempre più forte che non la faceva stare ferma in nessun luogo. La peluria bionda che aveva sulle braccia crebbe, si fece bianca, poi grigia e infine marrone. I bulbi dei peli si erano fatti d'osso; le stavano spuntando piccole piume, come quelle di un passero caduto dal nido. Nel giro di qualche ora il suo piumaggio crebbe tanto che potè iniziare a esercitarsi nelle prime prove di volo: correre e poi, raggiunta la velocità massima, saltare. I suoi salti la staccavano dal prato, la portavano sui rami più bassi degli alberi. Quando arrivò al tiglio, continuò a fare brevi voli dentro la sua chioma. A un tratto, si ritrovò sulla cima, si fermò a guardare il giardino, la casa dove aveva vissuto, e puntò dritta verso l'azzurro.

The Little Girl Who Learned How to Fly

A bird kept alighting on the windowsill and pecking the panes with its beak, brushing the glass with its wings, and then flying off. The rustling and the small beating sounds it made seemed letters of an alphabet to be deciphered. The bird would come at different times, sometimes in the morning and waking her, sometimes in the afternoon when she was bending over a sheet of paper and drawing. One day, after it had rained and she had gone down into the garden to look into the puddles, she saw a reflection of the little bird that came to the window. She turned around, looked at the highest branches of the trees, all the way to the top, then at the lawn and into the bushes, but couldn't spot the bird. She looked back into the biggest puddle: there it was, resting on something invisible. She couldn't help but touch it with her finger, slowly, so that it wouldn't fly away. But as soon as her finger broke the surface of the water, the bird vanished. She no longer knew where to search for it, whether on the roof or in the most hidden recesses of the garden. As she was thinking about where it might be, she began to feel, in her shoulders, an ever stronger restlessness that kept her from staying still anywhere. The blond hair on her arms grew, turned white, then gray and finally brown. The hair bulbs had become bone; small feathers were popping up, like those of a sparrow fallen from its nest. Within a few hours her plumage had grown so much that she could start practicing her first test flights: running and then, having reached the maximum speed, leaping. Her leaps brought her off the lawn, carried her to the lowest branches of the trees. When she arrived at the linden tree, she continued to make short flights inside its foliage. Suddenly she found herself at the top. She stopped to look down at the garden, the house where she had lived, and headed straight for the blue.

Un letto di sassi

Ora stai stringendo una maniglia. Le dita le ho già perse e quello che abbracciavi ora è una porta. Ferma un passo davanti a te. Devi aprirla e andare. Non capisci. Non vedi che non vivono animali in questa casa? Il mio cane rubava dai vicini. Cibo, come un randagio; non sarebbe morto di fame, certo, ma l'ho lasciato a degli amici tempo fa. E tu che quasi mi hai mangiato dalle mani come un cucciolo non ancora svezzato. Ti ha spogliato troppo presto la mia voce, ho dovuto vestirti d'acqua e cingerti al collo, o defluivi in un gorgo di capelli nella vasca. Ti ha portato la paura fino a me. Non potevo saperlo dall'inizio. Leggevo solo il passo silenzioso che ti aveva consegnata, con il tuo caldo carico di peso. Lo sapevi dove stavamo andando. Per questo appena mi allontanava un respiro, ti nascondevi. Sperando in una mimesi. Di uscire dalle tracce. Di rimanere confusa nella sedia. Ma non eri il bersaglio. Tu, così approssimata, così lontana da te stessa da non ricordare una donna; forse una forma umana sull'asfalto, in gesso bianco. Scampata alla morte, la contiene nella piega di un braccio, nella tensione spezzata di una gamba. Così ti ho vista nella luce della prima mattina, dormire. La persiana rotta non l'aggiusto, mi piace immaginare questo sud che si capovolge in un lontanissimo nord d'Europa. Ma è una luce più tiepida; ora è un laccio leggero alle caviglie. Le ore sono ancora poche, soltanto sei: è appena cresciuto il giorno, non c'è da temere; ma presto ruggirà come una belva. Finché non torniamo in piedi siamo salvi. Poi dovrò caricarti sulle spalle, e ripartire alla volta del lavandino, del corridoio, secondo la strada che ci aspetta.

Non eri il bersaglio... Le cose accadono semplicemente. Altri pesci si aggiravano lenti, sfiorandosi, nella piccola vasca del ristorante. Chi ha puntato il dito nel vetro ci ha stretti nello sguardo finché non siamo stati estratti. Ora sta a noi giocare la parte, una parte diversa e fraterna. Perché sono io che devo portarti, in cammino dal letto, per questi tre giorni, con la pressione del tuo peso che trema ad ogni mia scossa, sulle mie spalle. Lo capisco il silenzio, a cos'altro potevi affidarti? Ma ogni tanto parlavi nelle soste del viaggio: mi arrivava il suono lontano di uno scorrere d'acqua, che non traduceva interamente i riflessi di gioia e le ombre.

Chiudevo le orecchie nel sonno e ti accarezzavo di nuovo un piede, una mano che lasciavi dondolare nel vuoto. Se avessi parlato di più non avrei potuto ascoltarti. Dovevo ricordare la strada, tracciare di nuovo nella mente il cammino o ti avrei lasciato cadere a un tratto su una roccia, prima del tempo. Non devi rimproverarti il silenzio. Ti contenevi come un fascio di legna, io con le mani ti aiutavo a non perderti, a non abbandonare la stretta prima di arrivare nel luogo deciso. Un ago della mia voce l'aveva segnato appena ti ho visto:

A Bed of Stones

Now you're holding a handle. I have already lost my fingers and what you were hugging now is a door. It stands a step ahead of you. You must open it and go out. You don't understand. Can't you see that no animals live in this house? My dog would steal from the neighbors. Food, like a stray; it wouldn't have starved to death, of course, but I left it with friends long ago. And you who almost ate from my hands like a not-yet-weaned puppy. My voice stripped you too soon, I had to dress you in water and grip your neck, or you would drain away into a whirlpool of hair in the bathtub. Fear brought you all the way to me. I couldn't know this from the beginning. I was only reading into the silent footstep that had delivered you to me, with your warm burden of weight. You knew where we were going. For this reason, as soon you had gone a breath away from me, you would hide. Hoping for a mimesis. To leave no tracks behind. To remain confused on the chair. But you weren't the target. You, so approximate, so far from yourself that you didn't recall a woman; perhaps a human form on the asphalt, in white chalk. Having escaped death, she has it in the crease of an arm, in the broken tension of a leg. This is how I saw you sleeping in the early morning light. I don't repair the broken shutter, I like to imagine this South turned upside down into a very distant northern part of Europe. But it is a warmer light; now it's a weightless ankle strap. It's still early, only six o'clock: the daylight has just increased, there is no need to fear; but soon it will roar like a beast. Until we get back on our feet we are safe. Then I will have to load you on my shoulders, and leave for the washbasin, the hallway, depending on what lies ahead of us.

You weren't the target. . . Things just happen. Other fish were slowly swimming around, touching each other, in the small restaurant aquarium. The one who placed his finger on the pane held us in his gaze until we had been taken out. Now it's up to us to play the part, a different and friendly part. Because it is I who must carry you on my shoulders as I walk from the bed, for these three days, with the pressure of your weight that trembles with every one of my shakes. I understand the silence, what else could you rely on? But every now and then you would speak during the halts of the journey: I would hear the distant sound of flowing water, which did not fully translate the reflections of joy and the shadows.

I closed my ears when asleep and caressed your foot again, a hand that you let swing in the void. If I had spoken more I couldn't have listened to you. I had to remember the route, trace the path again in my mind or I would have suddenly dropped you on a rock, ahead of time. You don't have to blame yourself for the silence. You contained yourself like a bundle of wood; with

fra tre giorni, arriveremo fra tre giorni. Manon eri il bersaglio, tu... Se eri già ferita, la colpa è del tuo affidarti. In pochi passi di sonnambula hai spezzato la distanza. Io desideravo la tua sagoma, la tua fragilità. Sai quanta inconsapevolezza è necessaria perché una volontà si compia esattamente. Mi ero concentrato in questa leggerezza di piombo, calibravo e dondolavo internamente. Ma tu a un tratto hai oltrepassato la linea, come per ribadire che esistevi, che c'eri, tremante fuori della sagoma, in una forma diversa. O forse non ti eri affidata nel profondo, sussultavi nella tua fede bambina, per diventare altro. Ma non c'è tempo per crescere in questi giorni. E tu non puoi crescere oltre. Sono il padre che ti porta e la strada si fa sempre più in salita. È buio, il tuo peso inizia a curvarmi la schiena, a piegarmi le ginocchia. Non agitarti, non parlare, continua a sentire la mia stretta, le mie mani che ci sono.

Siamo arrivati. Non piangere, non sporgerti dalla rupe. Aspetta qui, seduta nell'erba umida.

Una volta un ragazzo è stato salvato, ma i miracoli non avvengono sempre. Io poi non ci credo.

Non guardarmi così. Ti abbraccio ora un'ultima volta.

Non eri tu il bersaglio. Ci hanno scelti. Hanno deciso così.

*

Spazzare mi piace. Puoi lasciarti cadere nei gesti e dimenticare tutto. Anche lavare i piatti mi piace. Avere le mani bagnate.

Tu ora mi aiuti un po', così facciamo prima. Hai capito che presto devi andare. Hai capito come? Guarda la polvere che si era accumulata, guarda queste macchie come spariscono.

Poi mi fai un massaggio sul collo. Qui, dove i piccoli gatti vengono sollevati dalle madri. Hai visto come piegano la schiena e si consegnano con le zampe al vuoto. Un ponte che non poggia su niente, un arco trasportato. Il peso concentrato negli occhi, consapevoli, mentre tutto il corpo è leggero. È questo che devi imparare. Guardami bene. Qualcosa mi sta portando da un luogo a un altro. E tu non puoi esserci.

*

È inutile che ti nascondi negli angoli della casa. Anche così sottile, attaccata alla parete o mimetizzata al pavimento, ti stanerei.

Vedi che ti ho trovata. Ecco dove sei. In un tremore appena percettibile, da minuscole antenne sembri avvertire quello che sta per accadere. Non posso schiacciarti. Non temere, non ne sono capace. Ti avvicino le mani perché,

my hands I helped you not to get lost, not to let go of your grip before reaching the determined place. A needle in my voice had indicated it as soon as I saw you: within three days, we will arrive within three days. But it wasn't you the target . . . If you were already wounded, the fault lies in your trusting. With a few sleepwalker's footsteps you broke down the distance. I desired your shape, your fragility. You know how much unawareness is required for a wish to be carried out exactly. I was concentrated in this lightness of lead, I was swinging and assaying inside. But you suddenly crossed the line, as if to hammer in the fact that you existed, that you were there, trembling outside of the shape, in a different form. Or perhaps you had not entrusted yourself to the depths, you jumped up with a child's faith, to become someone else. But these days, there's no time to grow. And you can't grow any further. I am the father who takes you and the road becomes ever steeper. It's dark, your weight starts to arch my back, bend my knees. Don't fret, don't talk, keep feeling my grasp, my hands that are there.

We have arrived. Don't cry, don't lean over the cliff. Wait here, sitting in the damp grass.

Once a boy was saved, but miracles don't always happen. Nor do I believe in them.

Don't look at me like that. I embrace you now one last time.

You weren't the target. They have chosen us. They have decided thus.

*

I like sweeping. You can let yourself fall into the movements and forget everything. I also like washing dishes. To have wet hands.

Now help me a little so we'll finish early. You've understood that soon you'll have to go. Have you understood how? Look at the dust that had piled up, look at how these stains disappear.

Then you massage my neck. Here, where small cats are lifted by their mothers. You've seen how they bend their backs and entrust themselves, their paws dangling in the void. A bridge standing on nothing, an arch borne along. The weight concentrated in the mindful eyes while the whole body is lightweight. This is what you must learn. Look at me well. Something is carrying me from one place to another. And you cannot be there.

*

It's useless for you to hide in the corners of the house. Even tiny as you are, attached to the wall or camouflaged on the floor, I'll hunt you down.

disorientata, nei tuoi movimenti minimi, tu possa lentamente salire su un mio dito ed essere trasportata fuori.

Non c'è più posto qui. Ti ho detto quale legge governa la mia vita: fuggire la pressione. I miei progetti, gli altri, tutto questo mondo che mi lega al collo e mi trascina come un cane zoppo. E io che voglio soltanto restare in casa, nel silenzio. Liberare le immagini intrappolate nella fronte, unire final mente le sillabe come vorrei. Te l'ho detto chiudendo gli occhi sul morbido che termina nelle tue ginocchia. Ma forse ti eri protetta le orecchie restando a lungo sottacqua ieri, vicino agli scogli. Non avevi ancora capito che la legge comprende anche te: non ci sono eccezioni o attenuanti. La pressione esercitata da un corpo, anche dal tuo, mi toglie il respiro.

*

Dice *la vasca, andiamo nella vasca.* È così che si uccidono i bambini. Le madri non se ne accorgono nemmeno. L'acqua uscita da loro in uno strappo, è arrivata a riempire un bacile, un lavandino, un lago. Superfici quiete che non contengono niente, aspettano qualcosa. Te lo chiedono allungandoti il viso in un riflesso mostruoso. Tagliandoti le braccia nella brezza. Piangevano i bambini, strideva senza fine qualcosa che stava per avvenire, che era avvenuto. Così si inquietano gli animali, strappano la catena, battono le sbarre, prima che si scateni un terremoto. Poi, a un tratto, il pianto si ferma: fluttuanti nel silenzio, gli occhi a catturare il movimento continuo di luce. Basta una mano a tenerli, una mano che leggermente prema sul petto, per non farli risorgere, per non farli rinascere più.

Una svolta, ed eravamo nel cuore del bosco. Più neri del buio i rami si contorcevano tra le foglie, salivano coprendo il cielo. «Hai un accendino?». E sei scomparso. Sei tornato e mi hai guidato fra i tronchi, fino a un luogo dove si apriva una piccola vasca. Era vuota. Hai acceso tre candele e non hai detto più niente.

Per questo fuori dal bosco mi avevi accarezzato la testa. Più a lungo, come dovessi dimenticare qualcosa. Avrei dovuto rimanere lì, a un lato della strada. Eppure avevo camminato. Sui miei piedi ti seguivo, ti avevo seguito fino alla soglia. La vasca si riempiva di serpi, di vermi e di tutte le zampe che brulicavano dal tuo petto peloso.

Andiamo a letto, ho detto appena ho potuto parlare di nuovo.

*

Fuori dalla vasca, in piedi, mi versi acqua sulla schiena. Inarcata sulle ginocchia piegate, le braccia tese, in precario equilibrio. Una tua mano ha il

You see that I've found you. Here's where you are. With a barely perceptible quivering of your minute antennae, you seem to sense what is about to happen. I can't crush you. Don't be afraid, I'm unable to do so. Because you're disoriented, I approach my hands so that you, with your slight movements, can slowly climb onto one of my fingers and be carried outside.

There's no place here anymore. I've told you which law rules my life: fleeing pressure. My projects, other people, this whole world that leashes me, dragging me along like a lame dog. I just want to stay home, in silence. To free the images trapped in my forehead, at last join the syllables as I wish. I've told you this, shutting my eyes on the soft spot that ends with your knees. But maybe you had shielded your ears by staying underwater for a long time yesterday, near the rocks. You hadn't yet understood that the law also includes you: there are no exceptions, no extenuating circumstances. The pressure exerted by a body, even yours, takes my breath away.

*

He says *the bathtub, let's go to the bathtub*. This is how children are killed. Mothers don't even notice. The water that flowed out of them in a start ended up filling a basin, a washbasin, a lake. Quiet surfaces that contain nothing, wait for something. They ask you about it, stretching your face into a monstrous reflection. By cutting off your arms in the breeze. The children were crying, something that was about to happen, that had happened, was relentlessly screaming. Just as animals become worried, breaking the chain, beating against the bars, before an earthquake is unleashed. Then, suddenly, the weeping stops: floating in the silence, the eyes capture the continuous movement of light. A hand is enough to hold down the children, a hand pushing down lightly on their chests, so that they will not re-emerge, not be reborn anymore.

A turning point, and we were in the heart of the woods. Blacker than dark, the branches were twisting among the leaves, rising and concealing the sky. "Do you have a lighter?" And you disappeared. You came back and guided me through the tree trunks, to a place opening onto a small bathtub. It was empty. You lit three candles and said nothing more.

This is why, outside of the woods, you caressed my head. For a long while, as if I had to forget something. I should have stayed there, on one side of the road. Yet I had walked. On my feet I was following you, I had followed you to the threshold. The bathtub filled with snakes, worms, and all the legs that swarmed from your hairy chest.

Let's go to bed, I said as soon as I could speak again.

*

sapone che cancella gli odori e le tracce. L'altra regge l'acqua che torna a riavvolgermi. Tiepida, dentro le fasce che stringevano le madri. Trattenendo il tremore dei gesti, liberando soltanto i movimenti del collo. La testa che può voltarsi da un lato e dall'altro. Gli occhi che si possono aprire e richiudere. La bocca che ti può chiamare, che può gridare, piangere, e tornare a dormire.

*

Dormiamo nel sangue della partenza. Dormiamo a un giorno di addio. Ma di nuovo qualcosa mi sveglia per prima e ti ritrovo affondato in te stesso, in un pozzo che non mi contiene. Così tu cadi davvero nel sonno e continui a capofitto a precipitare, mentre io ci scivolo lentamente, dopo essermi aggrappata e a lungo assicurata alla tua banchina. Mi allontano per un breve tratto, senza perdere alle spalle l'arco disteso dell'orizzonte. Respira. Sono le onde del mare che entrano ed escono da casa tua, gli ospiti dell'estate che accogli nella stanza accanto, nei letti che restano sempre: la casa è più grande di te, è per una famiglia che si compone e scompone, tra richiami e gridi, voli e ritorni improvvisi. Nell'inverno e per lunghi momenti deserta, poi, nella corrente della sera, d'improvviso affollata da una colonia di gabbiani. L'uno accanto all'altro cerchiano un'isola, un luogo prescelto nella rovina.

Resto ad ascoltare il mare nel tuo respiro e aspetto che la corrente riaffiori, e sia anche per te la chiara distesa della mattina. Tolgo spine dal corpo scrivendo ai bordi del letto, brevi frasi che bruciano subito. In viaggio ho visto campi di stoppie annerirsi a un margine di fuoco.

Se ti sveglia un sottile crepitare di fiamme sono io che lentamente avanzo. Brucio stecche appuntite, quello che resta di una mietitura. Ma tu non ascolti. Di questo nero che si avvicina senti forse soltanto un voltare di pagine. Il letto è pieno di sangue e tu dormi. Dormi nel sangue mio.

Tutto il giorno non parlo. Se parlo si deforma il viso. La bocca, una piega spaventosa. Cerco di camuffarla ma lo sento: ho già i tratti tumefatti. Tu nascondi nel tenero delle labbra, avvolgi di carezze. La partenza. Devo guardare i tuoi occhi chiusi. Si sta accorciando il respiro. Stai risalendo dal pozzo. Sei qui. Mi ritrovi voltata che segno la paura e le belve sulla parete della nostra caverna. E subito armato ti tendi per liberare il grido. Un grido che trapassa il soffitto, che fa crollare il cielo sulla terra. E piovono punte di freccia, grandi gocce di pioggia.

*

Standing outside the bathtub, you pour water on my back, while I'm squatting, my arms stretched out, in precarious balance. One hand soaps away smells and traces. The other hand holds the water that returns to envelop me. Lukewarm, inside the swaddling bands mothers would tighten. Restricting all trembling movements, freeing only the neck. The head that can be turned from side to side. Eyes that can be opened and closed. The mouth that can call out to you, that can scream, cry, and go back to sleep.

*

We sleep in the blood of the departure. We sleep one day away from farewell. But again something wakes me first and I find you sunk into yourself, inside a well not containing me. So you really do drop off to sleep and keep falling headlong while I slide slowly into it, after clinging and long securing myself to your quay. I slip away for a short distance, without losing the extended arc of the horizon behind me. It is breathing. Waves come in and go out of your home, summer guests you put up in the next room, in the beds that always remain there: the house is bigger than you, it's for a family that builds up and breaks down, amid calling and shouting, flying off and sudden returns. Deserted in winter and for long periods, then, in the flow of the evening, suddenly crowded with a colony of seagulls. All together they form an island, a place chosen within the ruins.

I linger, listening to the sea in your breathing, waiting for the flow to resurface and to be, for you as well, the clear expanse of morning. I remove thorns from my body by writing, on the edges of the bed, short sentences that burn immediately. On the trip I saw a blazing margin blackening stubble fields.

If a slight crackling of flames awakes you, it is I who am slowly moving forward. I am burning sharp stalks, whatever remains of a harvest. But you aren't listening. Of this approaching blackness, perhaps you hear only a page turning. The bed is full of blood and you are sleeping. You are sleeping in my blood.

All day long I do not speak. If I speak, my face becomes contorted. My mouth, a scary crease. I try to disguise it but I sense it: I already have the swollen features. You hide in the tender part of the lips, you envelop with caresses. The departure. I have to watch your closed eyes. Your breath shortens. You are coming up from the well. You are here. You find me turned away, marking the fear and the beasts on the wall of our cave. And immediately armed, you stretch out to free the cry. A cry that goes through the ceiling, making the sky collapse onto the earth. And arrowheads rain down, big drops of rain.

*

Cose che non puoi fare solo come questa: piegare le lenzuola. Consegna due angoli alle mie dita. E si tenderà nell'aria un cielo nostro, un sipario alzato e ridisceso sul viso. Ora bisogna flettere insieme, bruscamente, le braccia, in un'onda cancellare le pieghe. Più volte, lasciando che la nostra vela si gonfi e si svuoti nel vento. E navigare così, da questa lontananza che crea e muove ogni cosa.

E ancora prenderò un lato, mi allontanerò, e tornerò a renderlo. Finché tutto si chiude nella misura decisa, nella forma che vuole un cassetto.

*

Si è aperta una vena d'acqua nella fronte. Esce dagli occhi. Lentamente. Devo masticare in quest'ora. Nutrirmi contro me stessa. Contro la faglia. E questa corrente che preme e rovina. Cercava sbocco. Finalmente ha trovato.

Mangia questo cibo che dissolve in poltiglia. Porta ancora saliva. Versa lacrime e mangia. Spalanca la bocca: non ti contiene. Mostra l'impasto orribile che ci forma.

*

Non scrivo, non chiamo. Recupero forze. Ogni giorno. Viva, finalmente difesa. Le braccia a reggere questa barriera. Sei già stata travolta. È tardi. Ma il tempo continua. Si addensa altra aria al confine.

I tuoi occhi neri, oggi hanno il colore del mare. Ti ho tagliato i capelli e la barba. Non ti assomiglia più la foto all'entrata di casa. Sto lasciando scorrere la tua voce tra gli alberi.

La mattina siedo indolenzita alla finestra. La notte precipito in un torrente secco, in un letto di ciottoli e sassi. Chilometri senza una foce. Chilometri che spogliano di foglie e di rami, che scorticano. Fino alla chiara durezza che aspetti.

Things you cannot do alone, such as folding sheets. Give two corners to my fingers. And in the air our sky will be pulled tight, a curtain raised and lowered again over our faces. Now we have to flex our arms together, abruptly, with a wave remove the folds. Several times, letting our sail swell and slacken in the wind. And to navigate like this, from the distance that creates and moves everything.

And again I will take an edge, move off, then return to give it back. Until everything is folded up into the size decided upon, into the shape required by the drawer.

*

A vein of water has opened in my forehead. It comes out of my eyes. Slowly. I have to chew at this time of day. To feed myself against myself. Against the fault line. And this stream that pressures and devastates. It was seeking to flow out. It finally found a way.

Eat this food that dissolves into mush. Bring more saliva to it. Shed tears and eat. Open your mouth wide: it doesn't contain you. Show the horrible dough forming us.

*

I don't write, I don't call out. I recover my energy. Every day. I'm alive, defended at last. My arms for holding up this barrier. You've already been overwhelmed. It's late. But time goes on. Another air thickens at the border.

Today your black eyes have the color of the sea. I've cut your hair and beard. You no longer look like the photo in the entry of my house. I'm letting your voice flow through the trees.

In the morning I sit numb at the window. During the night I plummeted into a dried-up streambed of pebbles and stones. Kilometers without finding a way out. Kilometers which strip off leaves and branches, which flay. Until the harsh clarity you are waiting for.

Pareti, macerie

Una sorgente di calore, riserve accumulate di cibo. Sto accanto al fuoco azzurro che affiora dai fornelli e al respiro siderale del frigorifero. Chiusa nella cucina di una casa chiusa e vuota. Tra pareti cresciute senza che me ne accorgessi. Dormivo mentre la mia famiglia le costruiva. Ora vengono a portarmi il cibo alla porta, come a un uccellino in gabbia. Con il tempo le ali si sono fatte pesanti: sempre più faticoso saltare da un poggiolo all'altro, raggiungere la vaschetta dei semi.

La casa si chiude su di me, mi stringe le tempie. Di stanza in stanza una mano mi preme sul petto facendomi arretrare fino alla soglia. Un altro giorno per raccogliere le cose e partire. Le cose lasciate accumulare sui tavoli, sul pavimento, come in un bivacco. Il tepore si concentra tra la camera da letto e la cucina, nelle altre stanze è la desolazione di una terra abbandonata ai rovi.

Ogni tanto scende una pioggia sottile di pianti e di giochi. La vita della famiglia al piano di sopra è un albero che cresce. Posso sentire le radici che affondano oltre il soffitto, sospese diramano fino a farsi invisibili.

Forse basterebbe spostare un mobile per riconoscermi qui, con le mie forze e i miei gesti. Ho invece lasciato che fossero altri a scegliere i colori delle pareti, gli armadi e persino il mio letto. Sarei partita presto. Quell'appartamento mi avrebbe soltanto ospitato. E come ospite non potevo desiderare altro oltre allo stretto necessario. La bellezza è nell'aria, gli oggetti sono avvolti nel suo corpo luminoso. Se ci fosse la terra battuta e un manto di foglie, sarebbe il luogo migliore per una tana. Invece continuo a scontare questa pena: non potermi riconoscere in questo spazio e trovarmi in un tempo sospeso, rinviato. Una vita che non ha luogo non procede se non per sequenze indefinite, come da un treno con i finestrini velati di polvere. E mentre non prendo terra né corpo, qualcuno nel frattempo abita il mio vuoto. Il coinquilino avanza chiudendomi una dopo l'altra le porte alle spalle fino a farmi trovare fuori casa, senza chiavi. Sono anni che continuano a cadermi dalla borsa, dalle mani, quasi fossero di piombo. È una mia semina. Perché sparendo possano, nel tempo, germogliare.

Non sentirsi a casa è un male che dirama lentamente, fino ad affiorare come muffa alle pareti. Chiedo *se è possibile vivere, un altro giorno, qui*. Allora ci si alza dal letto con gesti ripetuti, come l'alfabeto di una lingua morta.

Dovrei prendere il martello nel ripostiglio e vedere quanto reggono questi muri. Colpirli come piantando qualcosa nel profondo: un chiodo a cui appendere ogni mattina il quadro che mi dedica la luce. Oppure auscultare ogni crepa fino a sentire il tremore della terra che vive. Distendermi sul pavimento e aspettare i disegni delle ombre sul soffitto.

Walls, Rubble

A source of heat, accumulated food supplies. I'm standing next to the blue fire, which emerges from the burner, and the sidereal breathing of the refrigerator. Closed up inside the kitchen of a closed and empty house. Between walls that have risen without my noticing. My family was building them while I was sleeping. Now they come and bring me food, to my door, as if for a caged bird. Over time, my wings have become heavy: it is ever more tiring to hop from one perch to another, to reach the tray of seeds.

The house closes in on me, presses against my temples. From room to room a hand pushes against my chest, causing me to step back to the threshold. Some other day, I'll pick up my things and leave. Pile up the things left behind on the tables, on the floor, as in a bivouac. The warmth is concentrated between the bedroom and the kitchen; the other rooms are desolate like a land abandoned to brambles.

Every now and then falls a light rain of crying and game playing. The family life upstairs is a growing tree. I can feel the roots sinking through the ceiling, hovering there and branching out until they become invisible.

Perhaps merely moving a piece of furniture would enable me to recognize myself here, with my own energy and daily movements. Instead, I have let others choose the colors of the walls, the wardrobes and even my bed. I might leave soon. The apartment would only have given me lodging. And as a guest I couldn't wish for anything other than strict necessities. The beauty is in the air, the objects are wrapped in its luminous body. If there were beaten earth and a blanket of leaves, it would be the best place for a den. Instead I continue to pay this penalty: not being able to recognize myself in this space, and finding myself in a suspended, postponed time. A life that has no place takes place only in indefinite sequences, as if from a train with dust-veiled windows. And while I neither land nor recover my body, in the meantime someone inhabits my void. My fellow tenant moves forward, closing the doors behind me, one after the other, until I find myself outside the house, without keys. For years they have continued to fall from my bag, from my hands, as if they were made of lead. It is one way I sow. So that, after a while, they can sprout.

Not feeling at home is an evil that slowly spreads, until it surfaces like mold on the walls. I ask if *it is possible to live another day here*. Then you get out of bed with your routine movements, like the alphabet of a dead language.

I should take the hammer into the closet and see how well these walls hold up. Hit them as if driving something in deep: a nail to hang the picture that the light devotes to me every morning. Or listen to every crack until I feel the tremor of the living earth. Lie on the floor and wait for the shadows to make designs on the ceiling.

Credo che questo spazio crollerà: un cataclisma si abbatterà su questo appartamento. Vivrò sotto le macerie in un interstizio d'aria, fino a riemergere, a ritornare libera.

I believe this space will collapse: a cataclysm will fall on this apartment. I will live under the rubble in an air gap, until I reemerge, come back out free.

Stazione centrale

Senza poggiare i piedi sono partita. La legge era quella di andare, seguire l'orario, il binario. Lasciarsi portare dalla corrente lontano dalle pareti chiuse. Andare obbedendo a ciò che è stabilito, piantato come un picchetto sulla ripida parete che devo risalire. 12.30, stazione centrale di Milano. Qualcosa alle spalle torna a chiamarmi: tutto può accadere così, abbandonando la presa, cedendo alla gravità che governa le cose. Resisto, appoggio un piede su quello che mi sembra un punto stabile. Il prossimo treno per Treviglio alle 14.20. Era questo lo spazio di attesa? Alcune cifre scarabocchiate su un foglietto lasciato sul comodino, contenevano ogni sequenza del viaggio. Ora che sono costretta a ricordarle a memoria sento il bianco tra un segno e l'altro espandersi. Siedo alla fine del binario, apro un libro. Ma sono subito raggiunta dal dolore attraverso una delle fratture che porto. Afferro il telefono, chiamo qualcuno che intreccia le sue parole alle mie in una fune che sembra tirarmi avanti. Il frastuono intorno si fa più forte. Gli addetti alle pulizie stanno passando con le loro spazzole meccaniche. Faccio qualche passo verso le scale d'uscita, intenta a seguire la fune che mi tiene.

È troppo tardi quando mi accorgo di non avere più lo zaino. Svanita quella pressione leggera che mi cingeva le spalle. Era stato scelto e riempito secondo uno scopo, accuratamente. Per questo avevo potuto sostenerlo, oltre la porta di casa, fino a destinazione e ritorno, negli spostamenti di questi anni. Ora è netto e profondo lo strappo. Il dolore confuso alla dolcezza di un dono. Come se le mani si aprissero e si mostrassero per quello che sono, scucite da ampie fenditure di vuoto.

Cinquanta centesimi, torna all'orecchio una voce. Ero intenta a digitare sullo schermo della biglietteria automatica, e quella cifra esatta, pronunciata senza tentennamenti, mi aveva raggiunto con il tono di un calcolo. Avevo proseguito i miei gesti, automatici come le procedure di quella macchina, come la richiesta di quella voce. Era la stazione centrale di Milano che mi parlava. Il suo volto che si compone e disperde a ogni arrivo e partenza, a ogni numero che affiora e si cancella sulla grande tabella. Con un ghigno sordo ora inghiottiva tutto quello che avevo dimenticato di avere. Il portatile e la possibilità di lavorare nei prossimi giorni, un paio di occhiali da sole, quattro libri, le ciabatte per entrare nelle case degli altri. La lista proseguiva fino ad assottigliarsi e raggiungere un punto che però non sentivo ancora tracciato: era un foro da cui continuava a fuoriuscire qualcosa, lentamente, come sabbia da una clessidra. Ogni oggetto appariva di fronte ai miei occhi, illuminato dalla propria presenza, come chiedendomi congedo. Ecco che cosa sono. Frammento dopo frammento si ricomponeva il mosaico della mia perdita. Ora potevo finalmente arrivare a

Central Station

Without putting my feet on the ground, I left. The law was to go, to follow the train timetable, the platform. To let myself be carried along by the flow, far from the closed walls. To go while obeying what had been decided upon, planted like a piton into the steep cliff that I have to scale. Half past noon, Milan Central Station. Something behind me again beckons to me: anything can happen like this—losing one's hold, yielding to the gravity that governs things. I resist, placing my foot on a spot that seems stable. The next train to Treviglio, at 2:20 p.m. Was this how long I had to wait? Some numbers scribbled on a piece of paper left on the bedside table detailed every step of the journey. Now that I have to recall them, I sense the blankness between one sign and the other one expanding. I sit down at the end of the tracks, open a book. But I am suddenly hit by the pain through one of my inner fractures. I grab my mobile, call someone who weaves his words with mine, into a rope that seems to pull me forward. The din around me increases. The cleaners are going by with their mechanical brushes. I take a few steps towards the exit stairs, intent on following the rope that holds me.

It's too late when I realize that I no longer have my backpack. Vanished is the light pressure around my shoulders. The backpack had been chosen and carefully filled, for a purpose. It was for this reason that I had been able to support it, beyond the door of my home, to my destinations and back on my trips during these past few years. The wrenching is now clear and deep. The pain mixed with the gentleness of a gift. As if my hands had opened and shown themselves for what they are, unstitched by wide rips of emptiness.

Fifty cents, a voice returns to my ear. I was concentrating on typing on the ticket machine screen, and that exact figure, uttered resolutely, had reached me with a calculating tone. I kept moving my fingers automatically, like the procedures of the machine, like the voice's request. It was Milan Central Station speaking to me. Its face, which is put together and taken apart with each arrival and departure, with each number that emerges and disappears on the large timetable. Sneering mutely, it now swallowed everything I had forgotten to have. The laptop and the possibility of working during the next few days, a pair of sunglasses, four books, slippers to enter others' homes. The list continued until it thinned out and reached a point which, however, I didn't yet sense as marked: it was a hole from which something kept trickling out, slowly, like sand from an hourglass. Illuminated by its own presence, each object appeared before my eyes as if asking to leave. *This is what I am.* Fragment after fragment was piecing back together the mosaic of my loss. Now I could finally manage to see it, to recognize it, to size it up. His arms emerged, his envel-

vedere, a riconoscerla e soppesarla nella sua entità. Affioravano le sue braccia, il suo corpo capace di avvolgere in cui ero affondata senza incrociarne gli occhi. Quella sequenza della mia vita era fatta di vuoto. Alle mie spalle non c'era la terra. A portarmi avanti, a segnare la strada, il filo d'acqua che mi attraversava il viso.

Non ti appartiene ciò che non custodisci. La stazione centrale mi aveva restituito al mio dolore, la destinazione unica del viaggio. Come se ogni andare non fosse che l'abbandonarsi a una forza che ci riconduce a noi stessi. *Quanto povera sei, neanche cinquanta centesimi.* Continua a biascicare la stazione, come la vecchia zingara accanto all'entrata, chiede spiccioli che nessuno concede. Lentamente la mia perdita mi veniva riconsegnata in dono: questa fede che si sta rinsaldando, che dovrò raccogliere per attraversare il vuoto e tornare in un punto della mia vita in cui cammino con uno zaino dove è tutto quello che mi sorreggerà fuori di casa. Tra un binario e l'altro si è aperto uno dei pozzi che collegano alle faglie della terra. Ho potuto così attingere all'acqua scura e ai minuscoli semi di luce che vi sono immersi. Sentirli germinanti, mi basta per riconoscere una traccia.

oping body in which I had sunk without my eyes meeting his. That sequence of my life was made of emptiness. Behind my back there was no ground. To bring me forward, to point out the road, the trickle of water crossing my face.

What you don't look after doesn't belong to you. The Central Station had given me back to my pain, the sole destination of the journey. As if every leaving meant merely abandoning ourselves to a force leading us back to ourselves. *How poor you are, not even fifty cents.* The station keeps mumbling, like the old gypsy woman near the entrance, asking for small change that no one gives. Slowly my loss was handed back to me as a gift: this trust that is strengthening, that I will have to muster to cross the void and go back to a point in my life when I walk with a backpack containing everything that will support me away from home. Between one platform and another, one of the wells connected to the earth's fault lines has opened. I have thus been able to draw off the dark water and the tiny seeds of light immersed in it. Feeling them germinating, it is enough for me to recognize a trace.

Sul traghetto Ancona-Igoumenitsa

L'estasi del non vedere più la terra si diffonde tra gli abitanti del ponte: la ragazza che sta montando una tenda, l'uomo che dondola sull'amaca, l'anziano che ha aperto una sdraia e si è coricato su un fianco. Tanti nel sacco a pelo attendono la notte. Girando senza sosta da prua a poppa, hai l'impressione che questa, sospesa tra due rive, sia una comunità ideale. Lo capisci dal modo in cui ognuno, a turno si allontana dagli altri e va dove il vento è così forte che impedisce di tenere un libro aperto, e può strapparti il cappello, gli occhiali dal viso. Là non puoi fare altro che guardare. Per pochi minuti o intere ore, ognuno resta appoggiato alla balaustra, legge qualcosa sulle onde scure, poi volta le spalle e torna nel brusio. Quando comparirà di nuovo la terra, saranno ad aspettarla, a chiedersi il suo nome, sentinelle di un popolo tra poco estinto.

On the Anconna-Igoumenitsa Ferryboat

The ecstasy of no longer seeing land spreads among the inhabitants of the bridge: the girl who is setting up a tent, the man swinging in the hammock, the elderly man who has opened out a deck chair and is lying on his side. Many in sleeping bags are waiting for the night. Wandering constantly from bow to stern, you have the impression that this community, suspended between two shores, is ideal. You understand this by the way everyone takes turns moving away from the others and going to where the wind is so strong that it prevents you from keeping a book open and can blow off your hat, your glasses from your face. There, you can do nothing but gaze. For a few minutes or whole hours, everyone keeps leaning against the railing, reading something into the dark waves, then turns around and goes back to the murmuring. When land reappears, they will be expecting it, wondering about its name, as sentinels of a people soon to be extinct.

Il ragazzo tra gli scogli

Vicino al porto di marina Gouvia c'è una piccola spiaggia da dove si vede il profilo dell'isola fino alla città di Corfù; di fronte, disabitati e brulli, i monti al confine tra Grecia e Albania sorgono dal blu del mare con il loro giallo ocra punteggiato di rade macchie sparse. È una striscia di sabbia coperta di alghe secche dove non vengono turisti ma solo qualche persona del posto. A fianco, oltre una recinzione sottile, inizia la spiaggia attrezzata con un grande bar e un ascensore che porta direttamente agli appartamenti cresciuti a pochi metri dal mare. Al lato opposto un promontorio roccioso copre la vista del porto; in alto, nel verde, si intravede qualche villa. A pochi metri dagli scogli sono attraccate piccole barche.

Tra quegli scogli si aggirava un pomeriggio un ragazzo. Lo ritrovavo ogni volta a testa china, indaffarato in qualche cosa, forse semplicemente a cercare i granchi negli anfratti o a mantenere l'equilibrio tra un masso e l'altro. Dal punto in cui si era fermato si apriva probabilmente la visuale sull'altro lato del promontorio e sul porto, così mi incamminai anch'io, lentamente, verso gli scogli. Appena iniziai ad avanzare in quel lembo di rocce sull'acqua, il ragazzo iniziò a camminare più avanti, allontanandomi. La sensazione di stare invadendo il suo territorio mi fece fermare. Anche il ragazzo smise di procedere. Lasciò passare qualche minuto come per assicurarsi che sarei rimasta lì, all'inizio degli scogli. Sotto il controllo del suo sguardo, mi girai a guardare la spiaggia che avevo lasciato alle spalle e a fare qualche passo nell'acqua più alta, come per tranquillizzarlo: *stavo facendo una passeggiata, come si fa spesso dopo avere nuotato, per asciugarsi al sole.* Il mio messaggio doveva essergli arrivato perché poco dopo lo vidi di nuovo armeggiare tra le rocce a testa china. Gli ero abbastanza vicina, ma non tanto da riuscire a capire cosa facesse: piegato com'era continuava a essere in parte coperto da uno scoglio. Forse per questo aveva accettato quella distanza pattuita insieme. Allora feci qualche altro passo verso l'acqua, per liberarmi la visuale senza avanzare verso di lui. Ed eccolo, di spalle, nel rigore dei gesti, sollevare con entrambe le braccia un masso fin sopra la testa e poi gettarlo, come stesse facendo una diga o compiendo un altro oscuro disegno. Quel ragazzo non aveva niente a che fare con le ville nel verde, né con le barche attraccate, né con la piccola spiaggia dove in pochi avevamo steso l'asciugamano. Ai miei occhi era bastata questa sequenza. Non avrei interrotto il suo rito. Ora potevo tornare ad osservarlo da lontano.

L'ombra del promontorio avanzava, costringendo i più ostinati a cambiare posto e a distendersi sempre più a ridosso della recinzione, verso l'ampia spiaggia dove i turisti sulle sdraie prendevano l'aperitivo, godendosi il giorno fino all'ultimo raggio. Un vento che alzava la rena e le alghe, spinse gli ultimi bagnanti a sollevarsi e infine ad andarsene. Finì che restammo soltanto io,

The Boy among the Rocks

Near the seaport of Gouvia there is a small beach from which one can see the profile of the island all the way to the city of Corfu; opposite, uninhabited and barren, the mountains on the Greek-Albanian border rise from the blue of the sea, their yellow-ocher color dotted with a few scattered woodsy spots. It is a sandy strip covered with dry seaweed to which no tourists come, only a few locals. Next to it, beyond a thin fence, the beach begins with a large bar and an elevator that goes directly up to the condominiums that have sprouted a few meters from the sea. On the other side, a rocky promontory conceals the view of the harbor; at the top, some villas can be glimpsed amidst the vegetation. Some small boats are moored a few meters from the rocks.

One afternoon, a boy was wandering among those rocks. I kept noticing him with his head bowed, preoccupied with something, perhaps simply looking for crabs in the cracks or balancing himself between one boulder and another. From the place at which he had stopped, the view probably opened out to the other side of the promontory and to the port, so I too walked slowly towards the rocks. As soon as I had begun to advance into that stretch of rocks within the water, the boy started to walk ahead, moving away from me. The sensation of invading his territory made me halt. The boy also stopped progressing. He let a few minutes go by as if to make sure I would stay there, at the beginning of the rocks. Under his intent gaze, I looked back at the beach that I had left behind and took a few steps into the higher water, as if to reassure him: *I was taking a walk, as is often done after swimming, to dry off in the sun.* My message must have reached him because shortly afterwards I saw him again, his head bowed, busying himself among the rocks. I was close enough to him, but not enough to understand what he was doing: bent over as he was, he continued to be partly concealed by a rock. Maybe this is why he had accepted that mutually agreed-upon distance. Then I took a few more steps towards the water to get a better view, but without nearing him. And there he was, his back turned, both arms precisely lifting a big rock up over his head and then throwing it as if he were making a dam or carrying out some other obscure project. The boy had nothing to do with the villas amidst the vegetation, nor with the moored boats, nor with the small beach on which a few people had spread their towels. To my eyes, this series of events sufficed. I would not interrupt his ritual. Now I could go back and observe him from afar.

The shadow of the promontory was advancing, forcing even the most obstinate sunbathers to move away and stretch out ever closer to the fence, towards the wide beach where tourists on deck chairs were having an aperitif and enjoying the daylight until the very last sunray. A wind swirling up the sand and the seaweed incited the last sunbathers to get up and finally leave. At the

portata dall'ombra al limite estremo della spiaggia, e il ragazzo tra gli scogli. Continuavo a leggere, nonostante la sabbia sugli occhi. In realtà continuavo ad osservarlo oltre le pagine; aspettavo che tornasse per incrociare il suo sguardo e cogliere qualcosa che mi dicesse di quel luogo, di quello che significava per lui.

La mia attesa fu premiata. Arrivò anche per lui la sera. Attraversava la spiaggia con passi cadenzati, come li stesse contando, lo sguardo basso e l'aria di chi deve portare a termine qualcosa. Soltanto ora mi accorsi che aveva nelle mani due bottiglie di birra vuote. Le buttò nel cestino a qualche metro alle mie spalle, poi si sedette su un muretto per togliersi la sabbia dai piedi. Stava per diradarsi quel qualcosa di indefinibile che lo aveva avvolto, nell'immagine di un adolescente venuto a passare un pomeriggio di solitudine. E invece in uno scatto si alza, torna al cestino, recupera le due bottiglie, riattraversa la spiaggia e si dirige verso gli scogli. Arrivato in quel punto in cui aveva gettato il masso, si ferma e scaglia deciso contro uno scoglio le bottiglie, infrangendole una dopo l'altra. Ora nessuno avrebbe più camminato scalzo tra quegli scogli. Nessuno oltre il ragazzo che, non appena ebbe sancito questo limite, tornò verso la spiaggia, prese la bicicletta e se ne andò.

end, after I had moved from the shadows to the far end of the beach, only the boy among the rocks and I remained. I was still reading, despite the sand in my eyes. In fact, I kept gazing at the boy beyond the pages. I was waiting for him to come back so I could catch his eye and grasp something that would tell me about that spot, what it meant for him.

My waiting was rewarded. The evening had arrived for him as well. He marched across the beach with cadenced footsteps, as if he were counting them, his eyes lowered and with the air of someone who has to accomplish something. Only now did I realize that he had two empty beer bottles in his hands. He threw them into the trashcan a few meters behind me, then sat down on a low wall to remove the sand from his feet. The indefinable something enveloping him was about to disperse into the image of a teenager who had come to spend a solitary afternoon. Instead, he sprung up, went back to the trashcan, retrieved the two bottles, crossed the beach again and headed for the rocks. Arriving at the spot where he had thrown the big rock, he stopped and hurled the bottles firmly against a rock, breaking them one after the other. Now no one would walk barefoot between those rocks anymore. Nobody besides the boy who, as soon as he had sanctioned this limit, returned to the beach, took his bicycle and rode off.

Mare, treno

Il luogo della nascita è coperto di macerie. La terra non respira. Dovrebbe essere il luogo di una fuga. Io ci vivo con gli orari del treno nel portafogli, tra andirivieni pendolari e strappi che ti portano a sentire com'è dura una catena, come resiste un gancio. Ho vissuto molti anni a occhi chiusi, come in un gioco dell'infanzia, lasciando spalancata la porta all'altro mondo, tastando una maniglia come un coltello, una parete come un viso, mentre gli altri ti sfiorano, ti pungono, respirano sulla tua bocca, si allontanano, in un balzo ti stringono e ti chiedono *chi sono chi sono*. Socchiudo gli occhi; li apro. Lascio che il ritmo dei passi mi porti. È così che vado verso il mare.

Vado a sfociare nel tratto di spiaggia accanto al torrente Arzilla. Qui l'Adriatico torna un lago preistorico. Contenuto dai frangiflutti entra disegnando baie che si susseguono tra Fano e Pesaro in dolci vasche di sabbia. Legni chiari si alzano tra gli scogli come segnali per i viaggiatori dei treni che scendendo dal nord vegliano questo tratto di mare, il primo ad aprirsi dopo la grande pianura e gli spettri delle città che si inseguono tra campi, periferie, sagome di fabbriche e grandi magazzini. Non so se questi tronchi siano stati piantati da mani umane, come segna-confine dai pescatori, o dagli schivi camminatori invernali, o se siano invece stati innalzati dalla violenza delle onde che ha finito per trovare un incastro, un punto di equilibrio elevando queste aste levigate come ossa di un grande mammifero smembrato dal mare. Sono monumenti del deserto che comincia oltre l'estate, colonne dell'aperto.

Non c'è stato treno che ho preso risalendo la penisola, senza seguire con lo sguardo questo tratto di mare. È percorso in dieci minuti da stazione a stazione, una tregua che mi permette di sentire che cosa sta accadendo, molto più che leggendo un giornale. Come guardando negli occhi chi abbiamo amato, nell'intervallo di tempo che si spalanca, prima del congedo: come sta, cosa transita nella sua fronte, quali tracce sta lasciando. Come respira oggi il mare, quante persone lo sfiorano di corsa, quante in cammino, in coppia, sole, con un cane al fianco. Cose che ogni mattino bisognerebbe sapere.

Appena fuori Fano la spiaggia si richiude in uno stretto corridoio tra la linea degli scogli e quella della ferrovia. Un sentiero sassoso ricoperto dai detriti portati dalle mareggiate e dal passaggio dei treni. Un luogo ultimo, solitario, di sterpaglie e condotti aperti come brevi tunnel. Qui almeno due vite hanno ubbidito al richiamo, risalendo il greto di sassi, nel tremito elettrico che attraversa i fili prima dell'arrivo del treno. Percorrendo questo tratto in auto, lungo l'Adriatica, si distinguono appena, tra i cespugli, le lapidi chiare sulla staccionata. Ai confini dell'estate, la bassa marea porta rari, pazienti raccoglitori di vongole:

Sea, Train

A birthplace covered with rubble. The earth doesn't breathe. It should be the place of an escape. I live there with train schedules in my wallet, between coming and going, and wrenching away, which make you feel how hard a chain is, how well a hook resists. I've lived for many years with my eyes closed, as in a childhood game, leaving the door wide open to the other world, touching a handle like a knife, a wall like a face, while others brush up against you, sting you, breathing on your mouth, moving off, then with a leap shaking you and asking *who am I who am I.* I close my eyes. I open them. I let the rhythm of my footsteps carry me. This is how I head to the sea.

I'm going to flow into the stretch of beach next to the Arzilla stream. Here the Adriatic turns back into a prehistoric lake. Contained by breakwaters, the sea comes in, outlining coves that follow each other in soft sandy basins between Fano and Pesaro. Between the rocks, bright woods rise up like signals for the train passengers coming down from the north and watching over this stretch of sea, the first one to open up after the great plain and the specters of towns chasing each other among the fields, the suburbs, the shapes of factories and shopping malls. I don't know if these boles have been planted by human hands, as landmarks for fishermen, or by shy strollers in winter, or if they have been raised, instead, by violent waves that have ended up finding a notch, a point of equilibrium, and erected these smoothed stakes like the bones of a large mammal dismembered by the sea. They are monuments of the desert that begins beyond the summer, columns of openness.

There has never been a train that I have taken back up the peninsula without my gazing at this stretch of sea. The distance is covered in ten minutes, from one station to other one, a respite that allows me to sense what is happening, much more than by reading a newspaper. It's like looking into the eyes of those we have loved, in the interval of time that opens before the farewell: how he is, what is moving across his forehead, what tracks it is leaving. How the sea is breathing today, how many people are touching it by running, how many by walking, in pairs, alone, with a dog at their side. Things you should know every morning.

Just outside of Fano, the beach closes up into a narrow corridor between the line of the rocks and that of the railway. It is a rocky path covered by debris washed up by the coastal storms and passing trains. There is a last remote area made up of brushwood and conduits open like short tunnels. Here at least two lives have obeyed the call and climbed the pebbly bank, amid the electric tremor that runs through the wires before the train arrives. If one drives along this stretch of the Adriatic, one barely makes out, among the bushes, the white gravestones against the fence. At the confines of summer, the low tide brings a few patient clam gatherers: with a stick and a bag they

con un bastone e un sacchetto avanzano lenti sul letto del mare; ogni tanto si chinano accarezzando la sabbia, come rimboccando un lenzuolo.

move slowly across the sea bed; every now and then they bend down, caressing the sand, as if turning down a bed sheet.

Piazza XX settembre – Fano. Seguendo le ammoniti

Questo spazio che vedo aprirsi lentamente, tra i tetti delle case, muri che dividono un'intimità da un'altra, proprietà, brevi giardini dal cemento, prende una forma definita, di una geometria dolce e imperfetta, come potrebbe tracciarla la matita di un bambino: un rettangolo smussato dagli anni, dai giorni di sole cocente, dalla pioggia fitta e sottile delle stagioni di mezzo. È la piazza. Posso vederla anche con gli occhi chiusi, o seduta alla finestra guardando la luce muovere gli alberi. C'è uno specchio lasciato sull'acciottolato e acqua che sgorga ininterrotta dal muso di leoni addomesticati dalla pietra: in una preistoria che si confonde con la fiaba sono scesi dalle colline ad abbeverarsi e come in un incantesimo sono rimasti, posati sulle zampe, mansueti, rilasciando dalle fauci un arco d'acqua. Sopra di loro, una donna liberata da un drappo, lascia che si gonfi nel vento. In un gioco mima l'asta di una bandiera, l'albero di una nave. Nuda come solo una divinità può essere. Senza malizia, indossando il suo corpo. Intorno inizia una città che potrei riconoscere e chiamare con due sillabe sole, quasi due note, o due opposte risposte, *fa no*. Il toponimo di un'inquietudine, di un'incertezza. Come qualcosa che appena pronunciato vorrebbe essere richiamato indietro, nel buio oltre la gola. È in questa lingua che parlo, la lingua che mi ha insegnato una terra increspata dal lagomare Adriatico. A una manciata di chilometri di distanza dalla riva, puoi ancora inseguire il suo velo come qualcosa di sommerso che si muove nell'aria. Sono di questa campagna, tra due orizzonti di colline, campi di grano e strade segnate dalle querce, antichi cippi di confine. Una spina dorsale d'acqua dolce l'attraversa, il Metauro. Da qualche parte, lungo le sue rive, in una banchina di rena, riposa il fratello chiamato in soccorso, caduto portando il germe della sconfitta. Asdrubale graffiato da un aratro, dai denti di una ruspa, derubato di armi e monete e subito ricoperto, oppure ancora affondato nel sonno, indisturbato, a qualche metro di terra dalla superficie. E sono dell'acqua, quasi mai limpida, di questo mare socchiuso, mite, furioso ogni tanto negli inverni, contro le rive che l'hanno costretto. Non sono di questa città. Ho un indirizzo, il nome di una via, un numero di casa a cui non risponde nessuno. È per questo che posso camminare fino al perimetro della piazza, sedermi sulla fontana come un fantasma e guardare. Qui, come bandierine in un gioco di conquista, stanno issati tutti i simboli di identità e possesso: la torre ricostruita dopo l'ultima guerra, l'orologio, e negli ultimi decenni banche, sempre più banche agli angoli, a reggere i confini. E questa donna che se ne sta lì, in piedi, nuda, al centro della vasca, forte del suo essere inerme, quasi orgogliosa del gesto che l'ha liberata dalla veste che ora, inarcata nell'aria, la restituisce alla sua armatura di carne. Per niente bella la direbbero oggi, con il ventre pronunciato e i piccoli seni. Ma se ti fermi a guardare la sua postura decisa, i suoi lineamenti affiorati come

Piazza XX Settembre — Fano: Following the Ammonites

This space that I see slowly opening up between the roofs of the houses, between walls dividing one intimacy from another, one property from another, tiny gardens from the concrete, takes on a definite shape with its pleasing imperfect geometry as might be drawn by a child's pencil: it's a rectangle softened by the years, by the scorching sunny days, by the dense drizzles of the intermediate seasons. It's the square. I can also see it with my eyes closed, or sitting at the window and watching the light move the trees. A mirror has been left on the cobblestones, and water flows incessantly from the muzzles of lions tamed by stone. In a prehistory blended with fairytales, they came down from the hills to drink and, as if in a spell, remained there meek and resting on their legs, releasing an arc of water from their jaws. Above them, a woman freed from a cloth lets it swell in the wind. As if in a game, it mimes a flagpole, the mast of a ship. She is naked as only a divinity can be. Without malice, she wears her own body. Around her extends a town that I could recognize and call with only two single syllables, almost two musical notes or two opposing answers: *fa no [do not]*. The place name denotes unrest, uncertainty— like something which, once pronounced, would like to be called back into the darkness beyond the throat. It is in this language that I speak, the language that I have been taught by an inland rippled by the Adriatic. At a handful of kilometers from the shore, you can still follow the veil as something that is submerged yet moving in the air. I am from this countryside between two horizons of hills, wheat fields, and roads signaled by oak trees, ancient boundary stones. A backbone of fresh water, the Metauro river, flows through it. Somewhere along its edges, in a sandbank, lies the brother who was called to the rescue and who fell, carrying the seed of the defeat. Hasdrubal, by now scratched by a plow, by the teeth of a bulldozer, robbed of weapons and coins, and immediately covered over again—or perhaps he is still sound asleep, lying undisturbed, a few meters of earth from the surface. And I am made of the almost never clear water of this mild, half-enclosed sea which becomes furious every so often in winter with the shores that have constricted it. I am not from this town. I have an address, a street name, a house number at which nobody answers. This is why I can walk to the perimeter of the square, sit on the fountain like a ghost and watch. Here, like little flags in a game of conquest, all the symbols of identity and possession have been hoisted: the tower rebuilt after the last war, the clock, and, in recent decades, banks—ever more banks at the corners to buttress the outer edges. And this woman who is standing there naked in the center of the basin, strong in her weaponless being, almost proud of the gesture that freed her from the very clothes which now, arched in the air, restores her to her armor of flesh. She is not beautiful at all, one

da un'antica moneta, puoi immaginarla alla guida di una processione rituale, dalla spiaggia fino al punto in cui sarebbe sorta una città. Lì ferma a richiamare su questa coordinata dello spazio gli occhi di un dio addormentato, avvolto tra infinite coltri di nubi. È una dea plasmata nel bronzo; la chiamano Fortuna, come un antico tempio di cui si sono perse le tracce.

Meno visibili, ma forse più di lei a segnare questo luogo, sono i piccoli cerchi delle ammoniti emersi dalle pietre. Un taglio nella roccia delle montagne ed è riaffiorato il seme che è sempre un antico messaggio d'acqua, una prima forma che la vita ha preso, indelebile. Le puoi cercare camminando con lo sguardo basso, assorto, seguendo le tracce di una spiaggia deserta, di un tempo che non conosceva l'uomo. Tutto è come allora, sono cambiati soltanto i contorni, le forme che abbiamo preso, quello che abbiamo imparato a costruire. Palafitte, case di terra, di paglia, di pietra tagliata, di cemento.

Continuo a camminare come avessi perso qualcosa, ma senza l'ansia di trovarlo, senza paura di averlo restituito per sempre. Ora sono su una pietra dalle striature chiare: sto calpestando delle ossa, animali o umane non importa; lo stratificarsi del tempo ha cancellato qualsiasi segno di calore, di pietà, per questa morte. È vissuto qualcosa capace di cambiare la pietra. Qualcosa che ha la forza di una scia luminosa nello spazio. Saremo una striatura chiara anche noi, non visti da nessuno, nel cuore chiuso di una montagna.

Vagando così, a occhi bassi, a un tratto mi ritrovo al centro della piazza, dove è disegnata una stella. Ho un vuoto che risuona dentro, sono fatta di carta e stracci incollati e dipinti. Mi guardano tutti, in cerchio; mi hanno fatta le loro mani durante l'inverno; ho nei tratti i sorrisi e le lacrime di tutto quello che è loro accaduto. Mi hanno beffato, hanno riso guardandomi, mi hanno portato sulle spalle come un santo. Ora qualcuno si avvicina portandomi il fuoco. Devo farmi di cenere, devo andarmene perché sia primavera. Sono il loro pupo di carnevale. Muoio ogni anno nel cuore della città, al centro della piazza. In realtà qui non si potrebbe stare: chi calpesta questa stella perde la fortuna, va nella mala sorte. Perché qui, al centro del centro della città, si è fuori; qui si brucia, si viene sacrificati perché la comunità possa continuare a riconoscersi in questo rettangolo sghembo di piazza, in queste costruzioni sorte dove sarebbe acqua salata e sabbia.

Documenti d'archivio della fine del '400 conservano due note contabili di spese sostenute per bruciare due streghe. Di una resta un nomignolo, «la Baronta», e la cifra servita per comprare i guanti al maestro di giustizia. Di un'altra un breve elenco più dettagliato di oggetti che sono serviti a cancellarla, come se la sua traccia scura sul selciato avesse resistito più a lungo, non se ne fosse voluta andare: «A voi Piero depoxitario livere tre, soldi dici nove, denari

would say today, with her protruding belly and small breasts. But if you stop to look at her resolute posture, with her features outlined like those on an ancient coin, you can imagine her driving a ritual procession from the beach to the place where a town would rise. There she stops to beckon, to this exact spot, the eyes of a sleeping god enveloped in infinite blankets of clouds. She is a goddess molded in bronze. She is called Fortuna, like an ancient temple whose traces have been lost.

Less visible, but perhaps signaling out this place more than she does, are the small circles of ammonites that have emerged from the stones. A slice in the rock of the mountains and resurfaces the seed that is always an ancient message from water—a first, indelible form taken on by life. You can search for ammonites while you are walking and looking down with an absorbed gaze, following the traces of a deserted beach, of an era that did not know man. Everything is as it was back then; only the contours have changed, the shapes we have taken on, what we have learned how to build: stilt houses, houses made of earth, straw, cut stone, concrete.

I keep walking as if I had lost something, but without the anxiety of having to find it, without the fear of having given it back forever. Now I am on a stone with pale streaks on it. That I am stepping on animal or human bones doesn't matter; the stratification of time has eliminated any sign of warmth, of pity for this death. Something capable of changing a stone has been alive—something that has the energy of a bright trail in space. We too will be a pale streak, unseen by anyone, in the closed heart of a mountain.

Wandering like this, with eyes looking downwards, I suddenly find myself in the center of the square, where a star has been drawn. I have a void that resonates inside me. I am made of paper and glued, painted rags. Standing in a circle, the townspeople are all looking at me; their hands made me during the winter; in my facial features I have the smiles and tears of everything that has happened to them. They have mocked me, laughed while looking at me, carried me on their shoulders like a saint. Now someone nears, bringing the fire to me. I must turn myself into ash, to go away so that spring can come. I am their carnival doll. I die every year in the heart of the town, in the center of the square. In fact, one shouldn't stand here: whoever treads on this star loses his good fortune, heads for bad luck. Because here, in the center of the center of town, one is outside: here one is burned, sacrificed, so that the community can continue to recognize itself in this skewed rectangle of the square, in these constructions which stand where there used to be only sand and saltwater.

de bolognini, sonno che fo speso per brusiare la striga, cioè legne e fascine, dui bochali d'olio, per corda, per confectione, per chiodi e per far levare quella bruttura che non se brusiò et bolognini vinte per el boio». Nell'esattezza anonima di un registro, dove ogni parola è composta della materia sorda dei soldi, «quella bruttura che non se brusiò» sembra quasi l'ultima sfida lanciata da un corpo, contro l'orrore della storia. La sua forza indifesa, la sua rivolta, è ancora in questa piega che ha portato nella lingua dei cadaveri, efficiente assassina lingua della burocrazia.

Archival documents from the end of the 15th century preserve two accounting records of expenses incurred to burn two witches. One record retains a nickname, "la Baronta," and the amount used to buy gloves for the executioner. For the other witch, there is a short, more detailed list of objects used to eliminate her, as if her dark stains on the pavement had lasted longer, unwilling to go away: "To you, Piero, the bailee, in total three *livere* and nineteen *bolognini*. This is what I have spent to burn the witch. That is, for wood and fagots, two jugs of oil, the rope, the preparations, the nails, and to remove that eyesore that wouldn't burn, and twenty *bolognini* for the executioner." In the anonymous exactness of a register, where each word consists of the deaf matter of currency, "that eyesore that wouldn't burn" seems almost the last defiance put forth by a body against the horror of history. Her defenseless strength, her revolt, is still present in this unexpected twist that entered the language of corpses, the efficient murderous language of bureaucracy.

Maria, verso Cartoceto

È scritto all'anagrafe e in ogni documento che mi appartiene: Maria, il nome che ho cancellato da questa Franca che rimane. Scomparso dalla mia firma. Un solo nome: due sillabe che mi pronunciano, che mi sottraggono al silenzio. Sono già molte per esistere. E anche la voce degli altri mi ha riconosciuto, mi ha chiamata Franca, semplicemente: si è fermata, come non ci fosse bisogno di dire ancora.

Maria è il nome della madre di mia madre. Mi piace sentire l'eco di questa parola, la profondità che apre indietro, nelle generazioni, come un filo che ci si passa nel buio. In questa ripetizione mi sembra di riportarla in vita, di donarle ciò che le appartiene, che le è dovuto; ha a che fare con qualcosa che non ha fine, che sprofonda alle mie spalle, fino a ciò che non mi è visibile né conosciuto. Da me, oltre me, non so come e se continuerà.

Lei è la madre di mia madre, di mia madre, di mia madre. Come scorrendo i grani di un rosario potrei ripeterlo ancora fino a renderla un'espressione muta, un'onda sonora che viene e ritorna nel silenzio. Maria è il nome che ogni donna porta. E davvero nelle nostre campagne marchigiane non c'era madre che non desse a sua figlia questo nome, come invocazione, come ringraziamento. Se non era il primo nome era il secondo, per custodirla.

Ma chiamerò Maria, la madre di mia madre, anche *nonna*, con l'affetto intatto dell'infanzia, incorniciandola in quegli anni della sua vita in cui ci siamo conosciute. Mi addormentavo spesso accanto a lei, nella metà del letto che era del marito, andato quando avevo quattro anni. Prima di chiudere gli occhi, distese su spesse lenzuola di lino, le sue parole si disegnavano come cerchi nel silenzio; il suo petto era un libro di pagine non numerate che terminavano a un passo dal sonno. Riprendeva la mattina, quando la seguivo nei suoi lavori di casa, in cucina, in cantina, nel pollaio. Tra le sequenze di suoni che ripeteva a memoria c'erano le preghiere. Insieme a queste mi ha insegnato un gesto che assomigliava a quello di legarsi le scarpe: un incrocio che si formava, se eseguito esattamente. Con la punta delle dita si tocca il centro della fronte, il centro del petto, la spalla sinistra e poi la destra. Come un laccio che ti tiene unita, che ti riporta al centro del tuo cuore che è sempre il cuore di un altro. Ogni volta che inizia qualcosa, che ti metti in cammino, segni questa croce su di te come faresti se ti trovassi su una riva, sulla terra bagnata, di fronte a un vetro umido e a ogni altra cosa che può essere scritta. Dice: *sono qui, in questo punto esatto*. E anche: *mi affido a questo tempo e a questo spazio, a questo momento e a questo luogo. Non farmi perdere, tienimi stretta nel tuo sguardo.*

Maria, towards Cartoceto

It is inscribed in the birth registry office and on every document that belongs to me: Maria, the name I have deleted from this Franca that remains. It has vanished from my signature. A single name: two syllables that express me, that remove me from silence. Two are already a lot in order to exist. And others' voices acknowledged me by simply calling me Franca: they stopped there, as if there were no need to say anything more.

Maria is the name of my mother's mother. I like listening to the echo of this word, the depths that open out, through the generations, like a thread passing through darkness. Through this repetition, I seem to bring her back to life, to give her what belongs to her, her due; it has to do with something endless that sinks behind me until it reaches that which is neither visible nor known to me. From me, beyond me, I do not know how and if it will continue.

She is the mother of my mother, of my mother, of my mother. As if telling rosary beads, I could keep repeating it until it turned into a speechless expression, a sound wave coming in and going back to silence. Maria is the name that every woman wears. And indeed in our Marches countryside there has never been a mother who did not give her daughter this name, as an invocation, as a thanksgiving. If it was not as a first name, then as a middle name, to keep watch over her.

But I will call Maria, my mother's mother, also *grandmother*, with my childhood affection intact, framing her in those years of her life when we knew each other. I would often fall asleep next to her, in the middle of the bed that belonged to her husband, who passed away when I was four. As I was lying on the thick linen sheets and before closing my eyes, her words would take on the shape of circles in silence; her bosom was a book of unnumbered pages that ended at one step from sleep. The book would begin again in the morning, as I followed her around while she was doing her housework in the kitchen, in the cellar, in the henhouse. Among the series of sounds that she repeated by heart were prayers. Besides these, she taught me a gesture that resembled that of tying shoes: a crisscrossing movement if performed exactly. The fingertips touch the center of the forehead, the center of the chest, the left shoulder and then the right one. Like a string that ties you together, that pulls you back to the center of your heart, which is always someone else's heart. Whenever something begins, whenever you head off somewhere, you make this sign of the cross, as if you were on a shore, on wet ground, in front of misty glass or anything else that might be written on. It means: *I'm here, at this exact point.* And also: *I entrust myself to this time and to this space, to this moment and to this place. Don't let me go astray, keep me closely in sight.*

Chi legga questo messaggio non so dirlo. So che è un segno che presto si cancella, che bisogna ripetere di nuovo. È un po' come con le scarpe allacciate la mattina per andare. Se le trovi slacciate poi durante il giorno, non puoi andare avanti molto, ti fermi un istante e ricominci.

Gli ultimi anni della sua vita, prima di addormentarsi, mia nonna aveva l'abitudine di chiedere "la benedizione": una piccola croce che un altro doveva segnarle sulla fronte. Una malattia molto dolorosa, alle ossa, la portava a chiamare a voce alta sua madre, ripetutamente. Accorrevamo a vedere che cosa volesse, di che cosa avesse bisogno; spesso chiedeva di spostare un po' la tenda, di avvicinarle qualcosa, spesso era soltanto un pretesto per vederci accanto a lei. Da adolescente mi ero quasi abituata a quella litania, e quando mi sembrava solo un capriccio tornavo presto alle mie cose. Chiamava sua madre, noi eravamo soltanto figli, figli dei figli, non potevamo consolarla, sollevarla tra le braccia, stringerla al petto, lontano dal dolore. Una notte, accorsa di malumore al suo richiamo di bambina, con un'irritazione trattenuta che chiedeva *che cosa c'è*, mi sono sentita chiedere per la prima volta la benedizione. Non c'era nessun altro in casa. Toccava a me. A me che già non credevo, che avevo perso quel gesto che mi aveva consegnato come una vecchia chiave di cui non si ricorda la porta. Potevo farlo io? Ne ero capace? Distesa a letto, non poteva abbandonarsi al sonno. Aspettava. Mi aspettava. Nel silenzio mi affidava un potere. Dal fondo della stanza mi sono avvicinata; con un dito le ho tracciato una piccola croce sulla fronte. Sembrava placata, rasserenata. Sono tornata in camera mia.

Ci sono due strade che da Lucrezia portano a Cartoceto. Si attraversa una zona di recenti case residenziali colorate a pastello e ci si ritrova a una biforcazione con due cartelli che indicano la stessa meta. Prendo sempre quella di sinistra, che sembra più breve. Prima di arrivare al paese si sale a Salomone, un nome che continua a ripetersi nella mente cercando qualcosa che richiami l'antico re della Bibbia fino a questa piccola frazione di case, mentre la strada svolta, inizia a costeggiare uliveti e un grande noceto. Si arriva presto a un incrocio a t: la strada da cui veniamo porta a Lucrezia, quella che prenderemo, sulla destra, a Cartoceto, quella a sinistra a Saltara e a Calcinelli. Qui è un monumento ai caduti della prima e seconda guerra: un tempietto chiaro con le pareti laterali interne piene di piccole foto ovali in bianco e nero e scritte che rinviano a una morte declinata in tre casi: per ferite, per malattia, in prigionia. Il luogo: dall'Albania all'Africa, dalla Russia a Creta. Nella parete centrale una lastra di pietra riproduce in rilievo l'immagine della Madonna delle Grazie. È per lei che oggi sono salita qui, a una quindicina di chilometri da

I cannot say who might read this message. I know it's a sign that soon fades away, that we have to repeat all over again. It's a bit like tying your shoes in the morning to go out. If later, during the day, you find them untied, you cannot go on very far; you have to stop for a moment and retie them.

During the last years of my grandmother's life, before falling asleep, she would ask for "the blessing," a small cross that another person had to mark on her forehead. A very painful bone disease made her call out for her mother, repeatedly. We would hurry in to see what she wanted, what she needed; she would often ask us to move the curtain a little, to bring something closer, but often it was just an excuse to see us next to her. When I was a teenager, I was almost used to this litany, and whenever it seemed a mere whim I soon returned to whatever I was doing. She would call out for her mother, but we were only children, children of children, and we could not console her, lift her up in our arms, hold her tight, away from the pain. One night, as I rushed over in a bad mood to her childlike cries, with my withheld irritation asking *what's the matter?*, I heard myself being beckoned to give the blessing for the first time. No one else was at home. It was up to me. To me who no longer believed, who had lost this gesture that she had handed down to me, as you might lose an old key whose door you cannot remember. Could I do it? Was I capable? Lying in bed, she could not give herself over to sleep. She was wait-ing. Waiting for me. Within the silence, she was entrusting me with a power. I approached from the back of the room and, with my finger, traced a small cross on her forehead. She seemed soothed, reassured. I returned to my room.

There are two roads that go from Lucretia to Cartoceto. You cross an area of recent pastel-colored residential houses, until a fork with two signs indicates the same destination. I always take the left route, which seems shorter. Before arriving at the village, the road rises to Salomone, a name that keeps repeating itself in the mind as it searches for something recalling the ancient Biblical king, all the way to the small cluster of houses where the road curves and begins skirting along olive orchards and a large walnut grove. Soon you arrive at a T-junction: the road from which we have come leads to Lucretia; the road we will take, on the right, to Cartoceto; the one on the left to Saltara and Calcinelli. Here there is a monument to soldiers fallen in the First and Second World Wars: a small palish temple whose inner walls are covered with small, oval, black-and-white photos and inscriptions referring to three kinds of death: from wounds, from illness, from captivity. The places: from Albania to Africa, from Russia to Crete. On the central wall a stone slab reproduces, in relief, the image of Our Lady of Graces. It is for her that I have come up here

Fano, seguendo in auto il cammino che mia nonna faceva a piedi fin da bambina. L'affresco miracoloso era proprio in questo incrocio, in un'edicola, prima di essere staccato e collocato nel Santuario accanto al paese. Riconosco le linee di quell'antico disegno, tante volte ritrovato a casa, sul comodino di mia nonna, dentro un libro, nella credenza. Un santino come un segnalibro, un fiore schiacciato tra le pagine: ricorda il punto fino a cui ti ha portato la vita, il punto da cui puoi continuare. I suoi colori di erba, di polvere e di terra li ritroverò presto nella piccola cappella costruita per lei, con le pareti adornate di cuori d'argento. Non resto a lungo. In questi monumenti ai caduti sento spesso qualcosa di estraneo: un fasto che a malapena riesce a coprire un inganno, un'impostura; i tratti mascherati, ufficiali, di una celebrazione che non riguarda davvero queste vite di uomini trascorse in un cerchio di case tra le colline prima di essere chiamati alle armi. Guardo gli occhi di tutti divenuti scuri nelle foto, seguo la data e il luogo di una stessa morte organizzata, diramata in divisioni e schiere. Qualcuno è stato disperso. Forse una forma di salvezza: non essere più trovati, riconosciuti accanto ai documenti. Finalmente liberi. Il tempo che passa, il vuoto che si apre e si disegna di strade che portano a casa o verso un'invisibile terra straniera, tra lingue sconosciute che arrivano all'orecchio, bisbigli che assomigliano a quelli dei morti. Ma sono tra i nomi dell'elenco. Non sono sfuggiti. Sono qui anche loro.

Faccio pochi passi fuori, verso l'incrocio; considero le tre direzioni possibili. Respiro per un attimo la vertigine di quel luogo che doveva essere sacro, difeso dai demoni che si nascondono nelle chiome degli alberi, nelle siepi ai margini delle strade, scuotendole come un vento; frantumano l'immagine che avevamo riconosciuto allo specchio, chiamandola con il nostro nome. Un soffio di voce all'orecchio ripete *io*, come la fiamma di una candela subito spenta dal vento. Bisogna proteggerla con il palmo di una mano e camminare fino all'immagine santa, alla madre dipinta.

Sono qui, nella cappella della Madonna delle Grazie. A quest'ora del pomeriggio in tutto il Santuario solo i miei passi e il silenzioso coro delle candele bianche. Le più grandi crepitano a tratti nel silenzio come ricadendo su se stesse. Chi le ha piantate qui conosce la durata della loro vita. Può venire a guardarle come un orologio, un calendario. Quando la più vecchia viene schiacciata dal tempo, ridotta al suolo come una buccia, un tappo, subito la fiamma passa a un'altra. Sono tre infatti, ognuna in un periodo diverso della vita: la prima è quasi intatta, la seconda è a metà, la terza verso la fine. In una colonnina d'acciaio se lasci cadere una moneta ne ricavi un tintinnio metallico come di salvadanaio: puoi portare con te un santino o prendere una candela piccola

today, about fifteen kilometers from Fano, following by car the road up which my grandmother walked ever since she was a child. The miraculous fresco painting was in fact originally located at this crossroads, in a shrine, before being detached and placed in the Sanctuary next to the village. I recognize the lineaments of that ancient painting, so often found at home on my grandmother's bedside table, in a book, or on a sideboard. A small holy picture like a bookmark, a flower crushed between pages: a reminder of the point to which life has brought you, the point from which you can continue. Soon I will find its colors of grass, dust, and earth in the small chapel built for the Madonna, its walls adorned with silver hearts. I do not stay long. In these monuments to soldiers fallen in battle, I often feel something strange: a pomp that barely covers over a deception, an imposture; the masked, official traits of a celebration that does not really concern these lives, which were carried out amid a circle of houses in the hills before the men were called to arms. I look at everyone's eyes, which have darkened in the photos; I examine the dates and places of the same organized death, shared out into divisions and troops. Someone is missing in action. Perhaps a form of salvation: no longer to be found, to be recognized alongside their identity papers. Free at last. The time that goes by, the emptiness that opens up and takes shape from roads leading home or to an invisible foreign land, between unknown languages that reach the ear, whispers that resemble those of the dead. But their names are on the list. They have not escaped. They are also here.

I take a few steps outside, towards the crossroads, and consider the three possible directions. I breathe for a moment the vertigo of this supposedly sacred place, defended from demons who are hiding in the foliage of the trees, in the hedges lining the streets, and who shake them like a wind; they shatter the image that we had recognized in the mirror, calling it by our name. A whisper repeats *I* in my ear, like the flame of a candle suddenly blown out by the wind. One needs to shelter it with the palm of a hand and walk to the holy image, to the painted mother.

I am here, in the chapel of Our Lady of Graces. At this hour of the afternoon, throughout the entire Sanctuary, only my footsteps and the silent choir of the white candles. The biggest candles crackle up at times, in the silence, as if falling back on themselves. Whoever plants them here knows how long their lives last. One can come and look at them as if they were a clock, a calendar. When the oldest one is crushed by time, reduced to the ground like a rind, a cork, suddenly the flame passes to another. In fact there are three candles, each in a different period of its life: the first is almost intact, the second

da piantare nell'aiuola insieme alle altre. Accanto è una colonia di ceri rossi; cimiteriali, è vero, ma basta guardarli pochi secondi per scorgere la minuscola fiamma protetta, quasi una vita che si muove lentamente nel loro grembo.

Dici che si può pregare anche così, con una mano che segna il bianco del foglio. È lo stesso bianco che è apparso a un lembo della tua veste, che si è portato via la bocca di un angelo che ti vegliava; è il bianco da cui ti hanno ritagliata, che ti contorna ancora. Noi torneremo lì, in quel vuoto da cui sei apparsa, da cui appari con occhi grandi e labbra minute, in boccio. Hai un'aureola intagliata di motivi geometrici, un antico disco solare; un velo ti nasconde i capelli. Su un ginocchio è seduto un bambino già uomo, vestito di verde come gli angeli e i prati, ti guarda stringendo una croce. Anche noi a cercare i tuoi occhi, a leggere il silenzio sul tuo viso.

Tra i cuori alle pareti cerco per gioco le iniziali del mio nome. So che sono venuti qui anche per me. Si sono inginocchiati al banco di legno, hanno acceso una candela. Andavo verso la morte, con l'istinto di un animale che migra. Ma anche le piccole divinità del cielo e dell'acqua si ingannano: le ritrovi spiaggiate, prese nelle reti, confuse dalle ferite.

Tutto quanto accade, è dentro i tuoi occhi quieti. Mentre il nostro piccolo cuore implode e si frantuma, non pompa più amore alle estremità del corpo.

Nel silenzio soltanto il rumore di un aspira-fumo e quello delle auto di fuori che spostano l'aria, come raffiche di vento. Prima di andare torno per un'ultima volta a guardare la tua immagine di muschio, ocra e sabbia bagnata. È come se fossi venuta dalla terra, vincendo la terra, il suo sgretolarsi. Resteranno i tuoi occhi, un segno su un muro scrostato.

is in the middle, the third towards the end. If you drop a coin into a small steel offering box, a clink resounds as if in a penny bank: you can take a little holy picture with you or a small candle to be planted in the flowerbed along with the others. Nearby is a colony of red candles; graveyards, indeed, but it suffices to look at them for a few seconds to glimpse the tiny protected flame, almost like a life moving slowly in their womb.

You say that praying can also be like this, with a hand making signs on the blank piece of paper. It is the same blankness that appeared on a hem of your dress, which erased the mouth of an angel watching over you; it is the blankness from which they have cut you out, which still surrounds you. There we will return, into that void from which you have appeared, from which you appear with big eyes and small lips, in bud. You have a halo carved with geometric patterns, an ancient solar disk; a veil hides your hair. On one knee is sitting a child who is already a man, dressed in green like angels and meadows, watching you clutch a cross. We also look for your eyes, to read the silence on your face.

Among the hearts on the walls, I search, in jest, the initials of my name. I know they have also come here for me. They have knelt at the wooden pew, lit a candle. I was heading towards death, with the instinct of a migrating animal. But even the tiny divinities of the water and the heavens can be tricked: you find them beached, caught in nets, bewildered by their wounds.

Everything that happens is inside your quiet eyes. While our little heart implodes and shatters, it no longer pumps love to the extremities of the body.

Within the silence, only the sounds of an exhaust fan and the cars outside stir the air, like gusts of wind. Before I leave, I return one last time to gaze at your image of moss, ocher, and wet sand. It is as if you had come from the earth, vanquishing the earth, its crumbling. Your eyes will remain, a sign on a peeling wall.

Dentro un orizzonte di colline

Chi non vede il mare impazzisce: c'è questo detto tra noi, disciolto nella saliva di generazioni. Dev'essere nato tra i contadini della costa e dell'immediato entroterra. Quelli che in poche ore di cammino potevano raggiungere la riva dell'Adriatico, la domenica o nei giorni di festa, preferendo l'acqua salata a quella del fiume e dei fossi. Dalle colline, lavorando, potevano avere uno sguardo alto, come i gabbiani richiamati all'interno dalle burrasche. Se non era l'intero nastro azzurro ad aprirsi, era almeno una sua breve sequenza, tra un crinale e l'altro. Durante il giorno, con lo sguardo chino sui campi, sapevano che da quel colle, da quella curva della strada, da quell'albero sulla cresta riappariva più celeste del cielo, come un premio che non si poteva meritare ma soltanto ricevere, fino a sentirsi inumidire gli occhi. Di paese in paese, di casolare in casolare, si custodiva questa parte di orizzonte, questa porzione quotidiana di bellezza, senza dire né mostrare nulla: nessun punto panoramico, nessun hotel miramare o ristorante con vista, soltanto un bagliore di azzurro e di verde e il suo disciogliersi nei gesti di ogni giorno, in un motivo cantato tra sé. Poi, a un certo punto, non è possibile dire esattamente a partire da quale campo o cerchio di case, il sipario si chiude. Inizia un'altra popolazione, un'altra stirpe di genti, quella dell'entroterra escluso dal mare, quella di chi si alza e si addormenta dentro un orizzonte di colline. Un mare di terra in cui si può sprofondare, scendendo in piccole valli coperte da una breve macchia. Nel punto più incavato, scorre sottile e nascosto da pioppi e rovi un fosso. Lì puoi sentire come la terra chiama ad ascoltare il suo respiro, mentre il tuo si apre, si rinsalda. Sono luoghi in cui puoi sparire alla vista di ogni essere umano e anche a te stesso. Sono pozzi aperti. Puoi discendere, come sott'acqua, mentre lo sguardo si libera e vede finalmente le cose nel loro nitore, sospese. Sosti in questa cuna del tempo fino a che qualcosa come l'umidità che si infiltra nelle ossa o il buio ti riporta alla ragione e ti rimette in piedi, suoi tuoi passi, ad affrontare la salita. Ci sono questi avvallamenti, come fenditure schiuse nel terreno e poi aperture del paesaggio dove lo sguardo può andare di crinale in crinale, da una terra arata a una macchia, da un casolare abbandonato a un borgo. Nessuna meta che potrebbe placare per un po' il desiderio, come un rifugio, una vetta. Il mare delle colline continua a cullare lo sguardo da una parte all'altra. C'è comunque sempre una riva, un confine: l'Adriatico, oppure il profilo scuro degli Appennini che inizia a increspare le colline fino a renderle indistinguibili alle proprie pendici. É proprio qui che inizierebbe la follia, tanto più fonda e radicale quanto la distanza dal mare è netta.

Inside a Horizon of Hills

If you don't see the sea you go crazy: we have this saying, dissolved in the saliva of generations. It must have been born among the peasants of the coast and the immediate hinterland. Those who in a few hours of walking could reach the Adriatic shore, on Sundays or on holidays, preferring salt water to that of the river and the ditches. From the hills, while working, they could have an overview, like seagulls called back inland by gales. If it wasn't the whole blue ribbon that opened out, it was at least a short segment between one ridge and another. During the day, as they gazed down at their fields, they knew that from that hill, from that curve of the road, from that tree on the ridge, the sea would reappear bluer than the sky, like a prize that could not be deserved but only received, until their eyes moistened. From village to village, from farmhouse to farmhouse, this part of the horizon, this daily portion of beauty, was cared for without saying or showing anything: no scenic overlook, no seaview hotel or panoramic restaurant, only a glow of blue and green and its dissolution in everyday gestures, in a tune sung to oneself. Then, at some point, it is not possible to say exactly at which field or circle of houses, the curtain closes. Another population begins, another stock of people, those of the hinterland excluded from the sea, those who get up and fall asleep inside a horizon of hills. A sea of land into which you can dive, descending into small valleys covered by a little scrubland. At the most sunken point runs a narrow ditch hidden by poplars and brambles. There you can sense how the land beckons to you to listen to its breath, while yours opens up, is strengthened. These are places where you can vanish from the sight of every human being and even from yourself. They are open wells. You can go down, as if under water, while your eyes are freed and finally see things suspended in all their limpidity. You come to a halt in this cradle of time until something like the humidity infiltrating your bones, or the darkness, brings you back to reason and puts you back on your feet, to face the ascent. In these hollows, like half-shut fissures in the ground and then openings in the landscape, your gaze can go from ridge to ridge, from plowed land to scrubland, from an abandoned farmhouse to a village. No goal that could satisfy desire for a while, like a refuge, a peak. The sea of the hills continues to cradle your gaze from one side to the other. However, there is always a shore, a border: the Adriatic, or the dark profile of the Apennines that starts to ripple the hills until their own slopes become indistinguishable. It is precisely here that the madness begins, all the deeper and more radical as the distance from the sea is distinct.

La terra della mia infanzia è attraversata da una sterrata di ghiaia senza uscita. Lì, a breve distanza l'uno dall'altro, sorgono due casolari che ap-partenevano a mio nonno. È una campagna a pochi chilometri dalla costa, una pianura da cui si distinguono le due linee di colline che delimitano la valle del Metauro: a nord quella guidata da Monte Giove con l'eremo che appare, risalendo in autostrada verso Fano, come un segnale di casa; a sud quella di Ferriano, ben riconoscibile per un tratto di ripe franose. Quest'ultima rimane in parte coperta da un cavalcavia e dai capannoni della zona industriale. L'altra invece si staglia sopra il piano dei campi come l'inizio di un mondo inscritto in altre geografie. Ogni volta il mio sguardo era richiamato da quella linea di colline che guardavo nelle diverse tonalità di luce. Come sorgessero dalla terra, che cosa le avesse fatte crescere o portate lì, docili come gusci rovesciati; appar-tenevano al mare, che le aveva abbandonate lasciando che la sabbia si mischiasse all'argilla e si coprisse di verde, o erano il margine ultimo, dolcissimo, delle nostre montagne? Avrei potuto camminare diritto davanti a me, attraversare il campo di mio zio e un altro paio di campi per arrivare dove la terra iniziava a salire, in quel punto di cui non riuscivo a capacitarmi. Non si lasciava rac-chiudere dalla ragione, continuava a sfuggirmi come le cose percorse dalla scossa della bellezza, come gli amori più grandi. Si conosce l'oggetto dell'amore riducendolo in parti più comprensibili e dominabili, si argina la piena rovinosa della passione incanalandola verso brani, dettagli. Così io di quella linea di colline isolavo spesso gli alberi: quelli che si stagliavano solitari sull'ultimo crinale, trattenendo tra i rami il cielo; quelli che comparivano ai margini dei campi o si riunivano nelle zone più scoscese; quelli che potevi distinguere in fila al centro di un terreno: sostenevano i filari di viti poi scomparsi, sostituiti da culture che richiedono meno presenza dell'uomo. Attraverso questi super-stiti affiora l'antico volto della terra: la pianta ritorta della vite, le grandi foglie che nascondono vespe, cavallette, grappoli d'uva, le schiene chine, le voci che si chiamano da un lato all'altro dei filari, le forbici che recidono, i secchi che si riempiono, il trattore che passa a raccogliere.

Di quella linea di colline che delimitava il mio orizzonte, lo sguardo ritagliava spesso l'immagine di un colle di una dolcezza disarmante: perfetta-mente disegnato come un cumulo di sabbia levigato dalla brezza o una ciotola rovesciata. Sulla sua cima si apriva la chioma di un albero, probabilmente una quercia. Trovarsi su quel crinale, accanto a quell'albero, al tramonto, era l'apice di una gioia possibile eppure continuamente rinviata. Lassù, guardando la valle, ci si sarebbe riempiti di luce come un canestro di frutta. Una riserva che sarebbe durata nei giorni. Forse era un luogo così inciso nello spazio che non

The land of my childhood is crossed by a gravel road with a dead end. There, at a short distance from each other, emerge two farmhouses that belonged to my grandfather. It is a countryside lying a few kilometers from the coast, a plain from which the two lines of hills that delimit the Metauro Valley can be distinguished: to the north, the one guided by Monte Giove with its hermitage which, as one heads up the motorway towards Fano, appears like a house sign; to the south, the Ferriano line, clearly recognizable by a stretch of steep eroded hillsides. The latter line remains partially covered by an over-pass and the warehouses of the industrial area. The other line, however, stands out above the level of the fields as the beginning of a world inscribed in other geographies. Each time my eyes would be drawn to that line of hills, which I would gaze at in the different shades of light. How had they surged forth from the earth, what had made them grow or brought them there, docile like over-turned shells? Did they belong to the sea, which had abandoned them by letting the sand mix with the clay and be covered with green, or were they the last, very gentle, edge of our mountains? I could have walked straight ahead, crossed my uncle's field and a couple of other fields to reach the place where the land started to rise, the point that I was unable to fathom. It did not allow itself to be embraced by reason; it kept eluding me like things traversed by the shock of beauty, like the greatest loves. The object of love is known by reducing it to more understandable and controllable parts; the ruinous flood of passion is held in check by channeling it towards fragments, details. This is why I often isolated trees from that line of hills: those that stood out, alone, on the last ridge, holding the sky between their branches; those that appeared at the edges of the fields or gathered together in the steepest areas; those that you could make out in rows in the center of a terrain: they once supported vines that had since then disappeared, replaced by cultures requiring less human presence. Through these survivors the ancient face of the land emerges: the twisted vinestocks; the large leaves that hide wasps, grasshoppers, bunches of grapes; the bent-over backs; the voices calling to each other from one side of the rows to the other; the shears that cut, the buckets that fill, the tractor that drives by to collect them.

From that line of hills that delimited my horizon, my gaze often carved out the image of a disarmingly gentle hill, perfectly designed like a turned-over bowl or a heap of sand smoothed by the breeze. At the summit the crown of a tree, probably an oak, opened out. To be on that ridge, next to that tree, at sunset, would be the acme of a joy that was possible yet constantly postponed. Up there, looking at the valley, one would be filled with light like

poteva tollerare un profilo umano. Un luogo dello sguardo, un luogo intatto: ciò che restava di un territorio che non avrei mai potuto raggiungere. Non sapevo quale strada vi portasse, e forse se mi fossi avvicinata quel luogo sarebbe sparito, sarebbe diventato invisibile, perso nell'aria, come gli arcobaleni. Di fatto non è mai apparso alcun uomo accanto a quella quercia, per quante sere la vegliassi, e non ho mai intravisto, nelle innumerevoli spedizioni sui colli, un sentiero o una sterrata di ghiaia che potesse condurre a quella mite onda della terra. Era un miraggio creato dalla lontananza? Sono sicura che al crepuscolo, indistinguibili ai miei occhi, gli animali usciti dalle selve vi transitassero, sostando più di un istante ad annusare la vallata, le nostre deboli costellazioni di luce.

Tutta la mia infanzia fu attratta da questo confine non segnato fra la pianura e i colli. La mia immaginazione gravitava attorno a questo punto di congiunzione fra due mondi. Ma non compii mai quel viaggio che poteva risolversi nell'avventura di un mattino: tagliare il breve tratto di pianura, salire per i campi o per una delle stradine tortuose e ridiscendere senza che nessuno gridasse il mio nome. Soltanto nella prima adolescenza, in una delle mie brevi fughe, arrivai sulla sommità di Monte Giove. In uno dei margini di tufo della strada scoprii un foro con il profilo di un muso. Scavai intorno alla tana per farlo riemergere: era un rospo in letargo. Lo portai via con me, con egoismo adolescenziale, lo segregai in un angolo del giardino, finché quell'interesse prese altre direzioni e forme. Qui la memoria ha uno strappo. Lascia entrare una parte di buio. (Forse sono questi i luoghi in cui penetra, attraverso i nostri gesti, l'assurdo, la sua crudeltà). Spero di averlo liberato nel fresco dell'erba, lontano dal ciglio della strada.

Nella mia esperienza delle colline, tra infanzia e adolescenza, si è disciolta la voce di Pavese. C'era qualcosa nelle sue parole di nudo e in cammino, che procedeva e scavava nel petto fino a una verità che affiorava nel sangue. Dalla prigione del Conte di Montecristo e dalla giungla delle tigri di Mompracem, fu lui a traghettarmi verso i libri che non contenevano più figure. Gli occhi dovevano seguire una dopo l'altra le frasi e aprire intorno il paesaggio, disegnare i volti, i gesti. Il primo suo libro fu *La luna e i falò*. Era mio padre a guidarmi tra le parole, leggendo per me prima del sonno, e ora scegliendo dalla sua biblioteca un libro che mi avrebbe parlato. C'era un messaggio indirizzato a me che avrei compreso leggendo. Mi precipitai subito: poche righe, la prima pagina, ma le parole restavano inerti. Glielo dissi e lui tornò con la sua voce a leggere. Immediatamente distinsi quella cadenza quasi ipnotica che non si

a basket of fruit. A supply that would last for days. Perhaps it was a place so engraved in space that it could not tolerate a human profile. A place for the eyes, an intact place: what remained of a territory that I could never have reached. I didn't know which road led there. Perhaps, if I had approached that place, it would have disappeared, become invisible, lost in the air, like rainbows. In fact, no man ever appeared next to that oak, no matter how many evenings I watched over it, and I had never glimpsed, during countless expeditions over the hills, a path or a gravel road that could lead to that mild wave of land. Was it a mirage created by distance? I am sure that at dusk the animals, indistinguishable to my eyes, would come out of the woods and pass across that land, pausing for more than a moment to sniff the valley, our weak constellations of light.

My whole childhood was attracted to this unmarked limit between the plain and the hills. My imagination gravitated around this point where two worlds joined. But I never made the journey that could have been resolved in one morning's adventure by cutting across the short stretch of plain, going up through the fields or one of the narrow winding roads and coming back down without anyone shouting my name. Only in my early adolescence, on one of my brief escapades, did I arrive at the top of Monte Giove. Along one of the tuff edges of the road I discovered a hole with a muzzle shape in it. I dug around this den to make it emerge: it was a hibernating toad. I took it away with me, out of adolescent selfishness, keeping it apart in a corner of the garden until that interest took on other forms and directions. Here, my memory is blank. It lets in a part of darkness. (Perhaps these are the places which, through our acts, are penetrated by absurdity, its cruelty.) I hope that I had freed it in the cool grass, far from the roadside.

Into my experience of the hills, between childhood and adolescence, Pavese's voice was blended. In his words there was something naked and ever in movement, advancing and digging into my chest all the way to a truth that would surface in blood. From the prison of the Count of Montecristo and from the jungle of the tigers of Mompracem, it was he who brought me to books that no longer contained illustrations. My eyes would have to follow the sentences, one after the other, and open up the landscape all around, draw faces, acts. His first book was *The Moon and the Bonfires*. It was my father who guided me through the words, reading to me before I fell asleep, and now choosing from his library a book that would speak to me. There was a message addressed to me that I would understand by reading. I rushed into it immediately: a few lines, the first page, but the words remained inert. I told him and again

può non seguire lasciandola risuonare dentro, quel mera viglioso modo che ha Pavese di narrare con l'andatura di chi ha deciso di non nascondere e non nascondersi niente. Una dopo l'altra si riversarono in me le sue frasi, tutti i suoi libri.

Da allora, nei miei occhi che guardavano le colline portavo anche i suoi, cupi e sfuggenti di adulto adolescente, che mi fissavano seri, dietro gli occhiali, dalla copertina di un libro che raccoglieva le sue poesie. Di fronte al mio orizzonte di colline mi chiedevo ogni volta chi avesse il privilegio di abitarci davvero in quelle piccole case che comparivano come tane nella terra, tra un campo arato e una macchia; soprattutto la notte, quando in quella massa più scura, affioravano punti di luce immersi nel buio compatto. In quegli anni, senza accorgermene, ero scivolata dentro ai pantaloni che dovevo stringere e rivoltare alla vita più volte, mentre le spalle spigolose e le costole che si contavano sembravano proteggermi da un qualche attacco esterno, come fossero la mia parte più dura e indistruttibile, l'armatura che mi era concessa. Nelle fitte di un dolore oscuro sbattevo tra le stanze come un insetto che non trova via di fuga.

Una sera d'inverno, con il buio già sceso, mi diressi con il motorino verso le colline di una zona più interna. Era un luogo che avevo appena iniziato a esplorare, perdendomi in alcune sterrate che diramavano dalla provinciale che sale verso Mombaroccio. Là i fili della luce sono ancora sostenuti da pali in legno che attraversano i campi inclinandosi leggermente. Quelle colline mi apparivano più vaste, più aperte al cielo di quelle dolci che contenevo negli occhi. Lasciai il motorino al margine della sterrata e continuai a piedi su un grande campo arato. Andavo verso il buio più folto, avanzando tra le zolle, nel cuore della terra. Camminai fino a che scomparve alla mia vista la strada. Il casolare del padrone era già tramontato alle spalle.

C'era soltanto la terra che si inclinava, perdendo ogni confine, entrando sempre più nella notte. Una terra così scura e sconvolta che dovevo seguire con gli occhi ogni passo: ogni istante sembrava sorgere sotto i miei piedi, emergere e ritirarsi. Ero all'inizio del mondo. Una strana grazia mi teneva le mani sollevate e aperte, come uno spaventapasseri attardato nel campo ormai deserto. Passarono alcuni minuti di vuoto purissimo. Poi mi sorprese l'ululato di un cane.

he read with his voice. Immediately I recognized that almost hypnotic cadence that cannot not be followed, letting it resonate inside, Pavese's wonderful way of narrating with the pace of one who has decided not to hide anything, nor from himself. One after the other his sentences poured into me, all his books.

From that moment on, my eyes would also carry, as they gazed at the hills, his own eyes, dark and elusive like those of the adolescent adult staring seriously at me, behind his eyeglasses, from the cover of his collected poems. Faced with my horizon of hills, I wondered each time who had the privilege of really living in those small houses that appeared to be burrows in the earth, between a plowed field and scrubland; especially at night, when from that darker mass emerged points of light immersed in compact darkness. In those years, without being aware of it, I had slipped inside trousers that I had to tighten, turning back the waistline several times, while my angular shoulders and countable ribs seemed to protect me from any outside attack, as if they were my hardest and most indestructible part, the armor that was granted to me. In the pangs of an obscure pain I would bash between the rooms like an insect that has no escape.

One winter evening, when darkness had already fallen, I rode my moped into the hills of a more inland area. It was a place that I had just begun to explore, losing my way on some gravel roads that branched off from the provincial highway that rises towards Mombaroccio. There, power lines are still supported by slightly slanting wooden utility poles that run across the fields. Those hills seemed vaster to me, more open to the sky than the gentle ones preserved in my eyes. I left my moped on the edge of the gravel road and continued walking over a large plowed field. I was heading for the thickest darkness, moving forward among the dirt clods, in the heart of the land. I walked until the road vanished from sight. The owner's farmhouse had already faded away behind me.

Only the land was tilting, losing all boundaries, entering more and more into the night. A land so dark and devastated that my eyes had to follow every footstep: every moment seemed to surge forth beneath my feet, emerge and withdraw. I was at the beginning of the world. A strange grace kept my hands raised and open, like a scarecrow lingering in the now deserted field. A few minutes of pure emptiness went by. Then I was surprised by the howl of a dog.

Abitare nella città ideale. Frammenti in forma di visione

Sorge quando chiudo gli occhi. Nitida come un'isola che appare a un tratto, oltre la foschia e le brume all'orizzonte. La vedi e non puoi che crederci anche se stai sognando e lo sai. Accade ogni volta in una luce diversa, come se quella piazza e quelle strade fossero la scenografia di una storia. Forse soltanto il fantasma di una voce che ha preso fiato, un vento radente sui ciottoli che attraversa in mulinelli di polvere lo spazio, che batte leggero alle finestre come un uccello che ha perso lo stormo.

Andavo diretta, a passi sicuri, verso la porta socchiusa. Quella della grande pagoda che un incantesimo ha fermato al centro di questo dolce deserto disegnato. Avanzavo sui grandi lastroni di marmo cenere e sabbia. Non potevo distogliere gli occhi da quella geometria che sembrava condurmi al centro, come una biglia che rotola prendendo velocità, avvicinandosi al foro dove deve cadere. Era quel buio oltre la porta e una paura che cresceva, che avrebbe potuto prendermi il corpo e bloccarmi; ma era impossibile, i miei passi continuavano verso il centro mentre il terrore sbocciava come un fiore nero. La porta avrebbe potuto aprirsi, lentamente, spalancarsi al soffio del vuoto coperto a stento da quelle costruzioni che ora mi sembravano di carta. Sono state appoggiate una accanto all'altra in una luce tiepida, ma non riescono, lo vedi, ad arrestare il nero senza fondo che preme dalle finestre e dalle porte accostate. Se entri nella pagoda sprofondi nel centro dell'universo, in una caduta senza fine. Ti scruta, ti aspetta, fingendo di dormire una bestia dagli occhi cavi: sei grandi quadrate pupille, in un cielo terso e sfumato che ti dice di non credere al buio, di non avere paura.

Puoi ripetere un gioco dell'infanzia e saltare solo sulle lastre chiare o solo su quelle scure. Precisamente, calibrando ogni movimento, come decidesse della tua vita. In questa concentrazione, obbediente, puoi avanzare fino ai piedi della scalinata. Ora sei lì, ferma di fronte al buio di quella fessura. Hai raccolto tutto il chiaro e la luce di questa scena; hai il tepore di un sole coperto dagli edifici ma caldo e sicuro, come in una mattinata tarda, senza scuola. Puoi vedere, lentamente, la pagoda girare su se stessa, come una giostra senza cavalli e senza musica, così lenta che sembra quasi immobile, ma ruota, ne sei sicura, ruota come la terra. Alla sommità il filo quasi invisibile che la sostiene potrebbe sollevarla di nuovo, ridonarle le sue fondamenta d'aria.

Ciò che vedi è stato fatto perché tu possa dormire, senza paura del vuoto tra le stelle. Lo abbiamo ritagliato nella forma di finestre e fenditure. Guardalo così, delimitato nel chiarore di questa nostra geometria. C'è ancora tempo prima che ogni linea scompaia. Prima che questa città si dissolva o si levi come una cortina sul vuoto. Abita ancora, credi a questo spazio, resta.

Living in the Ideal City: Fragments in the Form of Vision

It emerges when I close my eyes. As clearly as an island suddenly appearing beyond the haze and the mist on the horizon. You see it and can only believe your eyes even if you know you are daydreaming. It happens every time in a different light, as if that square and those streets were the setting of a story. Perhaps only the ghost of a voice that has taken a breath, a gust skimming over the cobblestones, whirlwinding dust across the space, beating lightly on the windows like a bird that has lost its flock.

With sure footsteps, I was heading towards the half-open door. That of the large pagoda a magic spell had brought to a stop at the center of this gently drawn desert. I was moving forward over the large, ash-and sand-colored marble slabs. I could not take my eyes off the geometry seemingly guiding me to the center, like a rolling marble that gathers speed, approaching the hole where it must fall. The darkness beyond the door and a growing fear could have gripped my body and kept me from moving, but it was impossible: my steps continued towards the center while my terror was blooming like a black flower. The door might have opened slowly, then widely, to the breath of the void barely covered by the constructions that now seemed made of cards. They have been aligned in a lukewarm light, but, as you see, they cannot halt the fathomless blackness pressing outwards from the windows and the half-open doors. If you enter the pagoda you sink into the center of the universe, in an endless fall. A beast looks at you with its hollow eyes, awaits you, pretending to sleep: six large square pupils in a clear mellow sky that tells you not to believe in the darkness, not to be afraid.

You can imitate a childhood game and jump only on the bright or the dark slabs. Precisely calibrating each movement as if your life depended on it. With such concentration, obediently, you can advance to the foot of the staircase. Now you're there, standing in front of the dark crack. You have gathered all the soft light of this scene; you have the balmy sun concealed by buildings but warm and sure, as in a late morning without school. You can see the pagoda slowly turning on its axis like a carousel without horses and without music, so slowly that it seems almost motionless; yet it rotates—of this you are sure—rotates like the earth. At the top, the almost invisible thread supporting it could lift it up again, restoring its airy foundations.

What you see has been done so that you can sleep without fearing the void between the stars. We have cut it out in the form of windows and slits. Look at it like this, delimited in the gleam of our geometry. There is still time before each line disappears. Before this city is scattered or rises like a curtain over the void. Keep living in it, believing in this space, stay.

La notte ha lavato via tutto. Una notte scura di pioggia che non finiva. Ne è rimasta una striscia più cupa nel cielo alto, lontano. Ogni abitante scomparso, scappato nel buio con l'acqua che aveva iniziato a sommergere la soglia delle case e continuava a scendere fitta. Avrebbe coperto ogni porta e finestra lasciando soltanto la piccola croce sulla cupola del battistero: come a indicare un sepolcro nel centro del lago che si estendeva, appena turbato da increspature sulla superficie. Insetti o qualcosa che si muoveva ancora, nelle profondità. Poi è tornato il sole e la luce, e giorno dopo giorno la città è riaffiorata così, come la vedi adesso. Quei due colombi bianchi sul cornicione sono stati i primi ad arrivare quando ancora i palazzi si specchiavano sull'acqua. Ora bagnata dalla luce la diresti di sabbia, così compiuta e fragile nelle mani del bambino che l'ha costruita e che potrebbe, per capriccio, calpestarla. Inizierebbe proprio dalla cupola del battistero: i contorni che si frangono e franano, le superfici che riaffondano nella materia.

Tornerà mai qualcuno a vivere qui? Chi è fuggito non ha avuto neanche la cura di chiudere a chiave le porte, accostare i battenti delle finestre. Uno per uno lentamente, o tutti insieme a un tratto: andati e non tornati mai più. Inutile aspettare, spiare segni nel fondo delle stanze. O fuori, sui balconi, ai davanzali tra i vasi non fioriti. È la mattina ad accudirli, con la sua pioggia leggera, la sua luce che sembra portare vita anche dove non è più possibile. Nel silenzio delle stanze una goccia penetrata è l'unica vicenda. Ne trema interamente lo spazio, il buio dove ogni cosa è rimasta com'era: i letti sfatti, la brocca sul tavolo, i piatti della colazione sporchi. Che cosa è accaduto lo sanno solamente le cose.

Inutile indagare il destino di questa città: è affidato alla luce. Per questo varia, come l'umore. Posso vederla spegnersi insieme all'azzurro che scende nel crepuscolo dalla finestra accanto al lettuccio. Posso sfiorarla con la nuca, o seduta avvertirla contro la schiena mentre nella mente il suo disegno si apre, figura per figura si compone e scompone. Oppure voltarmi e scorrere le sue linee come un bambino che sta imparando a leggere. A volte distesa all'altro capo del letto, l'accarezzo appena con la punta di un piede. Mi sembra di raggiungere, per un istante, l'altro polo del mondo, il rovescio liberato da ogni scoria, mondato dal tempo, come la metà vuota, limpida, di una clessidra. Oggi credo, oggi mi affido interamente al chiarore del pastello e penso che tutti sono ancora lì, tra le pareti, addormentati: è soltanto l'alba annuvolata di un giorno di festa, tra poco saranno di nuovo per le strade, i bambini accanto alle madri, nel vestito migliore, diretti verso la cattedrale in fondo alla piazza. facciate dei palazzi. Un linguaggio misterioso, fatto di vuoti che si lasciano coprire per misure diverse, di battenti da cui potresti intravedere una mano

The night has washed everything away. A dark rainy night that wouldn't end. A darker streak remains in the distant, high part of the sky. Every inhabitant vanished, ran away into the darkness, after the water started flooding the thresholds of the houses and kept pouring down heavily. It would have submerged every door and window, leaving only the small cross on the baptistery dome as if to indicate a sepulcher at the center of the lake that was expanding, barely disturbed by ripples on the surface. Insects or something that was still moving, in the depths. Then the sun and the light returned, and day after day the city resurfaced as you see it now. Those two white doves on the building ledge were the first to arrive, when the façades were still being reflected in the water. Now bathed in light, the city, you would say, was made of sand, so complete and fragile in the hands of the child who built it and who, on a whim, could trample it. He would indeed start with the baptistery dome, the contours breaking and collapsing, the surfaces sinking back into matter.

Will anyone ever come back here to live? Whoever fled did not even take care to lock the doors, to fasten the windows. One by one slowly, or everyone together all at once, they left and never returned. It's needless to wait, to peek at signs at the back of the rooms. Or outside, on the balconies, on the windowsills between the flowerless vases. It's the morning that attends to them with its light rain, its light seeming to bring life even where it is no longer possible. A raindrop penetrating into the silent rooms is the sole event. The whole space, the darkness in which everything has remained as it was, trembles because of this: the unmade beds, the jug on the table, the dirty breakfast dishes. Only these things know what has happened.

It's needless to investigate the fate of this city: it has been entrusted to the light. This is why the city varies, like moods. I can see it extinguished together with the blue that descends in the twilight from the window next to the day bed. I can brush up against it with the nape of my neck, or, when sitting, feel it against my back while its outline opens in my mind, putting itself together and then falling apart figure by figure. Or I can turn around and run my finger over its lines like a child learning to read. Sometimes lying on the other end of the bed, I barely caress it with the tip of my foot. For an instant, I seem to reach the other pole of the world, the back side freed from all dregs, cleansed by time, like the empty, transparent half of an hourglass. Today I believe, today I entirely entrust myself to, the gleam of the pastels. I think that everyone is still there, between the walls, asleep: it is only the cloudy dawn of a festive day; soon they will be out on the streets again, the children next to their mothers, in their best clothes, heading for the cathedral at the back of the square. This lasts only a few moments. The time in which something can

sporta, una nuca voltata, la metà di un viso che subito si nasconde. *Non credere agli abitanti del palazzo. Sono solo demoni che si rincorrono da un piano all'altro. Aspettano l'ora meridiana per allungarsi sul selciato della piazza. Questa è una città di morti; i suoi appartamenti sono loculi ordinati. È lasciata al governo del vento e della luce, incustodita perché possano entrare le vostre preghiere. Qui si può soltanto abitare il silenzio. Non abbandonarla. Non fuggire. Torna.*

Credi all'orizzonte che si apre oltre le vie, alle strade bianche che si perdono, agli alberi scuri che le accompagnano fedeli o si allontanano per un po' soli, in mezzo ai campi? Quei profili di colline sono il margine verde di un miraggio. Questo, costruito con la pietra dell'illusione, nel tremore sottile di una febbre che pervade l'aria. Oltre è l'aperto senza nome. Per questo continui a essere chiamata qui, in questa piazza, dove i confini sono segnati da due custodie d'acqua. Puoi avvicinarti e sporgerti sull'orlo per vedere se è vero che c'è ancora acqua in questa città deserta. Se è una vasca di pesci rossi o un pozzo in cui balugina qualcosa. Oppure è vuoto il fondo, illuminato da una pioggia di monete. Se ne hai una in tasca e getti anche la tua, dando le spalle al battistero, la sua porta si spalanca. Aspetta solo i tuoi passi. Se hai il coraggio di oltrepassare la soglia entri nel buio cavo e circolare come di un ventre che ti ha ripreso in sé. Lì ruotano le voci degli antichi abitanti; loro possono narrarti la storia della città. Quando a un tratto smettono di bisbigliare, come a volte i grilli nel mezzo di una notte d'estate, sei dalla loro parte anche tu, entrato tra loro a vegliare.

Dicono che puoi entrare e non morire. Non verrai inghiottito. Rimarrai nel centro del buio con le orecchie di un animale che trema. Poi sempre più quieto, fino a colmarti come un incavo d'acqua. Non saprai i passi per tornare fuori. Una volta raggiunto quel luogo lo spazio non conta. Ti muoverai, ma sarai sempre al centro di quel buio. Non parlare. Devi soltanto fare in modo che il soffio non sia ostruito. Risuonare come una canna vuota. Ora vai. Leggero come chi non può più dimenticare.

Sono sempre piccole le cose che salvano. Così piccole che spesso ci si scorda di loro. In questa tavola di legno appena oltre la tempera riaffiora il lavorio sottile di tarli che vissero nella penombra di una delle grandi stanze del Palazzo. Questo margine appena visibile oltre l'azzurro deciso del cielo, l'ocra e il grigio degli edifici e il chiaro della piazza, è come un confine leggero tra la veglia e il sonno. Quando a stento ti liberi dalla forza che dal centro del battistero si riverbera in ogni linea della città, e raggiungi infine il bordo di questo incanto, è come quando, dopo un tempo senza tempo a galleggiare sul dorso, ti riscuote il contatto con qualcosa di duro. Una brezza o l'inconsapevole

be avoided. Then the blackness of doors and windows returns, and it speaks for itself, as if sending signals from the building fronts. A mysterious language made of voids, which allow themselves to be concealed by different measures, and of doors and windows from which you might glimpse an outstretched hand emerging, or a turned neck, half of a face that immediately hides. *Don't believe the inhabitants of the building. They are just demons chasing each other from one floor to another. They are waiting for noon, to stretch out on the pavement of the square. This is a city of the dead; its apartments are orderly burial niches. It has been left to the government of the wind and the light, and left unattended so that your prayers can enter. Here one can only inhabit silence. Don't abandon the city. Don't run away. Come back.*

Do you believe in the horizon that opens out beyond the streets, in the white roads that vanish in the distance, in the dark trees that accompany them faithfully or move off for a while, alone, into the middle of the fields? Those outlines of hills form the green margin of a mirage, built with the stone of illusion, in the subtle tremor of a fever pervading the air. Beyond the mirage is a nameless openness. For this reason, you continue to be called here, to this square, whose edges are marked by two water receptacles. You can approach and lean over the rim to see if there is truly still water preserved in this deserted city. If it's a goldfish basin or a well in which something flickers. Or if the bottom is empty, illumined by a shower of coins. If you have one in your pocket and also toss it in, with your back to the baptistery, its door will open wide. It is waiting only for your footsteps. If you have the courage to cross the threshold, you will enter the darkness, hollow and round like a belly that has taken you back into itself. There, the voices of the former inhabitants are circulating; they can tell you the history of the city. When all of a sudden they stop whispering, as crickets sometimes do in the middle of a summer night, you are on their side too, having entered among them to keep watch.

They say you can go in and not die. You won't be swallowed up. You will remain in the center of the darkness with the ears of a trembling animal. Then ever quieter until you are filled with water, like something empty. You won't know what footsteps to take to get back out. Once you reach that place, space doesn't matter. You will move, but you will always be in the center of that darkness. Do not talk. You just have to make sure that your breathing is not obstructed. Resounding like a hollow reed. Now you go away. Lightweight like those who can no longer forget.

aportata dei tuoi movimenti ti ha condotto contro le pareti della vasca. Capisci llora di quale materia è fatto questo sogno che combatte contro i suoi sottili e invisibili distruttori. E forse sono proprio loro, gli insetti, i soli ad abitare la città, chiusi tra le linee, capaci di sfarinarla in un mucchietto di polvere.

Questo luogo ha un custode nascosto come un sole coperto dalla foschia. Lo senti sulla pelle, nell'aria, sei sicura della sua presenza eppure non lo trovi. Allo stesso modo so che non è stata abbandonata la città, che qualcuno continua a vegliarla, nascondendosi tra i portici e la fuga dei colonnati. È lui a indicarmi i due dettagli a cui mi devo aggrappare quando mi sembra di sentire cigolare la porta del battistero e le finestre dei palazzi spalancarsi nel buio, come a un colpo improvviso di vento. Lo stendardo azzurro che si leva sulla collina quasi come un enorme fiore chino sul suo stesso peso, un grande aquilone liberato che stenta a prendere il volo; se continui a guardarlo si pietrifica: è il versante di una montagna innevata che si confonde con il chiarore del cielo. Torno a cercare i colombi. Sono ancora lì, fermi sul primo cornicione del palazzo, come a ripararsi dalla luce che bagna interamente la facciata sulla piazza. Addossati alla parete, quasi mimetizzati agli intonaci, le uniche presenze animali in tutta la scena; gli unici cuori che pulsano in questo silenzio di pietre. Un attimo prima hanno sostato sul tetto del battistero. Un battito d'ali, il suo riverbero, e si modifica lentamente tutta la scena. Eccoli discendere in volo sull'acciottolato della piazza. Picchettano con il becco la scanalatura tra le lastre di marmo. Forse in quella intercapedine qualcosa è rimasto. Restano così, intenti per alcuni minuti, poi a un tratto si rialzano in volo, si posano sul balcone del palazzo stuccato di porpora. Tra le due piante che sporgono, il vaso di quercia bonsai e il cespo, si fermano alcuni secondi. Non fanno in tempo a raggiungere il giardino pensile vicino, che un battito improvviso li disperde, dissolvendoli dentro alle altre figure, sciogliendo ogni linea nel buio. Le mie palpebre si sono chiuse. La città è riaffondata.

Questo luogo è capace di condurti al delirio. Ti fa perdere come in una casa di specchi. Oggi ho intravisto il giardiniere sul terrazzo chinarsi furtivo sotto un cespuglio della siepe. Probabilmente lo stesso custode, due ombre che a volte si sovrappongono senza mai coincidere del tutto. D'altronde questo è lo spazio in cui non si distingue. Il sogno nel reale, il reale nel sogno. Due forze opposte si scontrano: il controllo geometrico e qualcosa di irriducibile a questa progettata armonia. Così il motivo della piccola quercia che si ripete,

Things that save are always small. So small that you often forget them. Inside this wooden panel just beyond the tempera, the subtle work of woodworms that lived in the semi-darkness of one of the great rooms of the Palazzo resurfaces. The slightly visible margin beyond the distinct blue of the sky, the ocher and gray of the buildings and the bright light of the square, is like a weightless border between wakefulness and sleep. When you barely free yourself from the force which, beginning with the center of the baptistery, reverberates in every line of the city, and finally you reach the edge of the enchantment, it is as when, after a timeless time spent floating on your back, you are roused by a collision with something hard. A breeze or the unconscious range of your movements has led you against the walls of the pool. You then understand what matter this daydream, which fights against its subtle and invisible destroyers, is made of. And perhaps insects really are the only inhabitants of the city, enclosed in its lines and capable of pulverizing it into a heap of dust.

This place has a custodian hidden like a haze-covered sun. You feel him on your skin, in the air; you are sure of his presence and yet you cannot find him. In the same way, I know that the city has not been abandoned, that someone continues to watch over it, hiding between the porticos and the converging lines of the colonnades. He is the one who points out the two details to which I must cling when I seem to hear the baptistery door and the building windows thrust open in the darkness, as if by a sudden gust of wind. The blue banner that rises on the hill almost like a huge flower bending over its own weight, a large freed kite that is struggling to take flight; if you continue to look at it, it turns to stone: it is a snowy mountain slope merging with the gleam of the sky. I go back to look for the doves. They are still there, sitting on the first ledge of the building as if taking refuge from the light completely bathing the façade looking onto the square. Sitting along the wall, almost camouflaged against the plaster, they are the only animal presences in the whole scene; the only hearts that pulse in this stony silence. A moment earlier they had made a halt on the baptistery roof. A beating of wings, its reverberation, and the whole scene slowly changes. Now they are flying down onto the cobblestones of the square. They are pecking at the grooves between the marble slabs. Perhaps something has remained in those gaps. For a few minutes, they remain intent like this, then suddenly fly up and alight on the balcony of the building with the purple stucco-work. Between the two protruding plants, the tuft and the pot with the bonsai oak, they come to a halt for a few

di davanzale in balcone per tre volte lungo la via a sinistra. Un capolavoro di contenimento così perfetto che l'occhio vorrebbe una lente. Sulla via opposta predomina invece il motivo del cespo che libera le sue fronde e torna per tre volte, in modo complementare. A un primo sguardo, da lontano, può essere scambiato con una di quelle erbe cresciute nell'incuria, nutrite dallo sgretolarsi dei muri, ma subito l'incanto dell'alberello dalla doppia chioma riporta alle forbici esatte del giardiniere, al suo sguardo che ha soppesato e voluto ogni cosa così come appare. L'abbandono è solo un pensiero. Qui non c'è natura liberata che possa prosperare nella desolazione. La città è presidiata da forze che contrastano lo sbiadirsi degli intonaci, il creparsi delle pareti.

Questo dipinto non permette di essere guardato. Non consente allo sguardo di avvicinarsi e andarsene come un visitatore qualunque. La città è sotto assedio. Chiusa in una grande stanza dorme la principessa bambina. Inizi a percorrere di piano in piano ogni appartamento. Apri tutte le porte. Spalanchi le finestre alla luce. Pensi di essere il principe che risveglia ogni cosa. Per un attimo la piazza e le vie si affollano di gente. Poi su tutto ridiscende il silenzio. Il mistero che governa questo luogo è più potente di qualsiasi immaginazione. Ogni storia inizia e finisce qui, in questo deserto di muri abbagliati dalla luce.

Continua a modificarsi sotto gli occhi la città, a schiudere figure che sottrae senza che te ne accorgi. Neanche ti accorgi di come il tuo sguardo sia diverso, ora, dopo avere soggiornato qui. Dietro queste linee è un campo di forza. Un solo punto, uno solo, come quello che i tuoi occhi, a volte, inavvertitamente fissano.

Non hai ancora visto niente, non hai saputo vedere. Qui ogni immagine è il duplicato di sé, ritorna come appare nel profondo, nell'acqua buia della mente. È il tuo pensiero che sta cercando un luogo dove potere albergare senza ogni volta entrare e uscire straniero, spossessato di tutto. Se riuscirà a fermarsi si aprirà come la città, contenitore di buio, custodia di silenzio.

*

Questi frammenti in forma di visione sono nati da lunghe immersioni nel lago della *Città ideale*. Sono un respiro fermo, un'apnea frammentata da brevi ritorni in superficie.

Quando ho saputo che questa tavola era probabilmente la testiera di un lettuccio meditativo non sono più riuscita a staccarmi da questa immagine da abitare distesi, tra veglia e sonno. Ho sostato a lungo perché non ho luogo, e come ogni cosa che non ha luogo non accade, così anch'io resto, entro ed

seconds. They don't have time to reach the nearby hanging garden when a sudden tapping scatters them inside the other forms, undoing every line in the darkness. My eyelids have closed. The city has sunk once again.

This place is capable of inducing delirium. It makes you get lost as if in a house of mirrors. Today I glimpsed the gardener on the terrace, bending furtively under a bush of the hedge. He is probably the same custodian—two shadows that sometimes overlap without ever coinciding completely. On the other hand, in this space everything blurs: a daydream within reality, reality within a daydream. Two opposing forces collide: the geometric control and something irreducible to this planned harmony. Hence, the recurrent motif of the small oak tree, from windowsill to balcony three times along the street to the left. A masterpiece of containment so perfect that the eye would be like a lens. On the opposite street, the tuft motif predominates, freeing its fronds and returning three times, in a complementary way. At first glance, from a distance, the tuft can be confused with one of those grasses that grow amid neglect, nourished by the crumbling of walls, but immediately the enchanting sapling with the double foliage recalls the gardener's precise scissors, his gaze that has pondered everything and wanted it to be as it appears. Abandonment is a mere thought. Here no liberated nature can thrive within the desolation. The city is guarded by forces that contrast with the fading plaster, the cracking walls.

This painting does not allow itself to be looked at. It does not allow one's gaze to approach and go away like any visitor. The city is under siege. Closed up in a large room, the little princess girl sleeps. You start to walk through each apartment slowly. You open all the doors. Open the windows wide to the light. You think you are the prince who awakens everything. For a moment the square and the streets are crowded with people. Then silence again falls over everything. The mystery that governs this place is more powerful than any imagination. Every story begins and ends here, in this desert of walls dazzled by light.

The city keeps changing before your eyes, half revealing figures that it removes without your noticing. You don't even notice how, after staying here, your gaze has now become different. Behind these lines is a force field. One single point, like the one at which your eyes sometimes inadvertently stare.

You haven't seen anything yet, you haven't known how to see. Here each image is the duplicate of itself, coming back as it appears in the depths, in the dark water of the mind. It is your thought that is seeking a place to lodge—

esco dalla soglia di questo spazio che appare e scompare. Trasportato e mutato dai pensieri come le nuvole dal vento.

Sono felice che questo dipinto non porti la firma di nessuno. Nel Palazzo Ducale di Urbino, dove nessun luogo sfugge al nome del suo padrone, dove ogni angolo ripete la gloria e l'ossessione di un'identità, dai soffitti alle soglie, dai camini agli stucchi alle pareti: *FD Fe Dux*, lo spazio anonimo della città ideale resta protetto da qualsiasi attribuzione. L'abbiamo disegnato in tanti, percorrendolo come la percorriamo ancora.

*

Le parole non hanno saputo staccarsi dall'immagine che le ha fatte nascere. Questo grande grembo al centro dello spazio, tradotto in linee e figure architettoniche. La città ideale, così sacra nel suo silenzio, accoglie come una madonna dentro il suo manto. Con la stessa misericordia contiene ciò che è umano, si apre donando un luogo protetto, avvolto dal cielo. Così lo spazio di questo abitare, di queste finestre e soglie che si rispecchiano e tornano ognuna a chiamarci, come a dire: fermati qui, è questa la tua casa, prenditi cura di questo vuoto. Qualcosa di magnetico ci riporta ogni volta al centro dello stesso mistero. Siamo noi, contenitori di memoria, di storie che ci appartengono, che ci hanno attraversato o che stanno sospese nell'aria in cui viviamo. Sono stata il battistero, la cattedrale in fondo alla piazza, la casa con il giardino pensile, quella con il colonnato all'ultimo piano, più aria che muri.

L'indirizzo che non ho mai riconosciuto è in te, in una delle tue vie si compone e ricompone un numero, un nome. Dove abito, dove sono.

Dove sono nata è scritto nei documenti. Dove vivo non lo scrivo. Non lo so, e forse non voglio saperlo. Per questo mia città dipinta nel legno ti prego ogni volta che i miei occhi si smarriscono e non riconosco la strada di casa, non riconoscono nessuna casa. La vorrei di paglia e di terra, sorta dalle mie mani, come in un pomeriggio senza tempo dell'infanzia. Quando racchiudi un luogo, lo cerchi con le braccia, come stringendolo a te, tracci confini. In quello spazio puoi cadere, abbandonarti al tuo peso come un seme. Così nella casa che avevo ricavato da un incavo formato tra la vigna e il campo arato. Ricoperto di rami e di frasche come un rifugio di cacciatori scavato nel terreno. Lì avrei depositato le mandorle e le noci raccolte per l'inverno. Lì mi sarei rannicchiata tra pareti scure scomparendo alla vista, recapitando i messaggi delle formiche, cogliendo sassi bianchi. Quando pulisco questa casa di marmo intonaci e vetri, questa casa dove vivo ora senza saperlo, la accarezzo come fosse

without entering and leaving every time like a dispossessed stranger. If your thought manages to come to a halt it will open out like the city, a receptacle of darkness, preserving silence.

*

These fragments in the form of a vision were born from long immersions in the lake of the *Ideal City*. They are one motionless breath, an apnea fragmented by brief returns to the surface.

When I learned that this panel was probably the headboard of a day bed for meditating, I was no longer able to detach myself from this image that could be inhabited while lying down, between wakefulness and sleep. I stopped off there for a long time because I have no place, and as something placeless cannot happen, therefore I also stay, going and coming back across the threshold of this space that appears and disappears. A space transported and transmuted by thoughts like clouds by the wind.

I am happy that this painting bears no one's signature. In the Ducal Palace of Urbino, where no place shuns its owner's name, where every corner reiterates the glory and obsession of an identity, from the ceilings to the thresholds, from the fireplaces to the stuccoes on the walls: *FD Fe Dux*, the anonymous space of the ideal city remains protected from any attribution. We have designed it in many ways, walking through it as we continue to do.

*

My words have not been able to detach themselves from the image that gave birth to them. This large womb in the center of the space, translated into architectural lines and figures. The ideal city, so sacred in its silence, gives welcome, like a Madonna into her mantle. With the same mercy, the ideal city contains what is human, opening itself up and providing a protected place enveloped by the sky. Such is this inhabitable space, where these windows and thresholds reflect each other, each again beckoning to us as if to say: stop here, this is your home, take care of this void. Something magnetic brings us back every time to the center of the same mystery. It is us, the receptacles of memories, of stories belonging to us, having passed through us or suspended in the air in which we live. I have been the baptistery, the cathedral at the end of the square, the house with the hanging garden, the house with the colonnade on the top floor, more air than walls.

The address that I have never acknowledged is in you; in one of your streets a number, and a name, is put together and put together again. Where I live, where I am.

di pietra e di terra viva, come sentisse le mie mani. Torno alla sua materia, prima della betoniera e dei passaggi di stato, prima delle trasformazioni dell'industria, alla sua materia semplice. Per questo mi piace ritrovare la polvere, quando è maturo il tempo e si può radunare in piccoli depositi scuri. Riunire l'inizio e la fine del mondo.

Mia città dipinta, mia città, voglio che tu sia nella mia stanza, a un capo del letto, come un'immagine sacra. Come il quadro con la madre e il bambino che ogni camera di contadini aveva insieme a un ramoscello di olivo benedetto, a una spiga secca di grano. Mia città, ogni volta che passo di fronte a un'agenzia di viaggi, quegli annunci di weekend e settimane da trascorrere in un punto come un altro della terra, mi avvolgono di un senso di morte. Assomigliano agli annunci con le date esatte di un'esistenza che ti saluta da una foto. Ho bisogno di un luogo, ho bisogno di te ogni volta che mi si cancella lo spazio sotto gli occhi. Questo spazio consunto, che non ho aperto con il mio desiderio, che non ho plasmato con la mia immaginazione. Non si regge più, può crollarmi addosso da un momento all'altro come un rudere. Si è cancellato il paesaggio. Non accoglie più i miei passi questa terra: mi pesa sulla lingua, mi ricopre dalle caviglie alla nuca. È una madre assopita, capace di rimangiarsi i suoi figli. Allora vado in stazione come in farmacia. Con lo stesso sollievo con cui si prende una medicina salgo su un treno. Tu, mia città dipinta, sei sul mio petto come un ciondolo. Ti posso toccare ogni tanto con una mano, sovrappensiero. Lo so che non mi abbandoni, e più che saperlo lo sento. Sei il luogo in cui può accadere ogni cosa, lo scenario in cui la mia vita torna a svolgersi. Si ferma, si addensa su di sé in un gomitolo di buio, poi rotola, finalmente si libera nello spazio aperto.

Where I was born is written down in documents. I don't write down where I live. I don't know where it is, and maybe I don't want to know. For this reason, I pray to you—my city painted on wood—every time that my eyes get lost and I can't find my way home, that I can't find any home. I would like it to be made of straw and earth, born from my hands, as in a timeless afternoon of childhood. When you enclose a place, you encircle it with your arms, as if holding it tightly; you draw up boundaries. You can fall into that space, abandoning yourself to your weight like a seed. So it was in the home I had made out of a hollow formed between the vineyard and the plowed field, and had covered with branches and brushwood like a hunters' refuge dug into the ground. There I would deposit the almonds and walnuts collected for the winter. There I would curl up between dark walls disappearing from view, delivering the messages of the ants, gathering white pebbles. When I clean this house made of marble, plaster and glass, this house where I now live without knowing so, I caress it as if it were made of stone and living earth, as if it felt my hands. I go back to its original matter—before the cement mixer and the changes of state, before the industrial transformations—to its simplest matter. This is why I like to find dust when the time is ripe and it can be gathered in small dark deposits. To bring together the beginning and the end of the world.

My painted city, my city, I want you to be in my room, at one end of the bed, like a sacred image. Like the painting with the mother and child that each peasant room had along with a blessed olive branch, a dry ear of corn. My city, every time I pass in front of a travel agency, the announcements of weekends and weeks to spend in a place like any other place on earth, envelop me with a sense of death. They resemble those announcements with the exact dates of an existence greeting you from a photo. I need a place, I need you every time that a space vanishes before my eyes. This worn-out space, which I have not opened with my desire, which I have not shaped with my imagination. Nothing holds up this space anymore; at any moment it can collapse on me like a ruin. The landscape has been eliminated. This earth no longer welcomes my footsteps: it weighs on my tongue, covering me from my ankles to my neck. The earth is a dozing mother, capable of devouring her offspring. So I go to the train station as I would to a pharmacy. With the same relief with which one takes a medicine, I hop on a train. You, my painted city, are on my chest like a pendant. Every now and then, distractedly, I can touch you with one hand. I know you won't abandon me, and the more I know this, the more I feel it. You are the place where anything can happen, the setting in which my life again evolves. It comes to a halt, thickens itself up into a ball of darkness, then rolls away, at last freeing itself in the open space.

La donna delle pulizie

Un giorno, un minimo gesto, e siamo da capo. Non esistono argini o dighe. Solo questa rete sottilissima che cade dall'alto senza fine e si fa scorgere nel sole, in un raggio che rimane in certi momenti sospeso nella stanza. Qualcosa lassù rovina incessantemente. Particelle discendono su di noi, invisibili piovono fitte, fino a consistere in un velo leggero, e grigie piume che si raccolgono agli angoli delle stanze. Il tempo è un animale che non ho mai visto. Non so che taglia abbia, quali abitudini, se sia addomesticabile. Ma si aggira nella vostra casa addensando le sue tracce nei luoghi più riposti. Mi piacerebbe incontrarlo, ma so che sarà lui a tagliarmi la strada, fissandomi negli occhi con la profondità di un bosco.

Ogni mattina, nella vostra sala deserta, un malinconico filo è abbandonato dal suo creatore. Fino a che arriva il mio giorno di turno. E posso rimanere a raccogliere questa finissima cenere illuminata che scende a seppellirci. Che ci chiuderà gli occhi, più dolcemente di quella esplosa da un vulcano, ma nello stesso irrimediabile modo. Continuiamo a compiere ciò che è dovuto, a versarci dalla prima all'ultima ora nei gesti, finché non iniziamo ad avvertire qualcosa e lentamente ci invade la paura. Chi cerca di raggiungere la riva, chi si inoltra nel verde, chi si ripara al chiuso delle pareti o fino all'ultimo continua a trascinarsi. A ogni modo tutti saremo ricoperti. L'ultimo pensiero è contenuto nella posizione dello scheletro. È per questo che mi fermo a lungo, il giovedì mattina, sotto il raggio. Voglio che venga prima per me. Vorrei guardare la trama del lenzuolo e respirare in quello spazio protetto, nascosta dai piedi alla nuca. Come da bambina, quando per lunghi momenti mi inabissavo per riemergere a un tratto. E poi va bene, resterò mezz'ora in più la sera, per finire quello che dovevo.

Questa polvere mi fa bene, mi ricopre di una strana eternità. Come se fossi già dalla sua parte. Così posso spostare le nuvole sul pavimento, o lasciare addensare il grigio che vi minaccia. Mentre voi correte a strofinarvi l'uno contro l'altro per salvarvi, per togliervi di dosso la polvere. Ma di che cosa siete fatti per lasciare le cose in questo modo. Precipitate da un dirupo a capo del letto, l'una avvinghiata all'altra, le tante salme che vi portate addosso, così sporti sul vuoto da attraversare in pochi minuti stagioni e identità. Neanche l'amore o qualcosa che gli rassomiglia può ripulire la vostra lordura. Ogni volta vi alzate ancora più sporchi, come se strofinandovi aveste accolto il fango dell'altro. Per questo si innalza lento e continuo il coro della centrifuga, come di acqua contro macigni, a renderli sassi arresi nel tempo. Non affidatemi più compiti inutili come ripiegarvi le maglie. Una veste rovesciata va indossata com'è: ecco una grande fortuna, un cambiamento vicino. E il giorno dopo vedrete

The Cleaning Lady

One day, a slight gesture, and we are back at the beginning. There are no embankments or dams. Only this very thin net that falls from on high, endlessly, and can be glimpsed in the sunlight, in a ray that keeps hovering, at certain moments, in the room. Something up there constantly decays. Invisible particles rain down heavily upon us until they form a light veil and gray feathers that gather in the corners of rooms. Time is an animal that I have never seen. I don't know its size, its habits, whether it can be tamed. But it roams through your homes, leaving ever-thicker tracks in the most hidden spots. I'd like to meet up with it, but I know that it will be the one to cut in front of me, staring into my eyes with the depths of a woods.

Every morning, in your deserted rooms, a melancholy thread from a spiderweb is left behind by its creator. Until my cleaning day comes. And I can stay to collect this fine shiny ash that comes down to bury us. That will close our eyes, more gently than the ash of an exploding volcano, but in the same irremediable way. We continue to do what must be done, to throw ourselves into our acts from the first to the last hour until we begin to sense something and slowly are invaded by fear. Some try to reach the shore, some slip into the vegetation, others take shelter within closed walls or, until the end, keep crawling away. In all events, we will be covered. One's last thought is contained in the position of the skeleton. This is why I stop for a long time, on Thursday mornings, in the ray of sunlight. I want it to come for me first. I would like to look at the weave of the bed sheet and, hidden from my feet to the nape of my neck, breathe in that protected space. As when, a child, I would sink into it for long moments only to surface suddenly. And then, all right, I'll stay a half-hour longer in the evening to finish what I have to finish.

This dust does me good, it covers me with a strange eternity. As if I were already on its side. I can thus move the clouds across the floor, or let the grayness threatening you thicken. While you all run to rub against each other to save yourself, to get rid of the dust. But what are you made of to leave things this way? Thrown off the cliff at the head of the bed, clinging to each other, are the many corpses you wear, and you lean out over the void to go through seasons and identities in a few minutes. Not even love or something that resembles it can cleanse your filth. Every time you get up even dirtier, as if by rubbing against each other you had accepted the filth of the other. For this reason the chorus of the centrifuge rises slowly and continuously, like water against boulders, turning them into pebbles that have surrendered over time. Don't entrust me with useless tasks like folding your shirts. A dress turned inside-out should be worn like that: how fortunate, a quick change. And the

che senza pensarci ritorna la tinta consueta. Quanti sforzi per cambiare senza successo. Basterebbe una mattina dimenticarsi. Allacciare una scarpa alla gamba del letto. O come capita a volte quando mi inginocchio a raccogliere qualcosa, rimanere prostrati di fronte alla potenza degli armadi.

next day you'll see, without thinking about it, that the usual color has returned. So many unsuccessful efforts to change. A morning would be enough to forget oneself. To tie a shoe to the bed leg. Or as sometimes happens when I kneel down to pick something up, to keep prostrating myself in front of the power of wardrobes.

Vigilando

Ferma a scrivere per strada, su un taccuino che per ossessione o abitudine ho sempre con me, sono stata scambiata da un passante per vigile urbano. «Ci fai la multa?» Ha chiesto vedendomi segnare in piedi qualcosa accanto a una fila di auto parcheggiate. Avrei dovuto ringraziare quell'uomo, ma ho soltanto sorriso, assorta a tracciare sul taccuino. Per qualche istante ho sentito le mie parole illuminarsi: se fossero lette con la stessa attenzione di quei fogli lasciati sul parabrezza. . . se le vite degli abitanti di questa via ne fossero, per qualche sequenza, modificate. . .

Camminando ho sempre ceduto al vizio che mi porta a scrivere, prendendo appunti dalle cose, ritrovandomi a un tratto sulla soglia di un segreto che mi chiama, come un cane, a muso chino, quando intercetta un punto in cui la vita affiora in un suo denso precipitato. Bisogna aspirarlo e filtrarlo, fino all'ultima molecola. Niente ha significato, fino a che non si è assolto quel compito di obbedienza a una presenza invisibile, capace di attenuare e annullare persino il dolore (qualcuno tenta di tirarti via a forza, arriva a prenderti a calci). Molte volte questo accade a chi è portato ad avvertire, nelle strade di ogni giorno, le tracce di un'altra vita. Bloccando per alcuni momenti il flusso di ciò che è usuale, compreso nei principi di utilità e commercio.

È per questo, credo, che con un senso di malcelato disagio, scrivo per strada, lasciando che il mio istinto si appaghi, il più velocemente possibile, sperando di passare inosservata.

Quest'uomo che oggi mi ha riconosciuta in un vigile urbano, ha intuito qualcosa: sto svolgendo il mio lavoro. Difficile comprendere per chi o per che cosa. Faccio rapporto, consegno il mio verbale.

Keeping Watch

Stopping to write on the street, in a notebook that out of habit or obsession I always have with me, I was taken for a traffic policewoman by a passerby. "Are you writing out a ticket?" he asked, watching me mark something down while I was standing next to a row of parked cars. I should have thanked the man, but I merely smiled, absorbed as I was in jotting in my notebook. For a few moments I sensed my words brightening: if they were read with the same attention as those slips of paper left on windshields. . . if the lives of the inhabitants of this street were, for some time sequence, modified. . .

While walking, I have always given into this vice that induces me to write, taking notes from things, suddenly finding myself on the threshold of a secret that calls out to me, as when a dog with its snout on the ground sniffs a point where one of life's thick precipitates is emerging. It's necessary to breathe it in, to filter it, up to the last molecule. Nothing has meaning until you have carried out this duty of obedience to an invisible presence, capable of attenuating and nullifying even pain (someone tries to pull you away by force, ends up kicking you). This often happens to one inclined to sense, in everyday streets, the traces of another life. Thwarting for a few moments the flow of what is usual, included in the principles of utility and trade.

This is why, I think, I write on the street with a feeling of ill-concealed unease, letting my instinct satisfy itself as quickly as possible, and hoping to go unnoticed.

The man who took me, today, for a traffic policewoman, intuited something: I'm doing my job. It's difficult to understand for whom or for what. I'm making a report, and delivering it.

Un verso è una vasca e altri appunti sulla poesia

Quando percorro avanti e indietro le vasche di una piscina, alla ricerca di quello stato di narcosi che mi coglie poco tempo dopo il ritorno all'asciutto, mi seguono inizialmente alcuni pensieri. Scorrono leggeri sulla superficie insieme alla mia chiglia, fluttuano appena sulla linea che guardo per non deviare. Per un'ora circa avrò soltanto alcuni gesti, con le braccia che a volte sembrano disegnare un arco deciso e tagliare l'acqua, oppure oscillare e cedere. Ripeterò gli stessi gesti fino a quando sentirò le spalle muoversi in un celeste che lentamente si solidifica. Allora risalirò dalla scaletta, ascolterò la doccia e il phon, e tornata a casa verrò richiamata nel fondo, dove si depone il governo delle mie forze.

Alle prime bracciate, quando ancora l'acqua non è stata dissodata e i miei archi procedono incerti, mi sembra di continuare a scrivere, su un foglio limpido, con tutto il corpo. Penso che si arrivi alla fine di un verso, come di una vasca, muovendosi all'interno di una misura. Una serie di gesti si ripete fino a che si raggiunge una sorta di equilibrio per cui sembra di non muoversi, ma di essere portati. Chi infrange il codice di movimenti e si dibatte oltre la forma stabilita, affatica il suo corpo e alla lunga lo addolora. I suoi schizzi suonano stonati, non necessari. Sbaglia per incapacità o per ignoranza. Ne vedo diversi avanzare sul dorso battendo le gambe con le ginocchia piegate, oppure andare di continuo a urtare i galleggianti delle corsie. Il fatto è che i movimenti sono già tutti scritti. L'unico pensiero è quello di aderire, di eliminare ogni intenzione che fuoriesce dal tracciato.

Anche se si arriva al bordo della vasca con un turbinio di rabbie e di rancori, nello stesso istante in cui ci si affida all'acqua le passioni come scorie tendono verso il fondo, liberano i propri riflessi nel gioco della superficie. Con il roteare delle braccia e il battere delle gambe, poi sembrano del tutto dissipate. In realtà hanno obbedito a leggi più grandi dell'istinto, e all'interno di quel rito di obbedienza si sono placate. Allo stesso modo, quando ci si affaccia alle soglie di un verso, non si arriva alla sua fine senza che lo stato emotivo che ci portava, non sia stato in qualche modo addomesticato. Si scrive con la stessa cieca consapevolezza con cui si nuota: ogni intenzione o slancio deve essere sorretto da tutto il corpo, approvato dalle sue forze e dalle sue riserve. Ogni gesto deve misurarsi con la necessità di toccare infine il bordo della vasca.

Non si sovverte la tradizione in un attimo, in un sussulto di immaginazione eccedente. Se mai nascerà un nuovo stile, o una variante all'interno di quello codificato, sarà per un progressivo e lento distacco dai movimenti precedenti, attraverso prove calibrate, minime infrazioni accolte.

Lo stile libero non esiste, non si è mai liberi se si vuole nuotare.

*

A Line is a Lap and Other Notes on Poetry

When I swim laps back and forth in a pool, seeking that narcotic state that hits me a little while after my return to dry ground, a few thoughts initially follow me. They skim lightly across the surface, along with my keel, barely floating along the line I watch to keep from veering. For about an hour I will make only a few kinds of movements, my arms sometimes seeming to draw a clear-cut arc and slice into the water, or to waver and give way. I will repeat the same movements until I feel my shoulders advancing through a slowly solidifying sky blue. Then I will climb the ladder, listen to the shower and the hairdryer, and, once home, be called back to the bottom, to which my governing forces sink.

With my first strokes, before the water has been plowed up and while my uncertain arcs are progressing, it seems to me that I continue to write with my whole body, on a transparent sheet of paper. I think that one comes to the end of a line as if it were a lap, while moving inside a measure. A series of movements is repeated until a kind of equilibrium is reached through which one seems not to pass, but rather to be carried. Whoever breaks the movement rules and flounders beyond the established form, wears down the body and, in the long run, makes it ache. The splashing sounds out of tune, unneeded. He or she errs out of inability or ignorance. I see several of them on their backs, kicking their legs with bent knees, or constantly running into the line buoys. Actually, all the movements are already written. One's unique thought is to comply, to eliminate any intention that swerves off course.

Even if one reaches the edge of the pool with a swirling of rage and rancor, once one's trust is placed in the water, passions sink like slag toward the bottom and free their own reflections to play on the surface. With the whirling of arms and thrashing of legs, the passions then seem completely dispersed. In fact, they have obeyed laws greater than instinct, and within this rite of obedience they have calmed down. In the same way, when one stands at the threshold of a line in a poem, the end is not reached without the emotional state, which has brought one there, having somehow been tamed. Writing is done with the same blind awareness as swimming: every intention or élan must be supported by the whole body, approved by its forces and reserves. Every movement must be measured by the necessity of finally touching the edge of the pool.

Tradition is not overturned in an instant, in a fit of excess imagination. Should a new style be born, or a variant within a codified style, this will take place through a slow, gradual detachment from previous movements, through carefully measured experiments, minimal infringements excepted.

Freestyle does not exist; you are never free if you want to swim.

*

Le uova ci sono e l'oca le cova. Forse è passato un mese, forse tre. Un vecchio che viene a potare la siepe dice che il tempo della cova è terminato, che là sotto, se c'è qualcosa, è tutto morto, e che se non si tolgono le uova l'oca continuerà ad avvolgerle nel ventre, fino a perdere le forze e ad ammalarsi. Il vecchio allora si china sul nido, prende le uova una a una, le avvicina all'orecchio e le scuote. Quelle che fanno un rumore sordo le spacca contro una pietra. Sulle zolle si apre un liquido rosso e marrone, gelatinoso e maleodorante. La maggior parte delle uova viene aperta, poche vengono rimesse nel nido. Assistiamo a questo rito consapevoli che una minima imperizia decide la vita.

Anche nello scrivere c'è un tempo oltre il quale ogni più premurosa costanza e dedizione non valgono a nulla: da quel testo non nascerà una poesia. Un lettore attento e con esperienza può aiutarci a riconoscere quale testo può avere ancora speranze. Forse con il tempo impareremo a distinguere da soli il suono della fissità e quello da cui può nascere la vita. Ma facilmente chi ha fatto le uova è portato ad aspettare oltre ogni limite, a riversare nella possibilità tutto se stesso. Certe cose invece non dipendono neanche del tutto da noi. A volte bisogna semplicemente alzarsi dal foglio, abbandonare il nido, e continuare a muovere passi nell'erba.

*

Senza un minimo di amore per se stessi non si parla, né tantomeno si scrive. Posso dirlo perché ho combattuto contro la mia statua di pietra, le ho lanciato calci e pugni. Forse, nella furia, l'ho appena scalfita. Poi ho smesso di fissarla con gli occhi bianchi di ostinazione. E lei si è lentamente sgretolata, fino a riprendere consistenza umana.

Contro noi stessi si può fare molto. Io ho desiderato e immaginato molto. Ma scivolava sul polso la lametta e la linea gialla non si faceva oltrepassare. Contro di me ho fallito, non ho portato a termine o compiuto. Poi ho impugnato la penna e ho iniziato ad aprire lunghi tagli sulle braccia. Più era profondo ed esatto il colpo, più stillava gioia.

*

È come quando si giocava da soli contro la parete. È dal modo in cui torna il pallone che ti accorgi se hai tirato bene. Solo che il tempo del rimbalzo è allungato a dismisura: non sai più se fidarti di te stesso, vorresti che a ricevere il pallone fosse un altro. Quando scrivi e non riesci ad ascoltarti, il gioco si fa sordo, senza ritmo, fino a che arriva il momento di smettere.

The eggs are there and the goose broods them. Perhaps a month has gone by, perhaps three. An old man who comes to prune the hedge says that the brooding time is over, that underneath her, if there's anything, it's all dead, that the eggs must be removed or she'll keep covering them until she loses strength and gets sick. The old man then bends over the nest, picks up the eggs one by one, brings them close to his ear, and shakes them. Those sounding dull are smashed against a stone. A reddish, brownish, gelatinous, foul-smelling liquid spreads over the dirt clods. Most of the eggs are broken open, a few are put back into the nest. We witness this rite, aware that the slightest incompetence determines life.

In writing, there is also a time beyond which the most thoughtful kinds of perseverance and dedication are worthless: from that text, no poem will be born. A careful, experienced reader can help us to recognize which text might still have hopes. Perhaps in time we will ourselves learn to distinguish an inert sound and that from which life can be born. Yet whoever has laid the eggs is easily led into waiting beyond all limits and throwing herself entirely into the possibility. Some things, however, do not wholly depend on us. Sometimes you just have to get up from the sheet of paper, leave the nest behind, and keep walking through the grass.

*

Without a minimum of self-love, one cannot speak, let alone write. I can say this because I fought against my stone statue, kicking and punching at it. Perhaps, in my fury, I barely scratched it. Then I stopped staring at it, my eyes white with obstinacy. And it slowly crumbled until it recovered its human substance.

Against ourselves much can be done. I myself wished for and imagined a lot. But the blade was gliding across the wrist and the yellow line didn't let itself be crossed. Against myself I failed, neither finished nor accomplished anything. Then I grasped the pen and started to open long cuts on my arms. The deeper and more exact the gash, the more joy dripped out.

*

It's as when one plays alone against a wall. From the way the ball bounces back you realize whether you've thrown it well. Yet the rebound starts taking too long: you no longer know if you can trust yourself; you'd like someone else to receive the ball. When you write and can't manage to listen to yourself, the game becomes dull, loses its rhythm, until the time comes to stop.

*

I versi sono i voli di un insetto imprigionato. Non si sa che cosa abbia portato l'insetto attraverso la fessura (un istinto innaturale forse, una bussola infranta). Una volta nella casa, si accorge presto che non è il suo luogo.

Un verso nasce quando l'insetto cerca la via d'uscita dirigendosi dove vede più luce. La fine di un verso è il battere dell'insetto contro la parete invisibile del vetro. Voli e versi si ripetono, a una cadenza che si fa più ossessiva con l'aumentare della consapevolezza che la vita continua fuori, da dove si è venuti. Voli e versi sono fallimenti.

La maggior parte degli insetti si consuma dentro la casa: si afflosciano alla fine arresi, si posano inebetiti dall'urto continuato.

*

Il lavoro del cameriere è fatto di sguardo. Il suo compito è fare in modo che nessuno chieda di lui. Invisibile compagno, mastica nel pensiero quello che i clienti hanno in bocca. È come se fosse seduto accanto a ognuno e invece è sempre in piedi, alle loro spalle, in qualche luogo imprecisato.

Ogni cameriere ha un suo ruolo e un suo settore della sala, ma sostanzialmente si lavora insieme, soprattutto quando c'è più afflusso. Allora puoi vederli aiutarsi con uno sguardo, con un cenno fare capire che porteranno loro un'altra bottiglia su quel tavolo. Così ogni tragitto dalla cucina alla sala non va perso.

Nei fine settimana di qualche anno trascorso, sono stata una cameriera mite e quasi muta. Lavoravo religiosamente chiusa in me stessa, riponendo la stanchezza in un mio luogo remoto. Quando ho riconosciuto la tela che univa e sorreggeva gli altri, il mio tempo era già trascorso. È bastato a comprendere in che modo si dovrebbe scrivere. O porteremo libri che rimangono chiusi, come bottiglie d'acqua su un tavolo in cui ne serviva soltanto una.

*

Cessate le fatiche e i ripensamenti, ci si ritrova con il proprio libro in mano. Anche quei versi che continuano a emanare un sottile stato di allarme, come non avessimo fatto il possibile per farli funzionare, tacciono come i grandi pilastri della corrente elettrica: più ci si avvicina, più si sente l'aria vibrare come per un'enorme arnia.

*

Lines in a poem are flights of an imprisoned insect. One doesn't know what has brought the insect through the crack (an unnatural instinct perhaps, a broken compass). Once in the house, it soon realizes that this is not its place.

A line is born when the insect seeks its way out, heading where it sees more light. The end of a line is the insect's beating against the invisible glass wall. Flights and lines are repeated at an increasingly obsessive pace as the awareness grows that life goes on outside, where one has come from. Flights and lines are failures.

Most insects wear themselves out inside the house: at the end they collapse, giving up, landing dazed from the continuous impacts.

*

A waiter's job consists of looking. His task is to ensure that nobody asks for him. An invisible companion, he chews in his mind what customers have in their mouths. It's as if he were sitting next to each and every one yet always standing behind their backs, at an unspecified place.

Every waiter has his own role and sector in the dining room, but basically they work together, especially when there is more influx. You can then see them helping each other out with a look, with a nod making it understood that they will bring another bottle over to that table. So no trip from the kitchen to the dining room will be wasted.

For a few years in the past, I was a meek, almost silent weekend waitress. I worked religiously closed up within myself, placing tiredness in one of my remote recesses. When I recognized the fabric weaving together and holding up the others, my time was already over. It sufficed to understand in what way one should write. Or else we will bring books that remain closed, like bottles of water on a table for which only one bottle was needed.

*

Once the work and second-guessing are over, there is a book in one's hands. Even those lines that keep emitting a slight state of alarm, as if we hadn't done all we could to make them work, are silent like tall power line poles: the closer one gets, the more one feels the air vibrating as from a huge beehive.

Un rischiosissimo gioco

Per quanto guardassi le cose dentro, non accadeva niente; mi piaceva dondolare in me le frasi, i loro inizi, immaginando nella scia che continuava, indicibili svolgimenti. Mi piaceva sostare dove la strada si dirama, come un enorme delta che si allarga fino a confondersi con un lago acquitrinoso, una marina, un mare dal fondo basso di sabbia, un mare. E intanto mi si avvolgeva tutto: le frasi appena lambite si arrotolavano al mio corpo impedendo i movimenti. Non riuscivo a parlare, a fare in modo che le parole uscissero nell'istante in cui nascevano, presenti e subito trascorse, subito pronte a generarne altre, in un discorso.

Ho sempre amato andarmene fino a lasciare del corpo due piccole fenditure per guardare. Immersa nella penombra che si allarga, assisto alle vicende, all'accadere. Ogni tanto vedo ricomparirmi un braccio che si agita, poi mezza gamba fino alla coscia, una spalla appuntita, un seno; il mio corpo si materializza a tratti, mai del tutto. Sono così libera da quello che succede, che a volte, dalla gioia, mi metterei a saltare, come un uccello piccolo che impara il volo. Eppure spesso, piccoli cerchi scuri macchiavano di sangue la terra, come chiamando qualcuno a seguire le mie tracce. Mi ferivo, sbattevo contro le pareti, come avessi potuto attraversarle. Con la stessa sicurezza guardavo qualcuno o qualcosa che mi si dirigeva contro, come stesse attraversando un antico arco di pietra, alle soglie di una città. Mi graffiavo, mi incidevo, aspettavo un segno che avrebbe rivelato la mia identità. E più mi accorgevo di essere sola, più mi lasciavo cadere con tutto il peso, su punteruoli e schegge. Un giorno avvenne la grande distruzione e mi fermai, a un passo dalla morte, attonita, gli occhi come vetri infranti, pensando che era finito tutto. Invece era finita soltanto la mia adolescenza. Lo capii quando, lentamente, uscii dalle macerie. Da allora avrei imparato a sostare sempre più a lungo, scrivendo, nello spazio del mio respiro.

Un pompiere, un medico, un giardiniere... Una notte della mia infanzia, prima di dormire, con gli occhi al soffitto, pensai a che cosa sarei diventata da grande. Non mi era chiaro dove battesse il cuore del mondo, dove avrei dovuto chinarmi ad ascoltare. Ma ero sicura che l'avrei capito, e che mi sarei precipitata dove i miei gesti fossero necessari, come acqua per le piante.

Con la strana ma precisa sensazione di essere stata mandata da qualcuno, osservavo, prendevo parte a quello che accadeva, ma rimanendo libera dal suo peso – qualcosa mi richiamava in alto, tra gli uccelli. Un pomeriggio, mentre mi aggiravo per le stanze della casa vuota, un libro che stava cadendo da una mensola mi sfiorò la coda di un occhio, e si aprirono di scatto le mie mani: lo trattenni, soppesandolo, e lo rimisi al suo posto, dandogli l'angolazione

A Very Risky Game

No matter how much I looked into things, nothing would happen; I liked to rock sentences inside me, their beginnings, imagining in their continuing wake the not yet formulated developments. I liked halting where the road branches off, like a huge delta that widens until it merges with a marshy lake, a marina, a sea with a shallow sandy bottom, a sea. And in the meantime everything enveloped me: hardly even formed, the sentences would wind around my body, preventing me from moving. I couldn't speak, couldn't get the sentences to come out the instant they were born—sentences that would be present and immediately passed by, immediately ready to generate others and assemble what I wanted to say.

I have always loved going away until my body has two tiny slits left to peer through. Immersed in the dim light that is spreading, I witness events, what is happening. Now and then I see my trembling arm reappear, then half a leg up to my thigh, a pointed shoulder, a breast; my body materializes now and then, never entirely. I am so free from what is going on that sometimes, out of joy, I could begin to jump like a small bird learning to fly. Yet often small dark circles would stain the ground with blood, as if calling out to someone to follow my tracks. I would often wound myself, crashing against the walls as if I had been able to go through them. With the same certainty, I would stare at someone or something heading toward me as if he, she, or it were passing under an ancient stone arch, at the threshold of a town. I was scratching myself, engraving myself, waiting for a sign that would reveal my identity. And the more I realized that I was alone, the more I let myself fall with all my weight on awls and splinters. One day the great destruction took place and I stopped, a step away from death, astonished, my eyes like shattered glass, thinking that it was all over now. However, it was only my adolescence that was over. I understood this when I slowly emerged from the ruins. From that day on, I would learn to stay ever longer, writing, in the space of my breathing.

A firewoman, a doctor, a veterinarian. . . One night during my childhood, before going to sleep, with my eyes on the ceiling, I thought about what I would become when I grew up. It was unclear to me where the heart of the world was beating, where I should bend down and listen. But I was sure that I would understand and that I would rush to wherever my acts would be needed, like water for plants.

With the strange but precise feeling of having been sent by someone, I would observe, taking part in what was happening, but I remained free from its burden—something was beckoning me upwards, among the birds. One afternoon, as I was wandering around the rooms of the empty house, I spotted out of the corner of my eye a book falling from a shelf and my hands snapped

esatta. Se non ci fossi stata io si sarebbe schiantato dando un forte schiaffo al pavimento.

In quei giorni sentivo parlare spesso del mare che avrebbe potuto crescere fino a sommergere la nostra regione. Forse una di quelle previsioni fatte ascoltando i ghiacci che ai poli si sciolgono. Così mi ritrovavo spesso in qualche angolo della casa, con in mano un piccolo oggetto e un gioco molto serio da fare. Potevano essere monete, carte, o qualcos'altro che trovavo. Se non restavano in equilibrio in una certa posizione, o un'altra determinata operazione falliva, il mare ci avrebbe raggiunti cancellando ogni cosa. Il destino di molti era nelle mie mani, anche se nessuno poteva sospettarlo. A volte, anzi tutte le volte, di fronte all'esito peggiore ero pronta a cambiare immediatamente il responso: «non avevo detto *se i due fili si intrecciavano*, avevo detto *se restavano vicini*», e tutto si ricombinava, rientrava tra le tessere di quel rischiosissimo gioco.

open. I caught it, felt its weight, then put it back in place, leaning it exactly. If I hadn't been there it would have crashed, hitting the floor hard.

Back then, I often heard that the sea could rise until it submerged our region. Perhaps one of those predictions made by paying attention to the ice melting at the poles. I thus often found myself in some corner of the house, holding a small object and with a very serious game to play. The objects might be coins, cards, balls, or anything else that I chanced upon. If they couldn't remain balanced in a certain position, or if some specific action failed, the sea would crash down upon us, wiping out everything. The fate of many people was in my hands, although no one could suspect this. At times, indeed at all times, facing the worst outcome, I was ready to change the response immediately: "I had not said *if the two threads became entwined*, I had said *if they remained close*." And everything would be recombined, slipping once again between the pieces of that very risky game.

Cedere la parola

Una parte di noi precipita in un luogo senza fondo. Piccole bolle risalgono verso la superficie: lievi increspature poi nulla, più nulla. Un sacrificio che compie qualcuno per noi esaudendo il nostro voto o che compiamo noi stessi bendati e inconsapevoli, spinti da invisibili mani.

Scrivo perché ho ceduto la parola. Cedo la parola alla bocca degli altri. La cedo fino a perderla, fino a ritrovarmi ammutolita, imbavagliata, a una frazione di secondo dalla possibilità di ritornare. Ma quel secondo è decisivo, in quel secondo si è già pattuita la visione delle cose, intessuta la discussione, riso e deciso anche per te: alla presenza di te che affondi in una delle tante scuciture, maglie allargate e strappi del reale. Sprofondi, lentamente perdi consistenza. Le parole si stagliano altissime, come nuvole bianche contro un cielo nitido. Appartengono agli adulti, a un mondo che continua ad accadere. Finché qualcuno ha la parola ascolti, persuasa del suo diritto a occupare uno spazio di senso e di suono, della sua ragione a esistere, nella forza di chi prende la parola, contenendosi entro i propri confini o cancellando anche i tuoi labili contorni. Perdendo la parola divento un animale docile, un albero che fruscia. Tutti i graffi e i segni che porto, le fratture, il sangue perso, vengono da questa sfasatura rispetto al presente. Una fenditura in cui è caduto anche qualche grano di polvere. Un giorno vi ho trovato un filo d'erba.

Una lunga tavola apparecchiata per il pranzo. Tutti i parenti seduti. Tu avanzi piccola accanto all'ombra paterna. Per un attimo intuisci: è questo il momento per dire. La frase si staglia. Hai trovato le parole, giuste come un vestito in cui provare a non sentirsi a disagio. È la tua occasione: puoi portare quella cosa finalmente là fuori, vedere la forma e la consistenza che prende al contatto dell'aria, nelle orecchie degli altri. Ma è rimasta dentro. La frase si è incisa nella mente, un soffio senza suono che non esce dal petto. Subito sono apparse le conseguenze che avrebbe portato se avesse raggiunto le labbra (domande, rimproveri, una colpa da spartire, sofferenza versata sugli altri). Ho deglutito. Quella sequenza di parole poteva scendere in me, tornare a sciogliersi lasciando intatto il suo significato. Come un forziere che avrebbe potuto essere riscoperto negli anni, oppure finire dimenticato. Per ora dovevo soltanto lasciarlo depositare. Avevo un grande spazio buio per accoglierlo, lì dove dormivano i piccoli animali morti che avevo nutrito, i semi che non potevano crescere. E in fondo i confini tra ciò che è reale e ciò che abbiamo immaginato sono così fragili che avrei potuto lasciare che fossero confusi dall'acqua e dal vento. Forse non era accaduto niente. Forse quella custodia sigillata era vuota.

Yielding Words

Something in us plummets into a bottomless place. Small bubbles rise to the surface: slight ripples then nothing, nothing more. A sacrifice that someone carries out for us by fulfilling our vow or that we ourselves make, blindfolded and unaware, driven by invisible hands.

I write because I have yielded my words. I yield my words to others' mouths. I yield my words until I lose them, until I find myself struck dumb, gagged, at a fraction of a second from the possibility of coming back. But that second is decisive; in that second, the vision of things has already been agreed upon, the discussion wrapped up, laughter, decisions, also for you: in your presence as you sink into one of the many split seams, stretched stitches and rips in the fabric of reality. You go under, slowly losing consistency. The words stand out very high, like white clouds against a clear sky. The words belong to adults, to a world that continues to take place. As long as someone is speaking, you listen, persuaded of his right to occupy a space of sound and meaning, of why he exists, with the strength of one who takes his turn to speak, confining himself within his own boundaries or effacing even your fleeting outlines. Losing my words, I become a docile animal, a rustling tree. All my scratches and marks, the cracks, the lost blood, come from my being out of phase with the present. A fissure in which a few grains of dust have also fallen. One day I found a blade of grass in there.

A long table set for lunch. All the relatives seated. You move forward, a little girl next to the paternal shadow. In an instant you sense it: the time to speak has come. The sentence stands out. You have found the words that fit, like a dress in which you try not to feel uncomfortable. It's your chance: you can at last bring that thing outside, watch the shape and consistency it takes on as it enters into contact with the air, in the ears of others. But it has remained inside. The sentence is engraved in your mind, a soundless breath that doesn't come out of your chest. Suddenly appeared the consequences that would have occurred if the sentence had reached my lips (questions, reproaches, a fault to share, suffering poured out on others). I swallowed. That sequence of words could go back down into me, come undone again, leaving its meaning intact. Like a strongbox that might be rediscovered years later, or end up forgotten. For now, I just had to let it settle to the bottom. To shelter it, I had a big dark place where the little dead animals I had fed were sleeping, the seeds that could not grow. And basically the boundaries between what is real and what we have imagined are so fragile that I might have let them be blurred by the water and the wind. Perhaps nothing had happened. Perhaps that sealed case was empty.

È stata questa la prima volta che ho scritto. Ho scritto in me, sul mio corpo così profondamente da prendere da allora la strada su cui cammino. Se avessi portato alla bocca quella frase oggi sarei un'altra persona. La parte di vita che ho trascorso finora sarebbe stata diversa. Per questo per me tutto continua a giocarsi con le parole. Con le parole ho un conto aperto.

Ho ceduto la parola così tante volte nella vita da entrare spesso a fare parte dei fantasmi, quelle presenze che si aggirano sfiorando gli altri e le cose, come scontando una loro forma di condanna. Nella prima adolescenza conoscevo centimetro per centimetro il fondo dell'autobus che scortava il mio gruppo di amici da scuola a casa. Ero sempre al margine del cerchio, sempre sulla soglia del non esserci. Mi sentivo così estranea da consolarmi al pensiero che comunque, accanto al bar in cui si ritrovava la mia compagnia c'era un grande pino e io ero tutto il tempo protetta dalla sua chioma. In quegli anni ho iniziato a prendere la parola nel silenzio della scrittura. Una grafia sottilissima che riempiva lentamente le pagine di quaderni: disegnavo con le parole quello che vedevo dalla finestra, annotavo quanto mi accadeva. Ma la vita era così forte, si incideva così profondamente da farmi sentire quanto fossero lievi quei miei segni sulla carta: quei quaderni avrebbero potuto essere lasciati al vento e alla pioggia senza che ciò avrebbe comportato una perdita per me. Non contenevano altro che qualcosa di debole e minimo che sfuggiva alla grande piena. Un sottile filo d'acqua di scolo accanto al fiume della vita. Erano solo i libri che andavo leggendo in quegli anni in lunghi pomeriggi ad abbassare i miei occhi dallo spettacolo dell'aria e della luce per guidarli dentro alle parole di Proust, Dostoevskij, Rilke, Pessoa, Eliot e delle altre grandi querce sotto a cui mi fermavo a guardare il mondo. Non rileggevo quasi mai le pagine dei miei quaderni, le voltavo insieme alla giornata trascorsa, con il senso che comunque qualcosa era rimasto, che avrei potuto tornare a rivedere quei momenti svolgersi sotto ai miei occhi come un filmino. A un tratto, verso gli ultimi anni della scuola superiore, quel filo d'acqua che aveva accompagnato la mia vita scomparve. Risucchiato dalla terra. Prosciugato da quella bestia meravigliosa e imprevedibile dell'esistenza.

Tornò quando, durante l'università, mi ritrovai spiaggiata. Una bussola capovolta mi aveva guidata a dirigermi verso la fine. Ritrovai l'acqua voltandomi indietro, riconoscendo una sequenza perduta dell'infanzia, e il silenzio che l'aveva avvolta. Tornai a prendere la parola nella scrittura. Con una sensazione che non avevo mai provato: quella di ritrovare una verità custodita dalle parole, protetta dal tempo e insieme sprigionata con la sua carica di emozioni

That was the first time I wrote. I wrote within myself, on my body so deeply that ever since, I have taken the road on which I now walk. If I had brought that sentence to my mouth, today I would be another person. The part of my life that I have spent up to now would have been different. This is why, for me, everything continues to be staked on words. With words I have an unsettled account.

I have yielded my words so many times in my life that I have often become one of the ghosts, those presences who wander around, lightly touching things and other people, as if serving a sentence. In my early adolescence, I knew inch by inch the floor of the bus that would transport my group of friends from school to home. I was always at the edge of the circle, always on the threshold of not being there. I felt so estranged that I would console myself at the thought that a big pine tree stood next to the bar where my friends and I would get together, and that I would be protected by its crown all the time. In those years, I began to speak within the silence of writing. A very thin handwriting slowly filled notebook pages: I would draw with words what I saw from the window, note down what happened to me. But life was so strong, so deeply engraved in me, that it made me feel how weightless my signs were on paper: those notebooks could have been left in the wind and rain without causing a loss for me. They just contained something weak and minimal that was escaping the great flood. A thin stream of drainage water next to the river of life. Only the books that I was reading back then, during the long afternoons, could lower my eyes from the spectacle of air and light and guide them inside the words of Proust, Dostoevsky, Rilke, Pessoa, Eliot, and the other great oaks below which I stopped to watch the world. I would hardly ever reread my notebook pages, would turn them along with the day gone by, with the sense, however, that something had remained, that I could go back and see again those moments unfolding before my eyes like a home movie. All of a sudden, towards the last years of high school, that thin stream of water that had accompanied my life disappeared. Sucked up by the earth. Drained by that marvelous and unpredictable beast of existence.

The thin stream of water came back when I found myself stranded during my university years. An upside-down compass had guided me toward the end. Turning back, I found the water again and recognized a lost sequence of my childhood and the silence that had enveloped it. I again started speaking through writing. With a feeling that I had never experienced: that of finding a truth guarded by words, both protected from time and released with its charge

nella lettura. Nacquero i testi che andarono a formare *Mala kruna*, il mio primo libro. In quel periodo ero bruciata dalla necessità di portare alla parola: sapevo esattamente che cosa volevo dire, mi mancava una lingua, la cercavo disperatamente, con un'incertezza ossessiva che mi portava a formare versi quasi marchiati sul corpo, nella sensazione costante di una frana, di un cedimento che poteva travolgere tutto. Inizialmente avevo steso i primi testi sull'infanzia in una forma vicina al racconto in versi. Poi li sacrificai con tagli e amputazioni. Avevo iniziato a considerare come, in realtà, non importasse a nessuno il contenuto di un vissuto per quanto traumatico. Se pretendevo ascolto da un altro dovevo essere pronta a perdere quanto di più personale avevo portato con me, dettagli che distoglievano soltanto l'attenzione. È stato sorprendente scoprire come potessi lasciare andare parte della mia vicenda, liberarmene per poterla salvare in una forma che chiamava gli occhi degli altri, come una terra umida fiutata da un muso. E scoprire anche come, quanto della mia vita non aveva preso parola e continuava ad essere protetto e trattenuto nel mio silenzio, si aprisse nella scrittura, riemergesse cicatrizzandosi. La lingua che avevo trovato mi liberava e insieme mi proteggeva. Dopo questo viaggio attraverso le mie ferite non avrei immaginato di scrivere un altro libro di poesia. Invece da un distacco doloroso e dalla crisi che ne è seguita è nato *Pasta madre*. Il dato biografico ora era quasi trasceso. Scrivendo ero finalmente in parte riuscita ad esaudire il desiderio più grande: liberarmi di me stessa, senza alcuna tragedia, sfiorando le corde della gioia. Lasciando che nei miei contorni rivivessero gli alberi e gli animali, che mi attraversassero e ricomprendessero nella loro corrente. L'ho fatto continuando ad occupare, come nella vita, lo spazio minimo di suono e di senso: i testi più ampi superano appena i dieci versi. E il silenzio è dappertutto, tra le parole e tra le sette parti che compongono il libro, come brevi isole nel bianco.

La scrittura non risarcisce nessuna perdita. I silenzi in cui cadi restano silenzi, con l'irrealtà che si avvicina e ti minaccia, gli altri che arretrano verso se stessi o avanzano a prendersi anche la tua parola, la tua possibilità di esistenza. La scrittura però ti nutre e cura come una madre. Prende con sé i tuoi balbettii, i tuoi mozziconi di frasi e rende loro il tempo e il calore di cui hanno bisogno.

Forse con *Pasta madre* ho iniziato a cedere la parola senza perderla. A donarla agli altri e alle cose che non hanno una lingua, ma possono riaffiorare nei silenzi della mia. Se penso a come scrivere mi ha formato negli anni riconosco come, lentamente, lo spazio dell'ascolto mi ha donato la parola e il coraggio di prenderla. È grande il debito che porto a fratelli e maestri che sono

of emotions by reading. The poems that would make up my first book, *Mala Kruna*, were born. At that time I was burned by the necessity of bringing what I wanted to say to words: I knew exactly what it was, I lacked a language, I was searching for it desperately, with an obsessive uncertainty that induced me to formulate lines of verse that were almost etched on my body with the constant feeling of a landslide, a collapse that could overwhelm everything. I had initially written my first texts on childhood in a form close to versified stories. Then I sacrificed them with cuts and amputations. I had begun to consider how the contents of an experience, however traumatic, actually mattered to no one. If I intended to be listened to by someone else, I had to be ready to lose the more personal things I had brought with me, details that only diverted attention. It was surprising to discover how I could let go of parts of my experience, freeing myself from it in order to save it in a form that beckoned to others' eyes, like wet land sniffed by a snout. And also to discover how the part of my life, which had not started speaking and continued to be protected and withheld in my silence, opened within writing, re-emerged healed. The language that I had found both freed and protected me. After this journey through my wounds, I would not have imagined writing another book of poetry. However, from a painful break-up and from the crisis that followed it, *Mother Dough* was born. Biographical facts were now almost transcended. By writing, I had finally managed to fulfill, in part, my greatest desire: to free myself from myself, without any tragedy, lightly touching the strings of joy. Letting trees and animals live again within my contours, come through me and include me again in their flow. I did this by continuing to occupy, as in life, the minimal space of sound and sense: the longest texts barely exceed ten lines. And silence is everywhere, between the words and the seven sections that are comprised in the book, like brief islands amid whiteness.

Writing compensates for no loss. The silences into which you fall remain silences, with unreality approaching and threatening you, with other people withdrawing towards themselves or coming forward to take your words as well, your possibility to exist. But writing nourishes you and cares for you like a mother. Writing takes on your stammers, your stubs of phrases, and gives back to them the time and the warmth that they need.

Perhaps with *Mother Dough* I have started to yield my words without losing them. To give my words to others, and to things, without language, yet able to resurface in the silence of mine. If I think about how writing has formed me over the years, I recognize how, slowly, the space of listening has given my words to me, as well as the courage to take them. Great is the debt that I owe to fellow writers and literary mentors who have been dams and

stati dighe e argini alla mia incertezza. Il loro sguardo lucido vedeva quello che avrei scorto soltanto con il tempo.

Sono loro le mani che ho portato e porto sul dorso della mia, scrivendo, come ora, custodita nel tepore. Nominarle una per una prenderebbe l'apparenza di un saluto, di un congedo. Preferisco continuare nel loro peso che preme, deciso e lieve, verso un'altra forma, un altro impasto.

embankments to my uncertainty. Their lucid gaze saw what I would glimpse only with time.

Theirs are the hands that I, safeguarded in their warmth while I write, have carried and carry on the back of mine. To name them one by one would take on the appearance of a greeting, of a leave-taking. I prefer to continue with the weight of their hands pressing down, firmly and lightly, towards another form, another dough.

Poesia, lingua madre

1

Si dice che a pochi istanti dalla fine scorrano davanti ai nostri occhi le sequenze fondamentali della nostra vita. Ogni vicenda e gesto appare in una densità che assume in sé gli altri cancellati nel tempo. Perché consegnare alla morte il significato della nostra esistenza? Forse è possibile avere quegli stessi occhi prima. La poesia è un colpo di fucile che può raggiungerci a un tratto, e precipitarci a terra, nel ritmo del respiro, nel battito del sangue. In quella caduta, non c'è più alcuna difesa o rinvio. Il tempo si concentra in un unico punto: ogni cosa ci viene incontro, nella sua danza.

2

Dall'inizio la fine. Dalla fine l'inizio. È in questo ritmo la poesia: un passo dopo l'altro su una terra che a un tratto precipita nel senza fondo. Ciò che si affida e consegna cecamente, a un certo punto della caduta si ritrova le ali, viene salvato: si ricongiunge al principio. Questo ritmo che detta i versi è lo stesso che presiede la vita. La forza che porta alla vita proviene dalla morte: dal cortocircuito, dallo scatto che si crea tra questi due poli. La corrente che li unisce genera armonia da quello che potrebbe essere un trauma. I versi obbediscono a questa corrente. Segnano la nostra direzione. Continuano a indicarci la strada, anche oggi, per quanto nascosti e quasi cancellati dalle reti pervasive della comunicazione. Sono la traccia sonora che possiamo custodire nella mente, mentre tutto intorno si accende di piccole luci intermittenti, esche e richiami commerciali, e bisogna lottare per mantenere aperta la visuale, per non perdere la rotta.

Viaggiando in autostrada capita di intravvedere oltre il guardrail, una parete trasparente su cui si stagliano sagome scure di uccelli in volo. Sono l'immagine stilizzata di un falco con le ali spiegate. Queste figure hanno un significato immediato per gli uccelli che transitano in quel tratto: li stornano, preservandoli dallo schianto. Qualcosa di simile produce in noi la scossa della bellezza. La poesia ne accoglie e traduce le vibrazioni. Per questo protegge la nostra specie, orientandoci verso qualcosa di autentico che ci appartiene e a cui siamo destinati venendo al mondo.

3

Ho sentito spesso di portare la scrittura nel mio corpo, di essere inscritta, nel

Poetry, Mother Tongue

1

It is said that at a few moments from the end the fundamental sequences of our life flow in front of our eyes. Every event and act appear in a density that has absorbed the others vanished over time. Why hand over the meaning of our existence to death? Maybe it's possible to have those same eyes earlier. Poetry is a rifle shot that can suddenly hit us and knock us to the ground, into the rhythm of breathing, into the beating of blood. As we fall, no defense or postponement is possible anymore. Time is concentrated in a single point: everything comes to meet us, in its dance.

2

From the beginning the end. From the end the beginning. This is the rhythm of poetry: one step after another on ground that suddenly sinks into bottomlessness. What is entrusted and handed over blindly, at a certain point of the fall, finds wings, is saved: the outset is rejoined. The rhythm that dictates poems is the same that presides over life. The force that leads to life comes from death: from the short-circuit, from the spark that is created between these two poles. The current that unites them generates harmony from what could be trauma. The poems obey this current. They point out our direction. They continue to show us the way, even today, however hidden and almost erased by the widespread communication networks. They are tracks left by sound that we can keep in mind whenever everything around lights up with small blinking lights, baits, and advertisements, and we must struggle to keep the view open, not to lose the route.

Traveling on the motorway, you happen to glimpse, beyond the guardrail, a transparent wall on which dark silhouettes of flying birds stand out. They are the stylized images of a hawk with spread wings. These figures have an immediate meaning for birds nearing this stretch of road: the figures turn them away, preserving them from a crash. Something similar produces a shock of beauty inside us. Poetry embraces and translates its vibrations. This is why poetry protects our species, directing us towards something authentic which belongs to us and to which we are destined by coming into the world.

3

I have often felt that I carry writing in my body, that I have been inscribed, in

buio, da qualcosa che preme e lascia segni in me, anche durante il giorno, inavvertitamente, mentre la vita con le sue azioni e gesti dovuti ci chiama. Nel momento in cui ci troviamo di fronte al foglio o allo schermo ciò che facciamo non è altro che cercare di tradurre quanto è stato scritto in noi. Siamo l'impronta del tempo che è stato, della vita che ci ha attraversato. Scrivendo portiamo alla luce questi segni che conteniamo, così come sono, oscuri e indecifrati a noi stessi. È come sporgersi su una soglia che dà nel vuoto. Siamo tramiti tra il non conosciuto e il nulla.

Credo che la poesia sia una voce che ci attraversa. Per questo scrivo sempre cominciando con il carattere minuscolo. Io non sto iniziando niente. Ho soltanto colto qualcosa che balbetto in questa lingua monca, che si sbriciola e spezza nel silenzio.

Prima delle parole c'è un ritmo: una cadenza che ci raggiunge a un tratto, nel silenzio, attraverso un'intercapedine che portiamo in noi. La sento a volte mentre cammino, lavo i capelli, riordino la casa, o sono immersa in una qualsiasi sequenza di gesti. Il ritmo ci ricongiunge alla nostra più autentica lingua, quella di un corpo che si muove cercando di accordarsi con ciò che lo circonda, entrando, attraverso questa sintonia, in quel punto in cui la realtà sta nascendo. Attingere al ritmo significa radicarsi nel continuo pulsare e scorrere della vita. È l'unica legge a cui dobbiamo obbedire, una legge che è insieme melodia (come in greco antico la parola *nómos*). Dobbiamo soltanto lasciarla affiorare, tornare a percepirla, ricongiungendoci a questo battito che ci attraversa, che è nel nostro sangue come nella natura.

La poesia è per me una pratica di salvezza quotidiana; una forma di rito, di radicamento nella vita. È come ritrovare i miei piedi sulla terra, in una direzione di cammino. È proprio questo un verso: la possibilità di dirigersi, di andare, vincendo la paura, lo smarrimento, l'incertezza. Una forza che ci guida e a cui ci affidiamo. C'è un modo di dire che appartiene a un'area dell'Italia centrale: "non hai un verso", per dire che non hai una forma, non si sa chi sei. Con la poesia siamo ricondotti a ciò che siamo veramente, al nostro più autentico volto, che è quello buio, aperto, in cui può affiorare una foglia, un muso.

Ci sono stati del nostro essere in cui i nostri confini si fanno così labili che possono essere facilmente attraversati. Per alcuni momenti siamo ciò che vediamo e sentiamo. È una condizione di fragilità estrema, in cui siamo esposti a un rischio enorme. Con il tempo, attraverso la scrittura, mi è stata donata la possibilità di invertire la direzione e il senso di questo ampio potenziale autodistruttivo attorno a cui gravitavo: è così che mi sono ritrovata nel *poiein*, nella possibilità di creare, di cambiare qualcosa attraverso di me. Nel

the darkness, by something that inadvertently presses down and leaves signs in me, even during the day, while life with its acts and duties is beckoning to us. When we find ourselves in front of the computer screen or the sheet of paper, what we do is merely try to translate what has been written in us. We are the imprint of the time that has been, of the life that has passed through us. By writing we bring to light these signs that we contain, as they are, obscure and indecipherable to us. It is like leaning over a threshold that looks into the void. We are between the unknown and nothingness.

I believe that poetry is a voice that passes through us. For this reason I always begin with a lowercase letter when I write. I'm not beginning anything. I've only caught something that I stammer in this broken language, which crumbles and breaks in silence.

Before words there is a rhythm: a cadence that suddenly reaches us, in silence, through a hollow space that we carry inside us. Sometimes I sense it as I am walking, washing my hair, tidying up my home, or am immersed in any sequence of acts. Rhythm reunites us with our most genuine language, that of a moving body seeking to be in tune with its surroundings, and entering, through this harmony, the point at which reality is being born. Drawing on rhythm means taking root in the continuous flow and pulsation of life. It is the only law that we must obey, a law that is also melody (as in the ancient Greek word *nómos*). We only have to let it surface, turn back to perceive it, rejoining this beat that passes through us, which is in our blood as in nature.

For me, poetry is a practice of daily salvation; a form of ritual, of taking root in life. It is like finding my feet on the ground, walking forward. A poem is precisely this: the possibility of guiding ourselves, of going forward, of overcoming fear, bewilderment, uncertainty. It is a force which guides us and to which we entrust ourselves. We have a saying in central Italy: "You don't have a poetic line." This means that you don't have a form, a direction, that no one knows who you are. With poetry, we are led back to who we really are, to our most genuine face, which is a dark open face in which a leaf, or the snout of an animal, can emerge.

There are states of our being in which our boundaries become so labile that they can be crossed easily. For a few moments we are what we see and hear. It is a condition of extreme fragility, in which we are exposed to an enormous risk. Over time, through writing, I have been given the opportunity to reverse the direction and the meaning of this broad self-destructive potential around which I was gravitating: this is how I found myself within the *poiein*, within the possibility of creating, of changing something through myself. By doing so, I draw on the force released from that short-circuit between death and

farlo attingo a questa forza che si sprigiona da quel cortocircuito tra morte e vita. È come una scossa elettrica che mi ricorda, in un istante, tutto ciò che ho dovuto sacrificare al buio. Mi ricorda l'altro lato dello specchio: i miei fratelli seppelliti, i dispersi e senza nome. Tutto ciò che ancora chiede voce e chiama.

4

Nel momento in cui un verso raggiunge le nostre labbra e viene pronunciato, ci ricongiunge alla vita e per questo ci salva. È una salvezza precaria, a cui dovremo riattingere, come un respiro che si ripete, confermandoci in vita.

C'è una forma di dolore che è baratro, distacco assoluto dal resto del mondo, scomparsa del mondo. Una voragine che ha una forza distruttiva e annientatrice enorme. L'intera nostra esistenza può concentrarsi attorno a questo punto di sprofondamento, mentre tutto il resto è cenere. Non ci sono allora più gesti o passi da compiere, si appartiene completamente al buio. O forse alla parte più chiusa e senza uscita di se stessi, a cui ci si consegna, come condannati: «dentro la prigionia di sé ch'è il vero inferno» (Mario Luzi). Eppure se siamo capaci di vivere pienamente questa condizione, senza risparmiarci, lasciando che questo tempo sospeso lavori in noi, ci ritroveremo a un tratto liberi, ricongiunti agli altri. La strada per uscire affonda in noi stessi, dobbiamo percorrerla anche se sembra condurci nella direzione opposta. È come se si apra a un tratto una porta murata, un antico passaggio che non sospettavamo di avere in noi. Questa esperienza è alla base dei testi che sono venuti a formare il mio secondo libro, *Pasta madre*. Mi sono ritrovata a vivere nella lingua la forza di metamorfosi che ha il dolore. Sentivo il mio corpo frantumarsi come una terra secca, senza amore. Avevo perso il radicamento nella vita; i gesti più quotidiani, come cucinare o vestirsi, mi chiedevano un senso. L'unico luogo sicuro per me era il sonno. Mi ci avvolgevo, indefinitamente, come in uno stato di narcosi, di anestesia prolungata. O forse obbedivo soltanto a un mio personale inverno, come un animale che cade in letargo per conservare le forze. Quando sono stata raggiunta dalle parole e da quel preciso ritmo che le scandiva, mi sono sentita liberata. Si era aperta una breccia, da cui sarebbero entrati altri versi. Quando ci si trova su un baratro, ogni parola che affiora deve sostenerci interamente, con tutto il nostro peso: allora un ponte inizia a costruirsi, a riportarci a casa. Ritrovando la lingua, torniamo nel movimento, nello scorrere della vita. Siamo già liberi dal dolore che è fissità, è un chiodo che ci trafigge e ci vorrebbe suoi per sempre, come insetti alla parete. Ma pronunciando una parola puoi sentire che non c'è niente che sia fermo: ogni cosa può essere guardata da un punto diverso, da una distanza o vicinanza.

life. It's like an electric shock that reminds me, in an instant, of everything that I have had to sacrifice to the darkness. It reminds me of the other side of the mirror: my buried loved ones, the missing, and the nameless. Everything that still asks for a voice and calls out.

4

The moment a poem reaches our lips and is pronounced, it reunites us with life and therefore saves us. It is a precarious salvation, on which we will have to draw again, like a breath that is repeated, confirming that we are alive.

There is a form of pain that is an abyss, an absolute detachment from the rest of the world, a disappearance of the world. A chasm that has an enormous destructive and annihilating power. Our entire existence can focus on this point of collapse, while all the rest is ash. There are no more acts to carry out or steps to take, one belongs completely to the darkness. Or perhaps to that most enclosed part of ourselves, which is without an exit and to which we surrender ourselves, as if we were convicts: "Within the prison of oneself which is true hell" (Mario Luzi). Yet if we are able to fully experience this condition, without sparing ourselves, and while letting this suspended time work in us, we will suddenly find ourselves free, reunited with others. The way out heads down into ourselves; we must follow it even if it seems to lead in the opposite direction. It's as if a walled door suddenly opens, an ancient passageway that we didn't suspect was inside us. This experience is the basis of the poems that compose my second book, *Mother Dough*. I found myself experiencing in language the metamorphosing force of pain. I felt my body breaking up like dry earth, without love. I had lost my roots in life, and the most everyday acts, like cooking or getting dressed, beckoned to me for meaning. The only safe place for me was sleep. I wrapped myself up in it indefinitely, as if I were in a state of narcosis, of prolonged anesthesia. Or perhaps I was obeying only my own winter, like an animal that hibernates to conserve its strength. When I was reached by words and the precise rhythm articulating them, I felt free. A breach had opened, from which other lines of verse entered me. When we find ourselves above an abyss, every emerging word must support us entirely, all our weight: then a bridge begins to be built, to bring us home. Recovering language, we return to the movement, the flow of life. We are already free from the pain that is fixedness; it is a nail that transfixes us and that would ike to make us its own, forever, like insects on the wall. But by pronouncing a word you can sense that nothing has halted: everything can be seen from a different vantage point, from afar or nearby. And while you

E mentre lo senti cambia il tuo sguardo, si trasformano i tuoi occhi, sei già un altro. Dimentichiamo così spesso questo antico cordone che ci nutre, dimentichiamo che abbiamo una lingua madre che si prende cura di noi, della nostra fragilità. Siamo figli della nostra lingua, siamo messi al mondo da lei. Lei ci fa nascere e rinascere alla vita.

5

Ciò che ricevo in dono dai sogni ha la forza di una scossa che a volte cerco di tradurre nei versi. Ma più spesso è in uno stato di dormiveglia che sono raggiunta da alcuni lampi di chiarore; semplici moniti come *ti sei scordata la valvola del gas*, oppure lacerti di frasi, barbagli di immagini che mi chiedono di essere subito appuntati, nel buio, cercando a tentoni il taccuino che tengo sempre accanto. Questi segni lasciati come da un estraneo, in una grafia a volte indecifrabile a me stessa, contengono le linee guida di quanto poi cercherò di portare a compimento, di tradurre alla realtà. È come se in quel tempo sospeso, ai margini della vita, la mente lavorasse in una sorta di accensione, di concentrazione aumentata dalla prossimità del buio. Più che nel sogno, l'origine della poesia mi sembra in questa soglia tra sonno e veglia, in cui siamo restituiti a noi stessi, nudi, interamente e solo sguardo, interamente e solo ascolto. È in questo stato di percezione limpida che veniamo a contatto con la parte più autentica e viva del reale, come un pulviscolo in eterno movimento. Ed è allora, con la forza della nostra attenzione concentrata, che ci è concesso di agire sul reale, trasformandolo. Come ai primordi l'uomo può attingere al "valore magico della parola" (Florenskij), alla possibilità di modificare se stesso e il mondo, attraverso la materia creatrice della lingua. La parola poetica (*poiein*: fare) ha in sé questa energia, questo movimento che porta nella realtà. Per questo perdere il seme poetico della lingua significa perdere la propria possibilità di agire nel mondo. La lingua a cui siamo assuefatti dalla comunicazione onnipervasiva ci rende inerti. Pasolini se ne era subito accorto alla metà degli anni Cinquanta, quando il diffondersi del linguaggio tecnico-aziendale veniva a formare il nostro italiano medio. Siamo parlati da una lingua che ha ben poco di umano. Anche la poesia sembra rifugiarsi in un significato il più possibile immediato. Eppure la forza della parola poetica è tale quanto più è capace di attingere alla sua valenza originaria, tornando a essere voce di un corpo che cerca, attraverso il ritmo, di stabilire un accordo con la realtà, per entrare nel suo mistero.

sense this, your way of looking changes, your eyes are transformed, you are already someone else. We often forget this ancient cord that feeds us, we forget that we have a mother tongue that takes care of us, of our fragility. We are children of our language, we are born into it. It gives us birth and rebirth into life.

5

What I receive as a gift from dreams has the strength of a shock that I sometimes try to translate into poems. But it is more often in a state of half-sleep that I am reached by a few glimmers; simple warnings such as *you forgot to close the gas valve*, or shreds of sentences, shimmering images that ask to be jotted down immediately, in the darkness, as I grope for the notebook that I always keep next to me. These signs left as if by a stranger, in a handwriting that I sometimes cannot decipher, contain the guidelines of what I will then try to carry out, to bring to reality. It is as if in that suspended time, at the edge of life, the mind were working in a state of being kindled, of concentration increased by the proximity of darkness. More than in dreaming, the origin of poetry seems to lie on this threshold between sleeping and wakefulness, in which we are given back to ourselves, naked, entirely and now only a gaze, entirely and only listening. It is in this state of clear perceiving that we come into contact with the most authentic and lively part of reality, like dust particles in perpetual movement. And it is then, with the strength of our concentrated attention, that we are allowed to act on reality, to transform it. As when in primordial times, human beings can reach "the magical value of the word" (Florensky), the possibility of modifying themselves and the world, through the creative matter of language. Poetic language (*poiein*: to make) possesses this energy, this movement that leads into reality. For this reason, losing the poetic seed of language means losing one's ability to act in the world. The language to which we are accustomed through pervasive "communicating" makes us inert. Pasolini was immediately aware of this in the mid-1950s, when the spread of techno-business language came to inform our standard Italian. We are spoken by a language that has very little humanness to it. Even poetry seems to take refuge in the most immediate meaning possible. Yet the power of poetic language is such that it is all the more able to draw on its original energy, becoming again the voice of a body that seeks, through rhythm, to establish harmony with reality, to enter its mystery.

6

Una poesia ha in sé una materia generativa di significato infinita. Sta a noi essere capaci di accoglierla e compiere quel lavoro che la consegna alla luce. In questo senso la poesia chiede a noi stessi una maternità. Ci chiama a prenderci cura di questo suo darsi inerme alla vita che sta cercando una forma, un senso che non le faccia violenza, che sappia approssimarsi con quella particolare attenzione e amore che lascia posto all'altro.

«Nessuno deve sapere che un segno riesce bene per caso... per caso, e tremando. E che appena un segno si presenta riuscito bene per miracolo, bisogna subito proteggerlo e custodirlo, come in una teca» scrive Pasolini nella sceneggiatura di *Teorema*. Credo che sia proprio questo il compito che spetta all'artista: creare dentro di sé lo spazio in cui l'altro può darsi, può essere accolto. Per questo bisogna farsi cavi come un contenitore che risuona. Fare ritorno alla corrente anonima della vita che preme entro i nostri confini come un torrente contro i massi sul suo cammino. Se siamo fedeli a questa forza originaria, qualcosa da lei giungerà. Allora non dovremo fare altro che esserne custodi. A questo dobbiamo dedicare tutto il nostro essere, tutta la nostra attenzione: la forma più alta e limpida di amore, il nostro atto di fedeltà alla vita. *Nostalghia*, uno dei film a cui sono più legata, ha al centro proprio questo. Come Gorcakòv attraverso la vasca di Bagno Vignoni, dobbiamo mantenere la fiamma della candela accesa portandola passo dopo passo. La fiamma vacilla, è ciò che c'è di più fragile e prezioso, va protetta con un palmo, con un lembo del cappotto. Si procede con la massima cautela. Nelle nostre mani ci sono le sorti del mondo. Come da bambini, soppesando il destino, in un gioco a cui ci siamo dedicati interamente. A questa stessa cura siamo chiamati lavorando nella lingua, come conducendo la nostra vita al bordo della vasca, al termine di ogni giornata.

7

La poesia è per me un'esperienza che non è possibile prevedere o circoscrivere all'interno di un progetto. Ogni verso affiora da una faglia che si apre in noi. Il nostro compito è vegliarla, fare in modo che non venga ricoperta dai doveri della giornata. Nutrirci di silenzio come le piante di luce. Sostare quanto più ci è concesso in una condizione di soglia, dove può affiorare la vita con il suo incanto. Per questo amo i lunghi treni regionali e la pioggia, il privilegio di potere essere solo sguardo.

6

A poem has a capacity to generate infinite meaning. It's up to us to take it in and carry out the work that will give it over to the light. In this sense, poetry requires a motherhood of us. It calls on us to take care of this giving of itself defenselessly to life that is seeking a form, a sense that does not violate it, that knows how to come close to the special attention and love that gives space to the other.

"No one must know that a sign is successful by chance . . . by chance and trembling," Pasolini writes in his screenplay *Theorem*, "and that as soon as a sign miraculously shows itself up as successful, one must immediately protect it, guard it, as in a showcase." I believe that this is precisely the task that belongs to the artist: to create within him- or herself the space in which the Other can exist, can be welcomed. For this, we need to become hollow like a resonating container. To return to the anonymous current of life that surges up to our boundaries like a torrent against the boulders in its path. If we are faithful to this primal force, something will come from it. Then all that we will have to do is to be its guardians. To this end, we must devote our whole being, all our attention: the highest and most limpid form of love, our act of faithfulness to life. This is indeed at the heart of *Nostalghia*, one of the films to which I am most attached. Like Gorchakov crossing the Bagno Vignoni hot springs pool, we must keep the flame of the candle lit by carrying it forward, step by step. The flame flickers: it is what is most fragile and precious, what must be protected with the palm of our hand, with the edge of our coat. We move forward with the utmost caution. In our hands lies the fate of the world. Like children, weighing destiny, in a game to which we have devoted ourselves entirely. We are called upon to take this same care when we work inside language, as when we lead our lives to the edge of that pool, at the end of every day.

7

For me, poetry is an experience that cannot be foreseen or circum-scribed within a project. Each poem emerges from a fault line that opens inside us. Our task is to watch over it, to make sure that it is not covered over by daily duties. To feed ourselves on silence, like plants on light. To halt as long as is allowed in a threshold condition, where life can emerge with its enchant-ment. This is why I love rainfall and long regional train rides, the privilege of being able to be merely a gaze.

È sempre in un tempo indefinito che viene a formarsi una poesia, come un lento smottamento che a un tratto mi raggiunge. Ogni libro poi si compone secondo un suo ritmo e una sua storia. I versi del mio esordio, *Mala kruna*, sono nati dentro il fuoco di un trauma. Sapevo esattamente che cosa avevo bisogno di attraversare, ma mi mancava una lingua. L'ho cercata disperatamente. Con un'incertezza a tratti ossessiva, affidandomi a versi o brandelli di versi che si erano accesi e poi cercando di portarne a compimento la scintilla, sillabando nel silenzio o scrivendo e cancellando sul mio taccuino. Ogni verso aveva per me il significato di un tatuaggio. Si imprimeva in me, si stampava sul mio corpo. Con la stessa sofferenza, lentamente, giustificato da una necessità assoluta. La mia esistenza doveva riconoscersi in quei segni. È stata una gioia quando, a un tratto, mi sono ritrovata dentro la materia della lingua: la sua forza mi liberava, mi denudava e proteggeva allo stesso tempo. Non c'era più alcuna ferita da nascondere. Si era cicatrizzata dentro le parole.

La poesia mi ha condotto a questa sorta di precisione assoluta che abdica a se stessa. Fissando esattamente, con tutta la tua concentrazione, il tuo bersaglio, lo manchi sempre ma giungi a un punto vicino che si apre indefinitamente. La parola a cui sei arrivato contiene molto di più di quanto tu stesso le chiedevi; l'esperienza a cui volevi dare una forma si schiude mostrandoti la traccia di altre vite che non avevi sospettato. Tornando poi a lavorare sui testi, ho lasciato che si aprissero altri occhi nei miei; con la misura di questo distacco, ho aspettato che cadessero, come foglie secche, tutte quelle immagini che parlavano della mia vita senza riscattarla. Il libro si è composto sul pavimento, come cercando fondamenta. Un foglio accanto all'altro, formando sequenze che si scioglievano e frantumavano. Da una parola o da un verso continuava a provenire un sottile richiamo, come una perdita di corrente. Fino a che a un tratto è sceso finalmente il silenzio. *Prometti di non farlo mai più*, mi sono detta. Qualche anno dopo si è aperta la fenditura che ha portato *Pasta madre*.

8

Scrivere un verso comporta un sacrificio. È come conservare soltanto il seme di un frutto. Puoi sentirne l'amaro. Ho avuto più volte la tentazione di scrivere in prosa proprio per raccogliere anche quanto stava attorno a quell'unico nucleo salvato.

La prosa chiede un ostinato e costante esercizio di volontà. Credo di non avere la forza per reggere a lungo una trama e di non essere capace di fingere. Ciò che creo sostenendolo con tutta me stessa, si interrompe a un tratto nel bianco, si spezza. Questa frantumazione mi appartiene, mi corrisponde

It's always in an indefinite time that a poem takes shape, like a slow landslide that suddenly reaches me. Each book is then composed according to its own rhythm and story. My debut poems, in *Mala Kruna*, were born within the fire of a trauma. I knew exactly what I needed to go through, but I lacked a language. I desperately searched for it. With sometimes obsessive uncertainty, entrusting myself to lines of verse or fragments of lines that had been kindled and then trying to make the spark catch fire, by spelling them out in silence or by writing them down and crossing them out in my notebook. Each poem had the meaning of a tattoo for me. It was etched on me, printed on my body. Slowly, with the same suffering, justified by an absolute necessity. My existence had to recognize itself in those signs. It was a joy when, suddenly, I found myself inside the matter of language: its force freed me, undressed me and protected me at the same time. There was no longer any wound to hide. It had healed within the words.

Poetry led me to this sort of absolute precision that abdicates itself. By staring exactly, with all your concentration, at your target, you always miss it but you reach a nearby point that opens indefinitely. The poetic language at which you have arrived contains much more than you asked for; the experience to which you wanted to give shape opens up, showing you the trace of other lives that you had not suspected. Returning then to work on my poems, I have let other eyes open in mine; from this remove, I have waited for all those images that spoke of my life, without redeeming it, to fall like dry leaves. The book was composed on the floor, as if it were seeking foundations. With one sheet of paper alongside the next one, forming sequences that dissolved and shattered. From a word or a line of verse a slight call continued to come, like the loss of an electric current. Until suddenly silence finally fell. *Promise yourself never to do this again*, I said to myself. A few years later opened the crack that led to *Mother Dough*.

8

Writing a poem involves a sacrifice. It's like keeping only the seed of a piece of fruit. You can sense its bitterness. I've often been tempted to write in prose precisely so that I could also collect what was around that single saved core.

Prose calls for an obstinate and constant exercise of willpower. I don't think that I have the strength to hold onto a plot for a long time and I'm unable to pretend. What I create by supporting it with my whole being, is suddenly stopped on the blank page, and breaks. This shattering belongs to me, intimately corresponds to me. A poem is also what I lack, my going forward

intimamente. Un verso è anche questa mia mancanza, questo mio procedere per pochi passi e arrestarmi in attesa dell'altro. La poesia mi concede di sostare nell'infanzia. In una lingua incompiuta, una "pasta madre" che solo se accolta dall'altro raggiunge una forma.

Con la prosa seguo il corso dei pensieri, con la poesia cerco di custodire il bagliore di qualcosa che è apparso. Prosa e poesia si generano l'una dall'altra. Un appunto può innescare un verso, così come una riflessione può crescere rami e foglie da un seme che aveva germogliato poesia. Ci sono immagini che giungono con un potenziale di significato che solo nel tempo, con lo stratificarsi delle letture, schiudono la loro profondità. Mi è capitato allora di scrivere in prosa, accompagnando questo processo, come restando a vegliare i carboni accesi di un fuoco. È forse anche un modo per prendere congedo da un libro. Le prose di *Un verso è una vasca e altri appunti sulla poesia*, sono nate ad esempio dopo la conclusione di *Mala kruna*, mentre sentivo l'esigenza di riflettere attorno al gesto e al significato della scrittura. La fine di un libro assomiglia alla fine di un mondo. Lascia ceneri e una lunga attesa. Mi è accaduto così con *Pasta madre*, quando mi sono ritrovata senza lingua. Quella che avevo mi era stata mozzata. Aspettavo che ricrescesse, come una lucertola che ha perso la metà del suo corpo. Mentre vivevo questo disagio, ho lasciato che ciò che affiorava proseguisse formando brevi frammenti in prosa. Li ho riconosciuti come *tasche finte*, luoghi di un incontro mancato, brevi spazi che si aprono soltanto per mostrare il loro carattere illusorio. Sono le tracce di un tentativo ripetuto di sentirsi accolti, di potersi riconoscere nel segno di un'autenticità che, dolorosamente, non è concessa.

9

È la forza di verità di un'esperienza a generare la parola poetica. Altrimenti siamo nella decorazione, in un gioco di tasselli, o nella superficie piatta del comunicare. Ciò che abbiamo vissuto plasma la materia della lingua. Nessuna immaginazione o finzione, soltanto un tentativo di aderire, e poi un lento lavoro di approssimazione. Non appena qualcosa si incide in noi, la tentazione è quella di lasciare subito un segno della sua incandescenza. Tentennamenti, bruciature, impronte sul fango. È il nostro modo di dare una forma alla bellezza che ci ha travolto, come cercando di colmare un debito che non potrà essere estinto. In una delle sue meravigliose lettere, dopo avere visto la chiesa di Auvers a cui poi dedicherà un quadro, Van Gogh scrive: «devo fare qualcosa per quei tetti azzurri». Questo monito fermo che la realtà ci manda, è insieme

my going forward for a few steps and stopping while I await the Other. Poetry allows me to make a halt in childhood. In an incomplete language, a "mother dough" that attains a form only if it is accepted by the Other.

   With prose, I follow the course of my thoughts; with poetry, I try to keep the glow of something that has appeared. Prose and poetry are generated from each other. A note can trigger a poem, just as a thought can grow its branches and leaves from a seed that had sprouted poetry. There are images with a potential of meaning which disclose their depth only over time and after stratified readings. In these cases, it has happened that I write in prose, accompanying this process as if I were lingering to watch over the burning coals of a fire. This is perhaps also a way to take leave of a book. The prose texts of "A Line is a Lap and Other Notes on Poetry" were born, for example, after the conclusion of *Mala Kruna*, while I was feeling the need to reflect on the act and the meaning of writing. The end of a book resembles the end of a world. It leaves ashes and a long wait. This happened to me with *Mother Dough*, when I found myself without a tongue. The one I had, had been cut off. I was waiting for it to grow back, like a lizard that has lost half of its body. While I was experiencing this uneasiness, I let whatever emerged continue to form short fragments in prose. I recognized them as *fake pockets*, places where an encounter is impossible, small spaces that open only to show their illusory character. They are the traces of a repeated attempt to feel welcomed, to be able to recognize oneself in the sign of an authenticity which, painfully, is not granted.

9

It is the forceful truth of an experience that generates poetic language. Otherwise we are involved in decoration, a tile-laying game, or on the flat surface of communicating. What we have experienced shapes the matter of language. No imagination or fiction, only an attempt to adhere, and then the slow work of coming closer. As soon as something is engraved in us, the temptation is to immediately leave a sign of its incandescence. Temptations, burns, footprints in the mud. It is our way of giving shape to the beauty that has overwhelmed us, as if trying to fill a debt that cannot be paid off. In one of his wonderful letters, after seeing the Auvers church to which he will later devote a painting, Van Gogh writes: "I have to do something for those blue roofs." This firm reminder that reality sends us is also a request for help that cannot be evaded or postponed. Because to exist, those blue roofs need him, his gaze that has

anche una richiesta di soccorso che non può essere elusa o rinviata. Perché per esistere quei tetti azzurri hanno bisogno di lui, del suo sguardo che li ha riconosciuti e accolti. «La realtà non è tenace, non è forte, ha bisogno della nostra protezione» (Hannah Arendt). Per questo non mi trovo mai senza un foglio e una penna. Dalla mia prima adolescenza mi aggiro sempre con un taccuino a portata di mano. E quando agli angoli delle strade mi fermo a un tratto a segnare qualcosa, lo faccio sempre vincendo un senso quasi di pudore. Sono l'inviata speciale di nessuno. Compio il mio lavoro di testimonianza.

Ho scatole piene di piccole agende, taccuini, foglietti spiegazzati, consunti dalle lavatrici. In fondo a un armadio raccolgono la mia adolescenza. Dentro una grafia sottile che si fa illeggibile, sono i contenuti più dolorosi. Resoconti dettagliati, frammenti di una guerra che ho sepolto in me stessa. Da anni ho ormai abbandonato il pensiero di rileggerli e riscattarli nella traccia di possibili racconti. Non pesano neanche più, sono semplicemente affondati. Continuo comunque a riempire taccuini di appunti, schegge. Nelle scatole più recenti, brandelli di immagini e di versi in formazione, sono intercalate a liste della spesa, orari di treni, elenchi di azioni. Dalla loro percentuale comprendo l'andamento della mia vita. Lo spazio di respiro che mantengo. Spesso, scorrendo le pagine indietro, mi accorgo di vivere inviando di continuo messaggi a qualcuno che è assente. Ma ho ancora la speranza che torni, e con la quieta costanza che porta a compimento le cose, ricomponga i versi e le frasi spezzate, ricongiunga i miei frammenti.

recognized and welcomed them. Hannah Arendt argued that reality was not tenacious, not strong, and that it needed our protection. This is why I never find myself without a pen and a sheet of paper. Ever since my early teenage years, I have always wandered around with a notebook at hand. And when I stop at street corners to note down something, I always do so by vanquishing almost a feeling of embarrassment. I'm no one's special envoy. I'm doing my job of witnessing.

I have boxes full of small diaries, notebooks, crumpled-up pieces of scratch paper faded by washing machines. At the bottom of a wardrobe, they have gathered my adolescence. Inside some thin handwriting that becomes illegible are the most painful contents. Detailed reports, fragments of a war that I have buried in myself. For years now, I have given up the thought of rereading them and redeeming them for possible stories. They no longer even weigh anything, they have simply sunk. However, I continue to fill notebooks with notes, fragments. In the most recent boxes, scraps of images and poems coming into form are interspersed with shopping lists, train timetables, lists of things to do. From their percentage I understand the progress of my life. The breathing space that I keep. Often, as I leaf back through the pages, I realize that I am living while constantly sending messages to someone who is absent. But I still have the hope that he will come back, with the quiet perseverance that brings things to completion, puts back together the lines and the broken sentences, and joins up my fragments.

Un libro di poesia, una struttura vivente

Scrivere poesia è come essere al timone di una barca a vela: possiamo avere una nostra rotta, un nostro itinerario di viaggio, ma ci sono forze molto più grandi che decidono per noi. Ciò che possiamo fare è riconoscerle, e non contrastarle, anche quando ci costringono a quella che sembra una sosta imprevista, o una deviazione che ci porta lontano da quella che credevamo la nostra meta. Chi ha guidato un timone ricorda la sensazione iniziale di completo spaesamento: per raggiungere un punto, bisogna virare nella direzione opposta. Spesso ce ne dimentichiamo, viriamo nella direzione in cui vorremmo andare e così vediamo quel punto allontanarsi, contro ogni nostra aspettativa e sforzo. In poesia è proprio così, come in un eterno apprendistato: le nostre intenzioni ci conducono dove meno ci aspettavamo. Chi potrebbe sostenere di avere quello che Heaney chiama «il governo della lingua»? Un poeta, come un bravo marinaio è capace di cedere il governo alle correnti e ai venti, adoperando queste energie per il suo viaggio.

*

Si può scrivere come innalzando solide pareti che proteggono dalle intemperie. In questo modo ci si sente al sicuro: sembra di possedere una lingua, di abitarla. Ma se questa casa non ha abbastanza finestre e crepe che permettono all'acqua e al vento di entrare, presto ci ritroviamo murati in noi stessi, sepolti dalle nostre stesse mani. L'unica forma che non tradisce la vita, è quella pericolante e aperta del rudere. Soltanto lì è possibile che la natura torni a crescere, gli animali a transitare. È uno spazio di soglia che contiene ciò che sopravvive al passato e ciò che sembra sorgere dal futuro. Le tracce di chi ci ha dimorato si confondono con quelle di un altrettanto lungo e indefinito abbandono. È questa la particolare forma di presenza che il nostro io dovrebbe avere nella scrittura.

*

Il giudice che vive in noi è il nostro stesso aguzzino. Ogni volta ci dichiara colpevoli. «La purezza è un vessillo luttuoso» ha scritto Remo Pagnanelli. La purezza, come la perfezione, è una condanna a morte. Ciò che riusciamo a compiere nella scrittura, avviene quando il giudice si lascia sprofondare nella materia della lingua, e nel suo ritmo chiude gli occhi, si addormenta.

*

In un periodo particolarmente critico della sua esistenza, una mia amica ha imparato a lavorare a maglia. Ricevevo ogni tanto in dono un piccolo pezzo di lana colorato, una sciarpa. Ogni volta ritrovavo più luce nel suo viso, fino a che si perse ogni traccia di quel suo lungo inverno. Mi ha raccontato

A Book of Poetry: A Living Structure

Writing poetry is like being at the helm of a sailboat: we can have chosen our route, mapped out our itinerary, but much greater forces decide for us. What we can do is acknowledge them, not opposing them even when they compel us to make what seems to be an unexpected halt or a detour taking us away from what we thought was our goal. Anyone who has steered a boat remembers an initial sensation of complete disorientation: to reach a point, you have to turn the wheel in the opposite direction. Often we forget this, steering in the direction we would like to go and thus watching the point moving away, against all our expectations and efforts. Poetry is exactly like this, an everlasting apprenticeship: our intentions lead us to where we least expected to go. Who could claim to have what Heaney calls "the government of the tongue"? Like a good sailor, a poet is capable of letting currents and winds govern, of using these energies for his or her voyage.

*

We can write as if we were raising solid walls to protect ourselves from the elements. In this way we feel safe: we seem to have a language, to inhabit it. But if this house doesn't have enough windows and cracks to let in water and wind, soon we are walled up inside ourselves, buried by our own hands. The only form that doesn't betray life is a perilous open ruin. Only a ruin allows nature to grow again inside it and animals to transit through it. It is a threshold zone that comprises what has survived the past and what seems to emerge from the future. The traces of those who have dwelled there mingle with those of an equally long, indefinite abandonment. This is the particular form of presence that our ego should have in writing.

*

The judge who lives inside us is our own persecutor. Every time he finds us guilty. "Purity is a flag of mourning," wrote Remo Pagnanelli. Purity, like perfection, is a death sentence. What we manage to accomplish in writing occurs when the judge lets himself sink into the matter of the language and, within its rhythm, closes his eyes, falls asleep.

*

In an especially critical period of her existence, a friend of mine learned how to knit. From time to time I would receive a small colorful piece of wool, or a scarf, as a gift. Every time I found more light in her face, until all traces of her long winter had vanished. She told me how, while the whole world remained closed for her, this simple movement of her fingers around a

come, mentre tutto il mondo per lei era fermo, questo semplice muovere le dita attorno a un disegno, verso un progetto, l'abbia salvata. Nell'antica metafora della scrittura come tessitura, c'è anche questo aspetto di una pratica benefica, rituale, come una liturgia quotidiana, che può quasi confondersi con un lavoro domestico, con i gesti che sostengono la vita ogni giorno. Hanno lo stesso significato per me le opere lente a cui ho contribuito da bambina, sgusciando insieme a mia nonna fagioli e piselli, tagliando la punta dei fagiolini. Scrivere poesia non comporta alcuna invenzione, piuttosto l'affidarsi a un fare, che in se stesso è un'arte, con le sue leggi: un campo di energia che si rilascia trasformando noi stessi e tutto ciò con cui viene a contatto.

*

> *Chi è morto non compie errori*
> *–non c'è luogo più sicuro di un sepolcro.*

Ci sono errori che condizionano un tratto della nostra esistenza. Come quando si sbaglia in autostrada: chilometri da percorrere prima della prossima uscita, e altrettanti prima di potere tornare nella direzione che riconoscevamo nostra. In questa sospensione, possono trascorrere anni. Continuiamo a compiere un viaggio che non avremmo voluto. La nostra rotta può essere anche visibile, a tratti, ma resta comunque irraggiungibile. Abbandonarla assomiglia a un lento silenzioso tradimento verso noi stessi. Una sorta di autocondanna. Mentre proseguiamo su questa strada che non ci appartiene, perdiamo lentamente il colore della vita: diventiamo pallidi come un foglio vuoto nel taccuino della nostra esistenza. Scrivere poesia ci permette di entrare in uno spazio in cui, in ogni istante, possiamo tornare dentro l'orizzonte che è nostro: verso l'aperto, fino a che inizia la fine, chiamandoci a ricominciare, ad andare a capo e riattingere a una stessa originaria forza.

*

Un libro di poesia è per me un punto luce, una possibilità di visione: una chiarezza che giunge su zone poco prima inaccessibili, franate sotto il cumulo del tempo e dei suoi accadimenti. Scrivo quando qualcosa dal buio chiede di essere guardato. Procedo così, a tentoni, giorno per giorno, con le pagine bianche di cui ha bisogno la vita, fino a che sento che è necessario fermarsi, cercare di comprendere dove mi trovo, voltarmi indietro e riconoscere la direzione che mi ha portato. È questo il momento in cui la scrittura torna alla terra, per ritrovare le sue fondamenta e crescere in una costruzione di senso. Come in un gioco dell'infanzia, seduta o inginocchiata sul pavimento della mia

pattern, towards a project, had saved her. In the ancient metaphor of writing as weaving, there is also this aspect of a beneficial, ritual practice, like a daily liturgy, which can almost be indistinguishable from a domestic chore, with the gestures that sustain life every day. For me, it has the same significance as the slow kinds of work to which I contributed as a child, by shelling beans and peas with my grandmother, or by cutting off the tips of green beans. Writing poetry involves no inventing, but rather a reliance on making, which is in itself an art with its laws: a field of energy is released, transforming ourselves and everything with which it comes into contact.

*

One who is dead makes no mistakes
—there is no safer place than a sepulcher.

Some mistakes mold a part of our existence. As when we make a mistake on the motorway: we must drive for miles before reaching the next exit, and just as many miles back, before we are able to turn off in the direction that we had recognized as ours. In the meantime, years can go by. We continue to make a journey that we wouldn't have wanted to make. Our route might also be visible at times, but it nonetheless remains unreachable. Abandoning it is like a slow silent betrayal of ourselves. A kind of self-condemnation. As we follow this road that doesn't belong to us, we slowly lose the color of life: we become pale like a blank page in the notebook of our existence. Writing poetry allows us to enter an area in which, in every moment, we can go back inside the horizon that is ours: towards what is open, until the ending begins, calling upon us to make a new start, to go back and draw again on the same original force.

*

For me, a book of poetry is a lighting point, a possibility of vision: a brightness that reaches zones which, just beforehand, were inaccessible, having caved in under the accumulation of time and its happenstances. I write when something from the darkness beckons to be watched. I proceed in this way, groping, day by day, with the blank pages that life needs, until I feel that I must stop, try to understand where I am, turn around and acknowledge the direction that has guided me. At this moment, writing returns to the earth, rediscovers its foundations and grows into a construct of meaning. As in a childhood game when, sitting or kneeling on the floor of my room, I begin to arrange the pieces of paper into sequences that come together and are taken

stanza, inizio a disporre i fogli in sequenze che si compongono e scompongono. Ci sono poesie architrave, poesie che costituiscono i muri portanti, e altre che hanno la funzione di cemento, calce e calcestruzzo. Annoto sul mio taccuino il legame che collega un testo all'altro e una sequenza all'altra: perlopiù vibrazioni rilasciate dai versi iniziali o finali di un testo, o da quella che emerge come un'immagine guida. Traccio così ipotetiche mappe, lascio che il senso che affiora possa prendere bivi e direzioni parallele, fino a che è possibile incontrare la forma in cui ogni tassello ha il suo posto, la sua più aperta e insieme esatta possibilità di significato. È una fase del lavoro in cui si scrive con ciò che si è scritto, distinguendo ciò che consiste, che può restare, da ciò che confonde e distrugge quanto si sta costruendo. Il progetto si delinea lentamente, attraverso la disposizione stessa dei testi, le concatenazioni di significato che si fanno via via indissolubili, donandoci consapevolezza, aprendoci gli occhi su ciò che abbiamo scritto. Mano a mano che questa traccia viene riconosciuta, diventa la nostra guida, ci orienta nella scelta dei tasselli che vanno abbandonati, se risultano nel disegno complessivo ornamenti o pesi non necessari. Spesso in questo movimento affiorano dalla scrittura messaggi che, solo grazie a questa particolare disposizione dei testi, si sono potuti affermare con chiarezza fino a raggiungerci. Altri, ancora avvolti nelle trame della lingua, verranno rilasciati nel tempo, dopo la pubblicazione del libro, intercettati da altri occhi che ce li restituiranno, in forma di dono inatteso.

Lo spazio che si sta creando assomiglia a una struttura vivente: non abbiamo fatto altro che assistere alla sua nascita e seguirla, nelle sue diramazioni, sacrificando tutto ciò che comportava una dispersione di energia. Un libro è compiuto quando può accogliere una traccia di significato e permettere un transito, e quindi una trasformazione, sia pure impercettibile, tra la sua prima e ultima pagina.

Nel momento in cui scrivevo i testi che avrebbero composto *Mala kruna*, *Pasta madre*, *Libretto di transito*, non avevo alcuna idea di quello che sarebbe stata la forma di questi libri. Il progetto resta, in una prima lunga fase dormiente, ma è in qualche modo già dentro le trame della lingua, così come il guscio delle uova si forma solo dopo che si è composto il tuorlo. *Tutti gli occhi che ho aperto* è nato in una maniera diversa, per me più sorprendente. Ho sempre dato poco credito ai testi scritti su invito, seguendo le piccole inaspettate occasioni che a volte nutrono la poesia; li guardavo in una luce sospetta, come fossero meno autentici, meno necessari. Ma negli ultimi anni, per una profonda personale esigenza di metamorfosi, ho accolto questi richiami alla scrittura con la certezza di un incontro con l'altro, qualcosa di importante per me dopo *Pasta madre*, un libro nato in una sorta di implosione, di crollo interiore. In

apart. There are lintel poems, poems that build the load-bearing walls, and others that take on the function of cement, lime, and concrete. I jot down in my notebook the link that connects one text to another and one sequence to another: most of these links are vibrations released by the opening or the closing lines of a text, or by what surfaces as a guiding image. I thus sketch out hypothetical maps, letting the emerging meaning take crossroads and parallel directions, until it is possible to meet up with the form in which each piece has its place, its most open and, at the same time, most exact possibility of meaning. This is a phase of the work in which we write with what we have written, determining what coheres, what can remain, and what confuses and destroys what is being built. The project takes shape slowly, through the very arrangement of the texts, the concatenations of meaning that gradually become indissoluble, giving us awareness, opening our eyes to what we have written. Little by little this trail is recognizable, becoming our guide, orienting us in our choice of the pieces to be abandoned if unnecessary weights or ornaments have resulted in the overall pattern. Often in this same movement, the particular order of the texts enables meanings to surface, from the writing, and to assert themselves clearly, therefore reaching us. Other meanings, still wrapped in the weave of language, will be released over time, after the publication of the book, and be intercepted by other eyes who will give them back to us in the form of unexpected gifts.

The space that is being created resembles a living structure: we have done nothing but witness its birth and follow it, in its ramifications, sacrificing everything that entailed a dispersion of energy. A book is completed when it can accommodate a trail of meaning and allow a passage, and therefore a transformation, albeit imperceptibly, between the first page and the last one.

When I was writing the texts that would make up *Mala Kruna*, *Mother Dough*, and *The Little Book of Passage*, I had no idea what form these books would have. The project remains dormant in a first long phase, but it is somehow already inside the weave of the language, just as the eggshell is formed only after the yolk is composed. *All the Eyes that I Have Opened* was born in a different, more surprising way. I had always given little credit to commissioned texts resulting from those small unexpected opportunities that sometimes nourish poetry; I would look at them in a suspicious light, as if they were less genuine, less necessary. Yet in recent years, due to a deep personal need for metamorphosis, I have accepted these commissions because of the certainty of meeting up with what is "other," something that has been important for me since the publication of *Mother Dough*, a book born in a sort of implosion, of inner collapse. Moreover, I recognized in these commissions

più, in questi appelli riconoscevo i resti di un tempo in cui la poesia faceva ancora parte della vita di una comunità: per precarie, circoscritte occasioni, qualcuno si rivolgeva alla forza creatrice della parola, le riconosceva un significato nella *polis*, e questo mi sembrava un piccolo vitale miracolo da custodire. Così è nato questo libro inaspettatamente plurale e aperto, dove la voce passa da una migrante al confine tra Serbia e Croazia, agli "alberi maestri", ad antiche statuette votive, alla santa custode della luce e della vista, a una donna nella sua quotidianità rarefatta: al centro ci sono le ferite-occhi aperti di una difficile relazione, il suo attraversamento grazie alle "luminescenze", e il suo ripresentarsi, nella "camera oscura" dove l'amore è errore. Nel momento in cui, sul pavimento, ho cercato la forma di questo libro, sequenze che mi apparivano inizialmente lontane e consegnate al progetto che le aveva fatte nascere, si sono ritrovate in un'unica scia di senso, dove tornava ad accendersi il motivo del vedere, del chiudere gli occhi e di aprirli, contenendo, attraverso voci diverse, il riverberarsi di una stessa identità aperta, come uno stormo in migrazione che può prendere altre forme, ma mai disperdersi. Questo libro, come i precedenti, è contenuto in una struttura circolare: la fine è anche un inizio, una possibilità per la presenza che ha preso voce di ricominciare, di riconoscersi in una vita, e per chi legge di tornare alla prima pagina, di riprendere il viaggio. Il cortocircuito di questa fine e inizio torna più volte nel libro, in particolare in quelle zone di transito, di forte tensione, che sono lasciate alle pagine bianche. La necessità di questa porzione di aperto mi accompagna da *Pasta madre*, strutturato, come il seguente *Libretto di transito*, proprio attraverso il bianco che scandisce il ritmo tra parole e silenzio, senza alcun titolo o numero né di sezione né di testo. In *Tutti gli occhi che ho aperto*, su suggerimento di Fabio Pusterla, ho lasciato che dalle pagine bianche affiorasse una piccola spirale: come dentro i tronchi degli alberi, e nelle nostre primordiali pagine di pietra.

the vestiges of an era when poetry still partook of community life: for temporary, limited occasions, someone would turn to the creative force of words, acknowledging their significance for the *polis*, and to me this seemed a vital little miracle to care for. This is how this unexpectedly plural and open book was born, with its voice moving from a migrant woman on the border between Serbia and Croatia to "master trees," to ancient votive statuettes, to the saintly guardian of light and eyesight, to a woman in her rarefied daily life: at the center are the wounds—the open eyes—of a difficult relationship, the ways in which it was overcome thanks to "gleams," and its recurrence in the "dark room" where love is error. While I was sitting on the floor and searching for the form of this book, sequences that initially seemed distant to me and consigned to the project that had given them birth, found themselves together in a single trail of meaning, where the motif of seeing, of closing eyes and opening them, had been kindled again, including, through different voices, the reverberation of the same open identity, like a flock of migrating birds that takes on other forms but is never scattered. This book, like the previous ones, is comprised in a circular structure: the ending is also a beginning, a possibility for the presence that has taken on a voice to begin again, to recognize itself in a life, and for the reader to go back to the first page, to resume the journey. The short circuit of this ending and beginning recurs several times in the book, especially in those transit zones, of high tension, which are left to the blank pages. The need for these open portions has accompanied me ever since *Mother Dough*, which is structured, as subsequently *The Little Book of Passage*, indeed through blank pages that create a rhythm between words and silence, and that bear neither a title and nor any section or text number. In *All the Eyes that I Have Opened*, I adopted Fabio Pusterla's suggestion and let a small spiral emerge from the blank pages: as if inside the trunks of the trees, and inside our primordial stone pages.

Una pratica di autochirurgia interiore

Qualche anno fa, camminavo in un bosco dell'Appennino, affidando il dolore a ogni passo, ascoltando la luce tra le chiome degli alberi, per ore, fino a disperdere i cerchi del mio tormento, come l'acqua che contiene un macigno levigato, caduto nel profondo. Quando a un tratto mi è venuto incontro un albero, dal tronco molto segnato. *Tutti gli occhi che ho aperto, sono i rami che ho perso* –mi ha detto. La sua chioma rada si apriva in alto, molto sopra il mio sguardo. Potevi leggere nella sua scorza la storia di tagli e amputazioni, cicatrizzata e trasformata in crescita, obbediente alla luce, oltre tutti gli impedimenti. Ho continuato a camminare con questa voce che si era scandita in me, e una sola immagine chiara: ci sono perdite che puoi piangere con tutte le lacrime, combattere con ogni sforzo, eppure sono necessarie. Daremmo tutta la vita perché non accadano, eppure stanno guidando la nostra linfa verso la forma e il luogo che le spetta.

Per vedere la realtà anche nella sua parte di tenebra, ci vuole molta forza. Ho sempre chiuso gli occhi di fronte all'orrore, come in un riflesso involontario. In quella frazione di tempo l'orrore non smette di esistere, accade. E tu non ne sei testimone, ne sei coinvolto. Le ferite sono occhi che non avremmo mai voluto aprire. E invece eccole, sul nostro corpo, sulla nostra scorza.

Mesi fa ho visto, a San Gimignano, alcuni disegni di Kiki Smith, dove occhi si aprono sulla pelle di una donna dai capelli sciolti, nuda come una santa del bosco. Questa figura torna in altri disegni e opere, come un autoritratto nel tempo, e insieme una sorta di archetipo, di immagine guida. In una di queste porta appese alle braccia due gabbie vuote e sulle spalle posate tre civette, gli uccelli che hanno l'intelligenza della notte. In un altro disegno, due volti di donne, o forse uno stesso volto in diverse età della vita, ha piccole tessere d'argento come polvere di specchio, polvere cosmica. Sono queste le lacrime, le nostre soglie, le nostre possibilità di visione. Ma c'è un'immagine di Kiki Smith che più di tutte resta come l'icona di una forza di trasformazione e ricongiungimento attraverso le lacrime che altro non sono che conduttori, cordoni attraverso cui scorre la vita. E non è un caso che questa immagine sia un arazzo, perché ci mostra proprio come siamo: intessuti nella stessa trama del cosmo. Seduta su un ramo di un albero, una donna nuda, forte del proprio stesso corpo, genera dagli occhi lacrime-filamenti colorati che si diramano congiungendosi agli occhi degli altri animali: un pipistrello, una civetta, due scoiattoli, un daino accucciato ai suoi piedi. Ha il volto sereno e fermo di una divinità antica: regale e inerme, governa le forze originarie. Sospesa in una notte senza tempo, ci guarda, vegliandoci, continuando a generare il filo che ci tiene uniti. Le lacrime che versiamo sono questa possibilità di uscire dai

An Act of Inner Self-Surgery

Once a few years ago in a woods in the Apennines, I was walking for hours, entrusting my sorrow to every footstep, listening to the light within the foliage of the trees, to disperse the circles of my torment like water enveloping a smooth boulder fallen to the bottom. When suddenly a tree with a very scarred trunk came to meet me. *All the eyes that I have opened are the branches that I have lost,* it said to me. Its sparse foliage opened out high, far above my eyes. You could read in its bark the history of cuts and amputations, healed and transformed into growth, obedient to light, beyond all obstacles. I continued to walk with this voice that had been articulated in me, and one clear image: there are losses that you can weep over with all your tears, fight with every effort, yet they are necessary. We would give our whole life so that they won't happen, yet they are guiding our sap towards the shape and the place that belongs to it.

It takes a lot of strength to see reality in its dark parts as well. I have always closed my eyes in the face of horror, as if by an involuntary reflex. In that fraction of time the horror does not stop existing, it happens. And you are not witness to it, you are involved in it. Wounds are eyes that we have never wanted to open. Instead, here they are, on our body, on our bark.

Months ago in San Gimignano, I saw some of Kiki Smith's drawings in which eyes open on the skin of a woman with undone hair and naked as a saint in the woods. This figure turns up in her other drawings and works, like a self-portrait over time, and at the same time a kind of archetype, a guiding image. In one of these images, the woman carries, hanging from her arms, two empty cages, and on her shoulders are perched three owls, those birds that have the intelligence of the night. In another drawing, two women's faces, or perhaps a same face in different ages of life, have small silvery tesserae like mirror dust, cosmic dust. These are tears, our thresholds, our possibilities of vision. But there is one of Kiki Smith's images which, more than all the others, remains the icon of a force of transformation and reunion through tears that are nothing more than conductors, cords through which life flows. And it is no coincidence that this image is a tapestry, because it shows us just as we are: woven into the same fabric of the cosmos. Sitting on the branch of a tree, a naked woman, strong in her own body, generates from her eyes colored filaments of tears that branch out to join the eyes of other animals: a bat, an owl, two squirrels, a fallow deer crouched at her feet. She has the serene and firm face of an ancient divinity: regal and unarmed, she rules over the primal forces. Suspended in a timeless night, she looks at us, keeping watch over us, continuing to generate the thread that holds us together. The tears we shed are this possibility

confini dell'identità, per tornare a essere attraversati dalla vita nella sua purezza. È questa l'immagine che vorrei di fronte al letto, l'immagine che può guidarmi ad affrontare il buio.

*

Non sono buoni i demoni che accompagnano il mio cammino; e quando li dimentico, si fanno ricordare. Scrivo per affrontarli, per ricomporre i miei frammenti. Devo creare per non essere distrutta. Le forze della distruzione vanno onorate. Onorarle significa riconoscere il loro potere, la loro presenza, concedere loro uno spazio dove possano ricevere il nostro sguardo, i doni di ogni giorno. Altrimenti si risvegliano, esigono il nostro tributo di sangue. Gli induisti hanno una divinità femminile che le incarna, Kali, la madre devastatrice. L'ho incontrata lo scorso inverno a Calcutta, in uno dei suoi templi più antichi, a poco più di un chilometro da dove vivevo. E ho sentito quanto fosse vitale riconoscere quella carica distruttrice che, lasciata dentro di noi, affiora nell'altro a cui prestiamo il coltello. Mentre se impariamo ad accoglierla, possiamo dirigerla verso ciò che ci limita, che ci sbarra il cammino, illuminando parti di noi che erano rimaste buie, avvicinandoci a ciò che siamo.

La scrittura ci porta dentro la nostra camera oscura, nel luogo del non conosciuto, lì dove si annidano i nostri demoni, le nostre più tenaci e impenetrabili ombre. È un luogo che ha precise leggi e scansioni del tempo, un fondamentale rapporto con il buio perché la visione si compia. La scrittura si nutre di questo buio, di questa possibilità di perdita e di distruzione che si fa conoscenza necessaria. Scriviamo per vedere dentro la nostra camera oscura.

*

Quando viviamo un trauma entriamo in una sorta di apnea, di sprofondamento e distacco dalla realtà: uno stato di stordimento, quasi di narcosi, che rende il mondo attutito, come sott'acqua, come in un'altra frequenza. Continua a svolgersi a pochi passi da noi eppure non ci riguarda. La realtà si riduce a un punto solo, quello in cui siamo stati uccisi: poche sequenze in cui è avvenuto qualcosa che continua a rilasciare il suo oscuro significato nel tempo. Se da una parte la nostra percezione è come sfuocata, affievolita, dall'altra si fa chiaro ciò che non possiamo perdere, ciò a cui dobbiamo tenerci saldi. È così che, nella tempesta, torno a guardare gli alberi: come "alberi maestri", miei riferimenti e guide, mie radici profonde e aperte al cielo.

of going beyond the boundaries of identity, to be crossed again by life in its purity. This is the image I would like to have on the headboard of my bed, the image that can guide me to face the darkness.

*

The demons that accompany my path are not good ones; and when I forget them, they bring themselves back to memory. I write to face them, to put my fragments back together. I have to create in order not to be destroyed. The forces of destruction are to be honored. Honoring them means acknowledging their power, their presence, yielding a space to them where they can receive our gaze, the gifts of every day. Otherwise they awaken, demand our tribute in blood. Hindus have a female deity who embodies them, Kali, the devastating mother. I met her last winter in Calcutta, in one of her oldest temples, just over a kilometer from where I was living. And I felt how vital it was to acknowledge that destructive charge which, left inside us, emerges in the other person to whom we lend the knife. While if we learn to welcome this charge, we can direct it towards whatever limits us, whatever blocks our way, illuminating parts of us that had remained dark and getting closer to what we are.

Writing takes us into our darkroom, to the place of the unknown, where our demons nestle, our most tenacious and impenetrable shadows. It is a place that has precise laws and rhythms, a fundamental relationship with darkness so that the vision is fulfilled. Writing feeds on this darkness, on this possibility of loss and destruction which becomes necessary knowledge. We write to see inside our darkroom.

*

When we experience a trauma, we enter into a sort of apnea, sinking and detaching ourselves from reality: an almost narcotic, stunned state that makes the world seem muffled, as if under water, as if in another frequency. It continues to take place a few steps away from us and yet it does not concern us. Reality is reduced to a single point, the one where we have been killed: a few sequences of events in which something has happened that continues to release its dark meaning over time. If, on the one hand, our perception seems blurry, weakened, then on the other it becomes clear what we cannot lose, what we must hold on to firmly. This is how, in the storm, I go back to looking at trees: like "master trees," my guides and references, my deep roots, open to the sky.

Le parti di noi che vengono ferite a morte, sono spesso le più fragili e inermi, quelle che si scontrano tragicamente con l'esistenza. Possiamo percorrerle con la scrittura, come in una pratica di autopsia interiore, riconoscere le cause della loro morte, e riuscire così a seppellirle. Attendono un rito che le liberi, che le consegni alla pace, perché la nostra vita possa continuare. La poesia può esserci di aiuto in questo: da sempre attraversa la fine-inizio, la necessità di sacrificare al silenzio, per andare a capo e ricominciare. «In my beginning is my end. […] In my end is my beginning» come ci ricorda Eliot.

*

La scrittura è una chirurgia dell'anima che chiede mano ferma, e un luogo profondo in cui convogliare l'incertezza e il tremore. È una pratica di autochirurgia interiore. Può condurci a riaprire condotti vitali che si erano intasati, donandoci energie e possibilità di conoscenza che non immaginavamo di avere. Può aiutarci ad abbandonare finalmente una parte di noi che comprometteva la nostra esistenza, o impiantarci l'organo che può salvarla. Per questo chiede soltanto noi stessi, la nostra più alta capacità di attenzione e di presenza.

Ciò che continua a vorticare in noi, prendendo altre forme e nomi, generando altri accadimenti che riverberano uno stesso dolore, potrebbe entrare nel nitore di una parola che è gesto compiuto nella piena presenza di noi stessi, gesto che ci salva. Quando ciò accade, siamo come un arciere di fronte al bersaglio. Prima che la freccia giunga a destinazione sente se è riuscito a essere lì dove è chiamato a essere, nella propria coordinata dello spazio; se ciò avviene, anche quei luoghi che portano a deviare lo sguardo, a chiudere gli occhi, sono stati attraversati dalla luce della presenza. Allora la freccia lanciata centra il bersaglio. L'operazione chirurgica ha buon esito.

The mortally wounded parts of us are often the most fragile and defenseless ones, those that clash tragically with existence. We can go through them by writing, as in an act of internal autopsy, recognize the causes of their deaths, and thus be able to bury them. They are waiting for a rite that will free them, that will hand them over to peace, so that our life can continue. Poetry can help us in this: it ever goes through the end-beginning, the need to sacrifice to silence, to return to the beginning and start over again. "In my beginning is my end. [. . .] In my end is my beginning," as Eliot reminds us.

*

Writing is a soul surgery that calls for a steady hand, and a deep place to which uncertainty and tremor can be convoked. It is an act of internal self-surgery. It can induce us to reopen vital conduits that had become clogged, giving us energies and possibilities of knowledge that we never imagined we had. It can help us to abandon at last a part of ourselves that was compromising our existence, or to implant the organ that can save it. This, however, is why it calls on us, on our highest capacities of attention and presence.

What continues to whirl in us, taking on other forms and names, generating other events from which the same pain reverberates, can enter the clarity of words, that is, an act carried out in the full presence of ourselves, an act that saves us. When this happens, we are like an archer facing the target. Before the arrow reaches its destination, he senses whether he has managed to be where he is required to be, in his own place in space; if this happens, even those places that tend to divert one's gaze, to close one's eyes, have been crossed by the light of presence. Then the shot arrow hits the target. The surgical operation is successful.

L'invisibile come testo a fronte

è una pianta la scrittura
l'inchiostro la sua radice.

L'inchiostro genera una pianta che può essere tossica, ma anche farmaco capace di curare, ricongiungendoci con ciò che sempre rinasce. Quando la radice dell'inchiostro non attinge agli strati primari, la scrittura si autogenera, prolifera come una pianta infestante: riempie gli scaffali delle librerie, gli schermi di computer e tv, le pagine dei quotidiani.

La scrittura che è farmaco è una pianta piuttosto rara. Per riconoscerla è necessaria attenzione, dedizione e un lento apprendistato. Questa pianta apre a un'esperienza che trasforma noi stessi e la realtà, rendendoci a nostra volta artefici e tramiti della creazione. Per questo non viene protetta né coltivata dalle istituzioni che detengono il sapere. Cresce in terreni marginali, connessi con gli strati più profondi, dove si deposita e rigenera un'antica originaria ricchezza, dove dormono i nostri antenati. Questa pianta si nutre della morte che si è fatta humus. Per le sue fibre non c'è fine che non sia inizio. Germoglia e dirama proprio in questo ritmo.

*

Chi scrive poesia in questo tempo, dovrebbe imparare dalle lucertole. Nutrirsi del calore che viene dal sole, e di fronte a ciò che assomiglia all'avvicinarsi della fine, accettare la perdita come sacrificio necessario. Un verso è la nostra estremità amputata, o che abbiamo dovuto abbandonare noi stessi, come strategia estrema, per confondere il nemico, per salvarci.

*

stringi la penna non scrive
come un ramo tagliato
altro che l'aria splendente.

È una sconfitta la scrittura, la presa d'atto di un limite, di un'impossibilità. La lingua non può restituirci pienamente la nostra esperienza del reale: la sua carica di bellezza sarà sempre limitata dalle parole che possono appena riverberarla. Restiamo debitori nei confronti dello splendore che ci è dato in ogni istante. Eppure non è a partire da una resa che può nascere un atto creativo. Nel momento in cui stringiamo la penna o posiamo le mani sulla tastiera, crediamo, come i nostri primi antenati, di potere raggiungere l'anima delle cose e di fare rivivere la loro presenza. Viviamo un lutto per tutto ciò che non abbiamo potuto portare alla luce della parola, come non fossimo stati capaci di salvarlo, come se fosse perso per sempre. Sappiamo l'odore, il fremito, il colore del cervo incontrato nella boscaglia, eppure, nei pochi segni che lasciamo sulla parete di roccia, sentiamo che vive l'animale e che continuerà a farlo, ogni

The Invisible as the Facing Page

writing is a plant
ink, its root.

Ink generates a plant that can be toxic, but also medicine capable of curing, reuniting us with what is ever reborn. When the root of the ink does not reach the primary layers, the writing is self-generated, proliferating like a weed: it fills the shelves of libraries, computer and TV screens, the pages of newspapers.

Writing that is medicine is a rather rare plant. To recognize it requires attention, dedication, and a slow apprenticeship. The plant opens out to an experience that transforms us and reality, turning us into the makers and means of creation. This is why the plant is neither protected nor cultivated by the institutions that house knowledge. It grows in marginal lands, connected with the deeper layers where an ancient original wealth is deposited and regenerated, where our ancestors sleep. The plant feeds on death that has become humus. For its fibers, there is no end that is not a beginning. It sprouts and branches out with this very rhythm.

*

Anyone writing poetry in our times should learn from lizards, feed on the heat that comes from the sun and, when the end seemingly nears, accept loss as a necessary sacrifice. A poem is our extremity that has been amputated, or that we ourselves had to abandon as an extreme strategy to confuse the enemy, to save ourselves.

*

clutch the pen it writes nothing
like a cut-off branch
nothing but the shining air.

Writing is a defeat, the acknowledgment of a limit, an impossibility. Language cannot fully restore to us our experience of reality: its charge of beauty will always be limited by the words that can barely reflect it. We remain indebted to the splendor that is given to us in every moment. Yet a creative act cannot be born from a surrender. The moment we clutch the pen or place our hands on the keyboard, we believe, like our first ancestors, that we can reach the soul of things and revive their presence. We live in mourning for all that we have been unable to bring to the light of the word, as if we had been unable to save it, as if it were lost forever. We know the smell, the quivering, the color of the deer encountered in the underbrush, yet we sense, in the few marks that we leave on the rock wall, that the animal lives and will continue to do so whenever our attention, through those engraved lines, returns to that point in life from which our experience was generated.

volta che la nostra attenzione, attraverso quelle linee impresse, tornerà in quel punto da cui si è generata la nostra esperienza.

*

La nostra vita si scrive nell'aria che attraversiamo, nell'aria che ci contiene, inconsapevoli, come il fondale d'oro di un antico dipinto, dove ogni essere appariva nella sua sacralità.

Ciò che accade lascia tracce nell'aria, e nel corpo che custodisce il nostro respiro come un baco. Rispetto a questa tessitura infinita, a questo irradiarsi del significato che regge ogni particella, che cosa può essere una pagina scritta?

I versi che ho riportato appartengono a *13 dicembre*, una sequenza che sta al centro del mio libro *Tutti gli occhi che ho aperto*. L'ho scritta raccogliendo rifrazioni di immagini della vita di Santa Lucia. Nei tanti dipinti che la raffigurano, Lucia, protettrice della luce e della vista, stringe in una mano la palma del martirio. Processata per la sua fede, sembra che non fu possibile spostarla né bruciarla (quale potere umano può muovere o distruggere la luce?), e che infine morì trafitta. La palma che stringe assomiglia a una grande penna caduta da un angelo. È un ramo tagliato con cui si può scrivere l'argilla; si può incidere la materia di segni visibili. Mantenendosi accanto all'origine: lasciando spazio all'invisibile, come testo a fronte.

Ogni volta che stringiamo una penna dobbiamo ricordare questo antico ramo con cui abbiamo scritto da bambini, quando traducevamo dall'invisibile (il nostro stesso corpo, la nostra presenza, era una traduzione recente dell'invisibile).

*

Our life is written in the air that we move through, in the air that contains us, in our unawareness, like the golden backdrop of an ancient painting in which every being appeared in his or her sacredness.

What happens leaves traces in the air, and in the body that houses our breathing like a silkworm. With respect to this infinite woven texture, to this radiating meaning that governs each particle, what can a written page be?

The lines that I have cited belong to "December 13th," a sequence that is at the heart of my book *All the Eyes that I Have Opened*. I wrote the sequence by collecting images refracted from the life of Saint Lucy. In the many paintings that depict Lucy, the protectress of light and sight, she holds the palm leaf of her martyrdom in one hand. After she was tried for her faith, it seems that it was impossible to move or burn her (what human power can move or destroy light?) and that she finally died transfixed. The palm leaf she holds resembles a large feather dropped by an angel. It is a cut branch which can write on clay; the substance can be engraved with visible signs. Staying close to the origin: leaving room for the invisible as the facing page.

Every time we hold a pen we must remember this ancient branch with which we wrote as children, when we were translating from the invisible (our own body, our presence, was a recent translation from the invisible).

Franca Mancinelli: Facing the Invisible

This precious and intricately structured book gathers the most important prose narratives and personal essays that Franca Mancinelli has written alongside her verse poetry and prose poetry during the years 2008-2021. It is also a unique volume, for English readers, in that the author has not yet collected the original texts into a book: several of the pieces are unpublished in Italian, whereas the others have appeared over the years in journals, in anthologies, and on websites. Several narratives are autobiographical and thereby disclose some of the personal sources of her writing, as she focuses on key events during her childhood and her passage into adolescence, while other texts raise questions about the self and its role in her poetics, notably the place of "the other" and the possibilities of an "open identity" that goes "beyond human contours." Readers of the prose poems of *The Little Book of Passage* and the verse poems of *At an Hour's Sleep from Here* know how crucial this issue of an open identity is to her. Her quest continues in her most recent Italian book, *Tutti gli occhi che ho aperto* (2020). In that collection, whose title means "All the Eyes that I Have Opened" and all of whose poems and prose poems have appeared in translation in various American journals, identity indeed opens up and the speaking subject becomes multiple. As its epigraph—"cannot scatter itself / puts itself back together at every turn [...]"—suggests, the presence that gives voice to her poems resembles the open plurality of birds in a "flock flying onwards."

Mancinelli was born in 1981 in Fano, located on the Adriatic coast in central Italy. After studying in Urbino and then living in Bologna for several years, and while often traveling throughout Italy to give readings and participate in literary festivals, she settled in Fano once again in 2020. Like Urbino, her hometown is situated in "Le Marche" region. This toponym is usually rendered as "The Marches" in English: the plural medieval Italian name indicates a borderland of the Holy Roman Empire. The area is known for its beautiful hills and the "dark profile" of the Apennines, as Mancinelli herself defines, in a text here, this high mountain range visible, as she looks inland, from her perspective on the Adriatic coast.

With the adjective "dark," it is clear that much more than a mere perception of a landscape is at stake. Writing about *At an Hour's Sleep from Here* in *Modern Poetry in Translation* (No. 1, 2021), the British poet Caroline Maldonado sees Mancinelli as having "absorbed and internalized [this] environment to express her deepest and most complex feelings." Maldonado notably links some of the geological features of The Marches to Mancinelli's poetry: "Central Italy is earthquake country and the fault-line metaphor is central to [her] work, even at the level of language itself which, she has said, can crumble

like chalky stone and *tufo* without warning." In addition, Mancinelli has herself explained, in an interview given to Lorenzo Franceschini, published in the journal *Scirocco* (No. 22, April-June 2008) and later republished on the website *Poetarum Silva*, how certain places dear to her heart are subject to landslides (another recurrent image), "such as the hills around Fano, near Mount Giove, the Ardizio area, and then also San Bartolo." Most importantly, these landscapes in her midst are transmuted into inner landscapes. In her poems and prose poems especially, she seems to have conjured them up from one of those states of awareness, both heightened and oneiric, that enable her to come into contact with inner realities emerging, transitorily, between sleep and wakefulness. The landslides and crumbling stones, the collapses and the ruins, are assimilated to those of the self. In *At an Hour's Sleep from Here*, for instance, she writes: "I've stopped holding up walls, / give myself over to the ruins." And in *All the Eyes that I Have Opened*, she remarks in one poem: "in the collapse, something sweet." As the publisher of this book, the American poet Paul B. Roth, has insightfully pointed out in regard to *At an Hour's Sleep from Here*, Mancinelli's texts are "introspective" and "border on biography," yet in fact "only touch the untouchable." Her "poems sway like waves," he comments, "back and forth, between water and shore. At times, you can pick things out floating along these waves that seem familiar, lost."

Whereas no place names appear in her verse poetry and poetic prose, in accordance with her poetics which, as she defines them in "Poetry, Mother Tongue," induce her to let all directly autobiographical details¬—"all images that [speak] of my life, without redeeming it"—"fall like dry leaves," in some of the narratives and personal essays in this book the references to the author's "places" and to her existence are more present. A key piece set in The Marches is "Inside a Horizon of Hills." The very title suggests confines, the search for a protective "home" within them, but also, arguably, the aspiration to cross them. Mancinelli defines a specific countryside that lies a few kilometers from the Adriatic coast, a plain from which the two lines of hills that delimit the Metauro Valley can be distinguished. "My whole childhood was attracted to his unmarked limit between the plain and the hills," she explains. "My imagination gravitated around this point where two worlds joined." In the same text, she recalls a difficult period during her adolescence when she experienced "the pangs of an obscure pain" and then, one winter evening, a life-changing event. She rode her moped further than usual into the hills. "I was heading for the thickest darkness," she writes, "[then] I walked until the road vanished from sight." At this point the land seemed to lose all its boundaries. It was "so dark and devastated that my eyes had to follow every footstep," she adds. "[. . .]

I was at the beginning of the world. A strange grace kept my hands raised and open, like a scarecrow lingering in the now deserted field."

Transformative moments like this, when an unexpected gift or blessing is received, coupled with a new awareness enabling her to reorient her perspective on her life, are often recorded in her writing. An example similar in imagery to the event recounted in "Inside a Horizon of Hills" is found in *Mala Kruna*, her first book (comprised in *At an Hour's Sleep from Here*):

> as the world was collapsing
> at night I would walk among the clods of dirt
> over a hill on which you cannot tell
> if it is slowly swelling into a mountain
> or swallowing you up in its hollow
>
> now a light lifts the soil
> or is it the whirl once the foot touches
> the rolling grains of earth within the darkness.

Mancinelli links her language and literary sensibility to this landscape and locality. It is an intimate connection which, in fact, interests her more generally. In an essay included in her doctoral thesis *Percorsi tra la poesia italiana e spagnola contemporanea*, she notes, with respect to the Italian writer Paolo Volponi (1924-1994), who was also from The Marches, that "perhaps language is nothing more than an exit from ourselves, an extension of our body that connects us to the landscape, to the reality in which we live." She adds that Volponi recognizes the origin of poetic speech in its relationship with landscape: "Its anchorage to reality is there, that 'nebulous root' towards which one extends, between seeing and vision, one's cognitive tension. The landscape that can be preserved by, or emerge in, the poems is always the mirror of a search for identity, of a truth about oneself and the world, which passes through one's gaze." In an interview given to Domenico Segna (*I martedì*, Vol. 42, No. 4.), who solicited Mancinelli's reaction to his impression that she seemed to "write under the dictation of the familiar and natural landscape of [her] homeland," she similarly replied: "The landscape writes our body. Writing is an imprint of the body, just like those hands in the Lascaux caves." The cover of the Italian edition of *At an Hour's Sleep from Here* in fact shows a hand from a Lascaux cave wall.

The present book provides several examples of this relationship between language and landscape. In "Piazza XX Settembre," Mancinelli describes the statue of Fortuna that stands in the central square of Fano, and then specifies: "Around her extends a town that I could recognize and call with

only two single syllables, almost two musical notes or two opposing answers: *fa no [do not]*. The place name denotes unrest, uncertainty—like something which, once pronounced, would like to be called back into the darkness beyond the throat. It is in this language that I speak, the language that I have been taught by an inland rippled by the Adriatic." In the same piece, she depicts herself as being "made of the almost never clear water of this mild, half-enclosed sea, which becomes furious every so often in winter with the shores that have constricted it."

As is already suggested by this analogy with water, Mancinelli often appeals to an imagery of metamorphosis between human forms and landscape features, natural elements, or the attributes of animals. Reviewing *At an Hour's Sleep from Here* in *The Fortnightly Review*, the British poet Peter Riley aptly comments: "During the poem, or sometimes prior to it, acts of affection and desire are transformed intact into scenes of metamorphosis so delicately and justly that you hardly notice it happening." Moreover, apropos of metamorphosis, in her aforementioned interview given to Domenico Segna, Mancinelli recalls her stay in Calcutta as the Chair Poet in Residence in January-February 2019: "This civilization with which I have just come into contact seems to recognize and to give body to things which, for us, remain impalpable or are rejected. This is why their divinities have more hands, more faces and snouts, are metamorphic presences which welcome human and animal natures, the strength of the masculine and the feminine. In contrast, our culture tends to assert individual identity, solid within its own confines. [In Indian civilization], one remains open to the forms of life from whence one comes and to those that await one."

Such quotations already reveal some of Mancinelli's central concerns: the dichotomies of limits and crossing limits (or of vanishing boundaries), of destruction (or collapse) and rebuilding, indeed sometimes of self-destructive forces and self-rebuilding potentialities, as well as her search for the unique personal language which was inside her when she was a little girl, and which later, through poetry, could also be lent to others' voices—as is detailed in the highly significant text "Yielding Words." The text elucidates the origins of her poetic language and her poetics. In a review of *At an Hour's Sleep from Here* published on his blog *Roughghosts*, the Canadian writer Joseph Schreiber had already been struck by her remarks (in her dialogue with me in the Autumn 2019 special feature issue of *The Bitter Oleander*) about "feeling the brand of one in exile, of the stranger." Schreiber saw in this "early awareness of an otherness," as he writes, a feeling "that drew her to sketch out her thoughts in words as a way of trying to connect." "One cannot help but recognize a kind of quiet

urgency motivating her perpetual need to re-connect," he commented, "this is writing as a vital act, as necessary as breathing." Now in this book, "Yielding Words" details an early scene, in the poet's life, which underlies this "awareness of an otherness."

This volume also makes known some of Mancinelli's literary references. One of them is T. S. Eliot. In fact, the pivot or crux of many writings, and even the very structure of her book *All the Eyes that I Have Opened*, parallels Eliot's lines from *East Coker:* "In my beginning is my end. / [. . .] In my end is my beginning," especially the second half of the equation. Other resonant poetic, philosophical, or spiritual elements emerge in her work. In "An Act of Inner Self-Surgery," she recalls her "meeting," while in Calcutta, with the Hindu female deity Kali, "the devastating mother." "I felt how vital it was to acknowledge that destructive charge," Mancinelli remembers in a revealing passage. "If we learn to welcome this charge, we can direct it towards whatever limits us, whatever blocks our way, illuminating parts of us that had remained dark and getting closer to what we are." Unmentioned in this book but sometimes mentioned in our conversations and e-mail exchanges is the French writer Christian Bobin, who, like Mancinelli, searches through writing to transform loss and suffering into a perspective that can at least teach, if not fully heal. In her own writing, Mancinelli similarly aims at acquiring "a possibility of vision." Her writing attempts to translate this vision into words in order to obtain a means of seeing even more distinctly what has been "given" to her by the wound. A striking image of this possibility is expressed in the very title of her recent book, *All the Eyes that I Have Opened.* The title is based on a distich in her sequence "Master Trees": "*all the eyes that I have opened / are the branches that I have lost.*" When a branch is removed, an "eye" remains. This new "eye" can enable one to see something else, or differently. Potentially, a positive transformation can take place.

Like this "tree eye" metaphor, another memorable recurrent image in Mancinelli's writing is that of "ruins." In Isabella Daddi's probing interview with Mancinelli in *L'urgenza del corpo: pratiche di resistenza e di esposizione attraverso il testo poetico: una destinazione femminile* (also available on Mancinelli's website), the poet elucidates the image in detail. Her response is worth translating at length:

> We are in a period of time in which the forms of living, in terms
> of both space and emotional ties, are undergoing profound trans-
> formations that still induce us to recognize more the remnants of
> the past than what resists or emerges in the present. For me, "the
> house is in ruins," as I wrote in *Mala Kruna*. But my viewpoint has

changed in recent years: more than a space of ruin and destruction, the remnants now appear to me as a space given to us so that we can inhabit it and cohere. It is only between precarious walls, ready to collapse, that nature can enter, animals make their lairs, rainwater gather, and other unpredictable events take place. Inhabiting means possessing something continuously until we recognize ourselves in it—in fact, the Italian verb *abitare* (to inhabit) comes from the frequentative form of the Latin verb *habere* (to have). I cannot recognize myself in anything that is itself closed and delimited. This is why, as [the poet] Antonella Anedda has noted, writing is often also for me "a reflection on non-belonging."

One thinks of Philippe Jaccottet's notion of poetry as a way of penetrating the existential dilemmas of "how to live?" However, in this at once literary and therapeutic context, centered upon the notion of a "space," a "place" or a "locus" that one can inhabit, indeed learn to inhabit through the writing of poetry, "darkness" is conspicuous in Mancinelli's work: it is an original and fundamental element in her own poetics of place. If for other poets, the privileged place is often a "place of light" or a "place of presence" discovered by chance, almost miraculously, as if through serendipity, Mancinelli in contrast often emphasizes the necessity of poetic labor, of concentration, of an inner struggle. Her poetics derive from her individual pain as well as from the pain of others; this kind of "darkness," as a source and resource, therefore forms the prerequisite to the affirming discovery or outcome. A striking example of this orientation is her use of photographic imagery, in particular of the "darkroom" in which a negative becomes a "positive": the photo, the poem. "Writing takes us into our darkroom," she explains in "An Act of Inner Self-Surgery," to the place of the unknown, where our demons nestle, our most tenacious and impenetrable shadows. It is a place that has precise laws and rhythms, a fundamental relationship with darkness so that the vision is fulfilled." For her, writing is nourished by this darkness, by "this possibility of loss and destruction which becomes necessary knowledge. We write to see inside our darkroom." In "A Book of Poetry: A Living Structure," she sums up this confrontation with what is dark and initially negative by asserting that she writes "when something from the darkness beckons to be watched."

Another insightful explanation of this essential aspect of her poetics can be found in our dialogue "Distance is a Root" (on the website *Hopscotch Translation*). During our conversation, I point out that the word "darkness," or one of its synonyms, appears at least twenty times in her book *All the Eyes that I Have Opened* and that the word "light," or a similar term, crops

up equally often. Asking her about the necessary role that darkness plays in our coming to awareness, to "enlightenment," she responds: "Being in darkness allows us to sharpen our eyesight, to recognize that part of things that becomes invisible in the light. It brings our eyes closer to animals' eyes, open to pick up the vibrations of matter. [...] The more we are able to open our eyes in the darkness that we carry within us, the more we are saved, even if in an always precarious and temporary way. Darkness feeds our demons, which grow and return to take power over our life."

"To open our eyes" is no mere metaphor here. The body is present in all its physicality. For there is a further sense in which darkness is evoked by Mancinelli, namely in regard to her oft-reiterated notion of writing "with" or "through" the body. "I have often felt that I carry writing in my body," she explains in "Poetry, Mother Tongue," "that I have been inscribed, in the darkness, by something that inadvertently presses down and leaves signs in me [...] When we find ourselves in front of the computer screen or the sheet of paper, what we do is merely try to translate what has been written in us." In "Distance is a Root," Mancinelli, responding to my question about her being, in this respect, a kind of "receptacle," observes: "What escapes through the mesh of language is precisely what beckons me. Poetry is born from what exists before and beyond words. It is the language of the unsayable and the untranslatable which, deep down, constitutes our existence. A pre-Babelic language, a primal language: the vibration that runs through matter."

Still another dimension of this issue—poetry as "born from what exists before and beyond words"—can be defined. As Mancinelli explains to the writer Roberto Lamantea in *Fare Voci* (December 2020), she perceives a kind of "love" passing through poetic language. For her, "our most fragile and wounded parts," which are "silenced and covered over" by daily life, can be "heard in poetry" and therefore "exist, relying on the strength of this original love that reaches us through our mother tongue." She also sees a responsibility, for the poet and in fact for all human beings, at this deep level. Because of language, we are distinguished from other beings who have no language, no "word"—no "parola"—who, as she states, "no longer have it because there is no one capable of stopping and bending over to listen." "Every time we speak," she concludes, "we also assume a responsibility: towards the silence we have interrupted and everything that has continued to live in that silence. Because of this, we can only seek a wider space for our individuality as much as possible, and open ourselves to other parts of our being, of our presence."

From such angles, Mancinelli peers into silence and into darkness in ways that address universal concerns. This is why many of her lines or sentences,

drawn from deep within herself and exhibiting her characteristic intensity and authenticity, ring so true with readers grappling with their own darknesses, however different they might seem to be. For there are common denominators among darknesses: opaqueness, obscurity, the absence of light in all senses of the term. Often citing Giorgio Agamben's essay *What is the Contemporary?*, she holds the view, like the Italian philosopher, that the poet is "he who firmly holds his gaze on his own time so as to perceive not its light, but rather its darkness." "All eras," continues Agamben, "are obscure—dark—for those who experience contemporaneity. One who is contemporary is precisely one who knows how to see this obscurity, who is able to write by dipping his pen into the obscurity of the present."

Agamben's remarks suggest how Mancinelli's exploration of darkness and light (sometimes formulated as "gleams" in *All the Eyes that I Have Opened*), of destruction and reconstruction, of collapse and re-composition, or of negativity and affirmation enables her to offer original vantage points on vital issues in modern and contemporary European poetry. Some of these thematic oppositions, which can in fact be in movement in Mancinelli's own texts, as one antipode evolves into the other one, or vice versa, are subjectivity and self-effacement, the self and the other, presence and absence, loss and recovery from loss, as well as origin and uprootedness as categories that are as onto-logical as they are existential and geographical. Her recent poetry shows an increased interest in anthropological archetypes as well as in rituals, artifacts, or symbolic figures from the ancient past as means for better grasping con-temporaneity and, above all, for casting unusual beams of light on being and existence. She offers insight into this aspect of her poetics, in her afore-mentioned interview given to Isabella Daddi, by underscoring her belief, "along with [the Russian thinker] Pavel Florensky, that poetry is formed from a psycho-physical energy that comes from the body and enters into contact with the deposit of meaning that the human community has kept alive through the generations." In "The Invisible as the Facing Page," she analogously equates writing to a plant that "grows in marginal lands, connected with the deeper layers where an ancient original wealth is deposited and regenerated, where our ancestors sleep. The plant feeds on death that has become humus. For its fibers, there is no end that is not a beginning." The same essay has a charac-teristic "mystical tension" or, to formulate this quality differently, a "religious" aspect (if one thinks of the etymology attributed to the adjective: that which "binds" or "links" us to something greater than ourselves). "Our life is written in the air that we move through," she posits, "in the air that contains us, in our unawareness, like the golden backdrop of an ancient painting in which every being appeared in his or her sacredness."

Informing her necessity to write is often the fact of having had a "home," in the various practical and metaphorical meanings of the word, and then of not having one. This theme is evidently related to the issue, delineated above, of a "space to inhabit" and nonetheless a state of "leaving" or, more precisely, of being "in transit," as she phrases it in *The Little Book of Passage*. Commenting on that book to the poet Giovanni Fierro (in *Fare voci*, June 2018), she revives the ancient conceit of life as a journey and defines traveling as the experience in which the trace of our existence is most recognizable. "We must not forget that we are passing through," she cautions, "even though everything around us leads us to believe in, and desire, stable and fixed forms." Being in transit can also imply a grave existential dilemma, as is the case in *The Little Book of Passage*. Yet in such a context, Mancinelli's originality stands out once again. The "dilemma" can also create a "threshold condition," as she has underscored, "from which writing and the acceptance of one's voice can be born." The "leaving" might indicate a voluntary process, even a desire to metamorphose into a bird as in "The Little Girl Who Learned How to Fly"—far from her family home, from her family ties, therefore away from childhood and towards new freedoms tendered by adolescence and adulthood. "Flight" in this book, or in her poetry and poetic prose, indicates an attempt to remove herself from a "place of pain," as she has stated, "and at the same time signifies metaphorically, perhaps, a kind of ascetic practice or spiritual exercise." This particular threshold condition, which brings together presence and absence, both nourishes her writing and defines her vantage point. "What I am is a window" is how she defines herself in a poem from her second book, *Mother Dough* (comprised in *At an Hour's Sleep from Here*), a line that she in fact chose for the title of our reading, from her work, at Oxford University (on 3 March 2021) as a part of the online series *Italian Poetry Today*. Still other narratives evoke crossing boundaries in an attempt to come back into contact with the most rudimentary natural elements. "When I clean this house made of marble, plaster and glass," she writes in "Living in the Ideal City: Fragments in the Form of Vision," "this house where I now live without knowing so, I caress it as if it were made of stone and living earth, as if it felt my hands. I go back to its original matter—before the cement mixer and the changes of state, before the industrial transformations—to its simplest matter. This is why I like to find dust when the time is ripe and it can be gathered in small dark deposits. To bring together the beginning and the end of the world."

More often in these cases of departure and displacement, darkness has once again fallen. Sometimes the breakup of a relationship causes the departure and, consequently, the search in transit for a transition, for self-

transformation. "Central Station" shows the author waiting to change trains in Milan and suddenly being "hit by the pain through one of [her] inner fractures." In addition, her backpack is stolen. She must henceforth find the force to exist away from what has been her home, and she manages to do so. "Slowly my loss was handed back to me as a gift," she concludes, "this trust that is strengthening, that I will have to muster to cross the void and go back to a point in my life when I walk with a backpack containing everything that will support me away from home." Appealing to her telltale geological metaphor involving fault lines and water tables, she adds: "Between one [train] platform and another, one of the wells connected to the earth's fault lines has opened. I have thus been able to draw off the dark water and the tiny seeds of light immersed in it." Water is often a symbolic healing element in her writing or a metaphor of moving—flowing—beyond the confines of the self, filling fissures and gaps in the process. In his review of *The Little Book of Passage* in *World Literature Today* (Vol. 93, No. 2, Spring 2019), Benjamin Myers notes that "throughout the book, images of water and of motion suggest a decentering of selfhood, a fluid consciousness." Similarly, the British critic Mark Glanville, writing in the *Times Literary Supplement* (27 February 2020) about *At an Hour's Sleep from Here*, perceives Mancinelli's work as coming "to life in Heraclitean flux, never at rest in its ceaseless endeavor to bridge gaps. [...] Her bridge-building appears to echo a kabbalistic desire to restore the universe to its original perfection."

These dualities of flux and the search for stability, of uprootedness and the quest of roots, of homelessness and seeking to be at home in the world and in oneself, inform many poems and prose texts. The poet Jerker Sagfors, who translated *The Little Book of Passage* into Swedish, perceived in that book "an unclear, split identity" in conflict "with the remaining fragments of its origin" and qualified the prose poems as being "about escape, independence and settlement," an aspiration "to catch oneself before anything else does." Several texts in this book also detail this desire. In "The Boy among the Rocks," Mancinelli watches a mysterious solitary boy, whom she spots on a beach, marking off a space for himself to exist. In other texts, a necessary departure from a "place of being," and sometimes from a place of "being together," transforms the once-reassuring and now-lost "home" into a "space of writing." "Living in the Ideal City" offers a prolonged meditation on this theme. Mancinelli refers to another kind of "home," one that would be our origin and our destination: a kind of void. "Such is this inhabitable space," she writes, imagining the interiors of an "ideal city" depicted in a fifteenth-century painting, "where these windows and thresholds reflect each other, each again

beckoning to us as if to say: stop here, this is your home, take care of this void." Elsewhere, another image related to this issue of "home" and "homelessness" crops up in the form of an insect that flies into a house and then tries to escape by banging itself into a windowpane. In "A Line is a Lap," Mancinelli extends the metaphor to writing. "The insects head towards the light," she explains to Grazia Calanna (in an interview on the website *L'EstroVerso*) about this recurrent image of which she is especially fond, "but with a kind of constant, self-damaging blindness. You find them exhausted, on their backs, inert, on the windowsill. In this crash I perceive writing, its beating against an insurmountable limit which, nonetheless, continues to call out to us, like the promise of a different dimension, of an air finally liberated and become ours."

This metaphor has ontological resonance. Coming into being can also imply finding oneself unwittingly in a "room," in a "house," within confines, indeed "inside a horizon of hills." Mancinelli faces up to the estrangement that we can feel in this "house." It is an estrangement which forms, of course, the counterpoint of the positive qualities that can result from learning to inhabit a space. Like the insect, we can feel ill at ease, that we are not in the right place, that we are literally "out of place." Then we spot some kind of light. But it seemingly emanates from the other side of a windowpane, a border, a barrier, a horizon, even perhaps from behind the face of another person. We try to reach the light, whatever it is—the remote promise—by attempting to cross the limit, to enter more deeply into the Other; but we fall, broken, and "end" in some way. Or, to cite another image, we hear a "call." This "call" has the same meaning as the one in Jack London's title, *The Call of the Wild*, but here "the wild" is another kind of wilderness. It is death and nothingness, the void; or, perhaps more precisely for Mancinelli, something "invisible" that beckons to us. "Sea, Train" associates the word "call" with suicide. "Here at least two lives have obeyed the call," she writes, "and climbed the pebbly bank, amid the electric tremor that runs through the wires before the train arrives." In one of her most candid and moving texts, "Maria, towards Cartoceto," she admits that at a certain moment in her life she herself "was heading towards death, with the instinct of a migrating animal." From this angle, Mancinelli's texts are about deeply understanding this "call," this inevitable "migration," and about facing up to it as the essential "given" in our human condition. Mancinelli is extremely attentive to that which is "given" to us: our "gifts." Even as she often recalls the etymology of the word "pharmacy," from the Greek *pharmakeia* or *pharmakon*, "a healing or harmful medicine, a healing or poisonous herb," our English word "gift" comes from Scandinavian and proto-Germanic root words indicating "that which is given" (and thus "inspiration") as well as "poison."

Such sentences about heading towards death embody pain, but they are never lamentations. Nor do they express "death wishes" in the common psychological or psychoanalytical senses of the expression. Mancinelli's "call," "instinct," and insect-windowpane analogy suggest a different, even stoical, viewpoint that inverts our habitual way of looking at death, at non-being— at what is "invisible," the term that is probably the most appropriate for the metaphysical entity, or space, or concept, on which she often focuses. We have come into being: we find ourselves in the world. We must live, survive, on various levels of experience. It is a commonplace for us to invoke an "instinct for survival" in a hostile environment, of whatever kind it might be. But in contrast to this instinct, Mancinelli perceives a second one, which is not exactly a desire or a wish. It is the instinct, or the "call," to return to whence we came, therefore to an origin that is now in front of us even as it remains behind us. It is thus also a destination. The beginning is the end, even as the end is the beginning. Moreover, this "end-beginning," as she sometimes phrases it, is inside us at all times. It is inside our bodies, even as Mancinelli senses that writing takes place "inside," with," or "through" her body.

The remarkable first text in this book already shows how the poet, as a little girl, came into contact with death, in spite of herself at first, by catching butterflies and holding them between her thumb and forefinger: "It was enough for her to talk to them, barely moving her lips or murmuring in her mind, until the butterflies, resting on her shoulder, no longer fluttered off: they had become attached to her. And yet not long afterwards, they would be inert, enfeebled leaves." "The Butterfly Cemetery," as Mancinelli has explained, "is a place steeped in the memory of childhood, whose boundaries have blurred over time, and at the same time it is the space of writing: the page on which we place the beauty that we have managed to capture and, inevitably, to kill. As in a children's game in which life, held in the hands, dies, each symbolic creation asks for a sacrifice, a burial, to enter a form, to become writing. In this sense, each page is a cemetery of butterflies: the space to which we have delivered the beauty that we have pursued, as it passes through the air."

The butterfly metaphor in fact structures this book. As Mancinelli and I were preparing the manuscript, she came up with an order of texts that did not respond to a chronological criterion, but rather to internal references which, beginning with "The Butterfly Cemetery," lead to the construction of this space, with three slight subdivisions marked by a blank page, on which she wanted a butterfly to fly again. "It is an ancient symbol of the vital breath that passes through us," she specifies, "and of the metamorphosis to which we are called." Butterflies, birds, flocks of birds, even insects unwittingly flying into

rooms—Mancinelli's vision is full of flights, acutely perceived flights, significant and revelatory flights, not mere "flights of the imagination" for this author whose texts always take wing from concrete images or occurrences.

When reading her poems, prose poems, narratives and personal essays, we are compelled to face up to the hypothesis that our true home is not, or not only, the here-and-now. And that our true form, or at least one of our true forms, is equally the previous one and the next one, both of which we can attempt to picture. This is why death, when it is invoked by Mancinelli, is not morbid, tragic, or dramatic. Non-being can be viewed as an "origin." So can non-hereness and non-nowness, that is, our prior and future "non-presence" in time and space as we know them. Personally, and not just as the translator of her clearsighted and deep-probing prose and poetry, I would like to say that Mancinelli's writings have helped me to open my own eyes to "the invisible" in a different way. Whatever intimidating darkness might have initially "inscribed" the words in her body, these texts often have a luminous and calming effect. "Staying close to the origin," she observes in "The Invisible as the Facing Page," "leaving room for the invisible as the facing page. Every time we hold a pen we must remember this ancient branch with which we wrote as children, when we were translating from the invisible (our own body, our presence, was a recent translation from the invisible)."

John Taylor
Saint-Barthélemy d'Anjou
17 April—31 July 2021

Acknowledgments

Franca Mancinelli and I would like to express our gratitude to the artist Kiki Smith, who generously granted us the permission to reproduce her tapestry "Congregation" on the cover. For their help and kindness in regard to this cover image, we also thank Era Farnsworth (of Magnolia Editions), Pace Gallery, and the French writer and art critic Jean Frémon.

As with Mancinelli's two previous books in translation, *The Little Book of Passage* and *At an Hour's Sleep from Here*, the poet Paul B. Roth, the publisher of The Bitter Oleander Press, has attended to this volume with sensitivity, insight, and precision. Indeed, from the onset of our work together, he has supported our projects with great care and enthusiasm. Some of these texts were initially published in the special feature, on Mancinelli's work, which appeared in the Autumn 2019 issue of *The Bitter Oleander*.

Let us now recognize the journals and literary websites who first published these Italian texts and their translations (sometimes in shortened or different versions):

"The Butterfly Cemetery"—*Trafika Europe* (No. 17, 2020). In Italian: *La Poesia e lo spirito* (25 June 2010).

"How the Fire Loves"—*One Hand Clapping* (October 2020). Unpublished in Italian.

"The Form of a Gift"—*Eurolitkrant* (January 2021). Unpublished in Italian.

"Sap"—*Eurolitkrant* (January 2021). In Italian: *Fiabesca* (18 December 2014).

"The Enchantment of Death: Briar Rose"— Unpublished in English. In Italian: *Fiabesca* and the book *Di là dal bosco: Dal blog di fiabe di Francesca Matteoni* (edited by Marilena Renda, Le Voci della Luna, 2012).

"An Earthquake Story"—*One Hand Clapping* (September 2020). Unpublished in Italian.

"The Little Girl Who Learned How to Fly"—*One Hand Clapping* (December 2020). Unpublished in Italian.

"A Bed of Stones"—*The Bitter Oleander* (Autumn 2019). In Italian: *Punto: Almanacco della poesia italiana* (No. 3, 2013), *Nuovi Argomenti* (8 July 2014), and in Mancinelli's *A un'ora di sonno da qui* (Italic Pequod, 2018).

"Walls, Rubble"—forthcoming in *Gargoyle* (No. 75). Unpublished in Italian.

*　*　*

"Central Station"—*The Bitter Oleander* (Autumn 2020). In Italian: *Erodoto108* (No. 20, Autumn 2017).

"On the Ancona-Igoumenitsa Ferryboat"—unpublished in English and Italian.

"The Boy among the Rocks"—*The Trouvaille Review* (June 2020). Unpublished in Italian.

"Sea, Train"—*The Bitter Oleander* (Spring 2021). In Italian: *L'Ulisse: Poetiche per il XXI secolo* (No. 18, 2015).

"Piazza XX Settembre—Fano: Following the Ammonites"—*Word City Monthly* (November 2020). In Italian: *Femminile plurale. Le donne scrivono le Marche* (edited by Cristina Babino, Vydia Editore, 2014).

"Maria, towards Cartoceto"—*The Fortnightly Review* (December 2018). In Italian: *Femminile plurale: Le donne scrivono le Marche* (edited by Cristina Babino, Vydia editore, 2014).

"Inside a Horizon of Hills"—*National Translation Month* (September 2020). In Italian: *Femminile plurale: Le donne scrivono le Marche* (edited by Cristina Babino, Vydia editore, 2014).

"Living in the Ideal City: Fragments in the Form of a Vision"—*Asymptote* (April 2020). In Italian: *S'agli occhi credi: Le Marche dell'arte nello sguardo dei poeti* (edited by Cristina Babino, Vydia Editore, 2015).

*　*　*

"The Cleaning Lady"—forthcoming in *Gargoyle* (No. 75). In Italian: *Semicerchio* (XLVIII-XLIX, 2013/1-2).

"Keeping Watch"—*The Bitter Oleander* (Autumn 2019). In Italian, this is a revised version of "Scrivendo per strada," *Atelier* (Vol. XIX, No. 74, June 2014); republished as "Vigilando" in Mancinelli's *A un'ora di sonno da qui* (Italic Pequod, 2018).

"A Line is a Lap and Other Notes on Poetry"—*The Bitter Oleander* (Autumn 2019). In Italian: *clanDestino* (Vol. XXI, No. 4, 2008), then in Mancinelli's *A un'ora di sonno da qui* (Italic Pequod, 2018).

"A Very Risky Game"—*Trafika Europe* (No. 17, 2020). In Italian: *La Voce di Romagna* (16 August 2011).

"Yielding Words"—*Trafika Europe* (No. 17, 2020). In Italian, on the website *Vibrisse, bollettino* and in *La formazione della scrittrice* (edited by Chicca Gagliardo, and based on an idea by Giulio Mozzi, Laurana editore, 2015).

"Poetry, Mother Tongue"—*Journal of Italian Translation* (spring 2021). Part 2 appeared in Italian only in *Ends of Poetry: Forty Italian Poets on their Ends* (edited by Thomas Harrison and Gian Maria Annovi, *California Italian Studies*, Volume 8, Issue 1, 2018). Parts 3-9 were published in Italian as "Risposte al Questionario" in *Poeti e prosatori alla corte dell'es* (edited by Giancarlo Stoccoro, Anima Mundi Edizioni, 2017).

"A Book of Poetry: A Living Structure"—*The High Window* (Autumn 2021). In Italian: "Materiali di Estetica," *Poesia* (edited by Stefano Raimondi, No. 7.2, 2020).

"An Act of Inner Self-Surgery"—*Irish Poetry Therapy Network Journal* (Volume 6, Issue 1, Spring 2021). In Italian: *Poetry Therapy Italia* (No. 1, June 2020).

"The Invisible as the Facing Page"—*Former People* (21 April 2021). In Italian: *La radice dell'inchiostro: Dialoghi sulla poesia* (edited by Giorgio Maria Cornelio, Argolibri, 2021).

Notes

Piazza XX Settembre — Fano: Following the Ammonites

For the archival documents mentioned in this text, see this book about women in Fano: *Le donne a Fano: Documenti d'archivio dal XIV al XX secolo: Proposte per un'indagine storica.* (Fano: Edizioni Fortuna, 1992, p. 17). The quotation in the last paragraph comes from an accounting register listing, among supplementary communal expenses, those made to burn a witch in the square. The *bolognino* is the name of various kinds of currency minted in Bologna between the end of the twelfth and the seventeenth centuries. *Livere* were also coins from the same period. A *boccale*, which is rendered here as "jug," is an ancient measure for liquids.

Living in the Ideal City: Fragments in the Form of Vision

The painting "Ideal City" ("Città ideale") is by an artist from central Italy and was formerly attributed to Luciano Laurana. Oil painting on wood, 67.7 cm x 239.4 cm, date uncertain (1480-1490), Urbino, Galleria Nazionale delle Marche.

Franca Mancinelli was born in 1981 in Fano, Italy, where she currently lives. Known for her acutely crafted and existentially incisive poems and poetic prose, she is considered to be one of the most original poets to have emerged in Italy during the past fifteen years. In English, her prose poems are available in *The Little Book of Passage* (The Bitter Oleander Press, 2018) and her verse poetry in *At an Hour's Sleep from Here* (The Bitter Oleander Press, 2019), both books translated by John Taylor. In 2020, Marcos y Marcos published a new collection of her poems and poetic prose texts, *Tutti gli occhi che ho aperto* (All the Eyes that I Have Opened), which was awarded the Europa in Versi Prize. Taylor and Mancinelli also carry on a dialogue about literary, philosophical, and spiritual issues: the first part was published in the special feature, on her writing, in the Autumn 2019 issue of *The Bitter Oleander;* a second part appeared online in *Hopscotch Translation* (July 2021). Mancinelli's poems and prose poems have been translated into many languages. She was the Chair Poet in Residence (Calcutta, India) in January-February 2019. She is frequently invited to read from her work at European literary festivals, has been selected for the ongoing European poetry project "Versopolis," and participated in the European program "Refest: Images and Words on Refugee Routes" in February 2018. From this latter experience was born her *Taccuino croato* (Croatian Notebook), now published in *Come tradurre la neve* (How to Translate the Snow, AnimaMundi, 2019). Her website: francamancinelli.com

---

John Taylor was born in Des Moines in 1952. He has lived in France since 1977. He has translated many key French, Italian, and Modern Greek poets, including, for The Bitter Oleander Press, books by Jacques Dupin, José-Flore Tappy, and Pierre Voélin. He is the author of several volumes of short prose and poetry, most recently *If Night is Falling* (The Bitter Oleander Press), *The Dark Brightness* (Xenos Books), *Grassy Stairways* (The MadHat Press), *Remembrance of Water & Twenty-Five Trees* (The Bitter Oleander Press) and a "double book" co-authored with the Swiss poet Pierre Chappuis, *A Notebook of Clouds & A Notebook of Ridges* (The Fortnightly Review Press). His first two books, *The Presence of Things Past* (Story Line Press, 1992) and *Mysteries of the Body and the Mind* (Story Line Press, 1998), were republished in new editions by Red Hen Press in 2020. His website: johntaylor-author.com

THE BITTER OLEANDER PRESS
Library of Poetry

TRANSLATION SERIES

Torn Apart by Joyce Mansour —translated by Serge Gavronsky
(France)

Children of the Quadrilateral by Benjamin Péret —translated by Jane Barnard
(France) & Albert Frank Moritz

Edible Amazonia by Nicomedes Suárez-Araúz —translated by Steven Ford Brown
(Bolivia)

A Cage of Transparent Words by Alberto Blanco —a bilingual edition with multiple translators
(Mexico)

Afterglow by Alberto Blanco —translated by Jennifer Rathbun
(Mexico)

Of Flies and Monkeys by Jacques Dupin —translated by John Taylor
(France)

1001 Winters by Kristiina Ehin —translated by Ilmar Lehtpere
(Estonia)

Tobacco Dogs by Ana Minga —translated by Alexis Levitin
(Ecuador)

Sheds by José-Flore Tappy * —translated by John Taylor
(Switzerland)

Puppets in the Wind by Karl Krolow —translated by Stuart Friebert
(Germany)

Movement Through the End by Philippe Rahmy —translated by Rosemary Lloyd
(Switzerland)

Ripened Wheat: Selected Poems of Hai Zi ** —translated by Ye Chun
(China)

Confetti-Ash: Selected Poems of Salvador Novo —translated by Anthony Seidman
(Mexico) & David Shook

Territory of Dawn: Selected Poems of Eunice Odio —translated by Keith Ekiss, Sonia P. Ticas
(Costa Rica) & Mauricio Espinoza

The Hunchbacks' Bus by Nora Iuga *** —translated by Adam J. Sorkin
(Romania) & Diana Manole

To Each Unfolding Leaf: Selected Poems (1976-2015) by Pierre Voélin
(Switzerland) —translated by John Taylor

Shatter the Bell in My Ear by Christine Lavant
(Austria) —translated by David Chorlton

The Little Book of Passage by Franca Mancinelli
(Italy) —translated by John Taylor

Forty-One Objects by Carsten René Nielsen
(Denmark) —translated by David Keplinger

At an Hour's Sleep from Here by Franca Mancinelli
(Italy) —translated by John Taylor

Outside by André du Bouchet
(France) —translated by Eric Fishman & Hoyt Rogers

I wander around gathering up my garden for the night
by Marie Lundquist —translated by Kristina Andersson Bicher
(Sweden)

Consecration of the Wolves by Salgado Maranhão
(Brazil) —translated by Alexis Levitin

Tango Below a Narrow Ceiling by Riad Saleh Hussein
(Syria) —translated by Saleh Razzouk with Philip Terman

The Butterfly Cemetery by Franca Mancinelli
(Italy) —translated by John Taylor

* Finalist for National Translation Award from American Literary Translators Association (ALTA)—2015
** Finalist for Lucien Stryk Asian Translation Award from American Literary Translators Association (ALTA)—2016
*** Long-Listed for National Translation Award from American Literary Translators Association (ALTA)—2017

ORIGINAL POETRY SERIES

The Moon Rises in the Rattlesnake's Mouth by Silvia Scheibli

On Carbon-Dating Hunger by Anthony Seidman

Where Thirsts Intersect by Anthony Seidman

Festival of Stone by Steve Barfield

Infinite Days by Alan Britt

Vermilion by Alan Britt

Teaching Bones to Fly by Christine Boyka Kluge

Stirring the Mirror by Christine Boyka Kluge

Travel Over Water by Ye Chun

Gold Carp Jack Fruit Mirrors by George Kalamaras

Van Gogh in Poems by Carol Dine

Giving Way by Shawn Fawson **

If Night is Falling by John Taylor

The First Decade: 1968-1978 by Duane Locke

Empire in the Shade of a Grass Blade by Rob Cook

* *Painting the Egret's Echo* by Patty Dickson Pieczka 2012

Parabola Dreams by Alan Britt & Silvia Scheibli

Child Sings in the Womb by Patrick Lawler

* *The Cave* by Tom Holmes 2013

Light from a Small Brown Bird by Rich Ives

* *The Sky's Dustbin* by Katherine Sánchez Espano 2014

* *All the Beautiful Dead* by Christien Gholson 2015

* *Call Me When You Get to Rosie's* by Austin LaGrone 2016

Wondering the Alphabet by Roderick Martinez ***

Kissing the Bee by Lara Gularte

* *Night Farming in Bosnia* by Ray Keifetz 2017

Remembrance of Water / Twenty-Five Trees by John Taylor

The Stella Poems by Duane Locke

* *Ancient Maps & a Tarot Pack* by Serena Fusek 2018

**Not All Saints* by Sean Thomas Dougherty 2019

* *Blue Swan, Black Swan: The Trakl Diaries* by Stephanie Dickinson 2020

Weightless Earth by Paul B. Roth

* Winner of The Bitter Oleander Press Library of Poetry Award (BOPLOPA)
** Utah Book Award Winner (2012)
*** Typography, Graphic Design & Poetry

All back issues and single copies of *The Bitter Oleander* are available for $15.00
For more information, contact us at info@bitteroleander.com
Visit us on Facebook or www.bitteroleander.com

The font used in this issue is the digital representation of a family of type developed by William Caslon (1692-1766). Printer Benjamin Franklin introduced Caslon into the American colonies, where it was used extensively, including the official printing of The Declaration of Independence by a Baltimore printer. Caslon's fonts have a variety of design, giving them an uneven, rhythmic texture that adds to their visual interest and appeal. The Caslon foundry continued under his heirs and operated until the 1960s